I0553240

SAVAGE ONE

BORN WILD BOOK TWO

DONNA AUGUSTINE

Copyright © 2019 by Donna Augustine

All rights reserved.

No part of this book may be reproduced in any form or by any electronic or mechanical means, including information storage and retrieval systems, without written permission from the author, except for the use of brief quotations in a book review.

ONE

My heart pounded so hard that it echoed in my ears and threatened to break out of my ribcage. The face of the clock beside my bed was visible by the light of the full moon. Thirty minutes this time. That was how long before the nightmares came. How long it took for the Magician to haunt my sleep, ax in hand, chopping off my legs and arms and trapping me forever. No chance of escape. The walls of my room felt like the sides of a jail cell, my bed a device of torture.

I closed my eyes but couldn't stop seeing him. *Breathe, slow and steady. He doesn't have me. He won't get me. I'll do whatever needed to avoid that fate, including my own death. Some futures are worse than never waking again.*

The breathing wasn't working, but then again, it never did. Unable to shed the cloying fear of being stuck, I shot out of bed. I pulled on my boots and threw on the heaviest sweater I had. I closed the door of my bedroom, holding on to the doorknob as it clicked home. The place was silent as I tiptoed through the halls, avoiding the spots that creaked.

I stepped out the front door. The air hit my skin and the smell of the trees infused the air with life, freedom, helping my lungs inflate again. I took off at a run because I could. The trees whipped past, branches scraping my flesh, rocks underfoot making me slip. I'd hit the ground and get right back up again. I didn't care. I'd run until the nightmares faded or the invisible bond that chained me to Callon yanked me back. I'd run until I felt like I was free, truly free. I wouldn't be caught, not again. Not ever.

I didn't stop until my limbs were loose as my back hit bark. My lungs burned worse than my legs, and a pain stabbed my side; I welcomed it gladly.

I listened for steps behind me but didn't hear anything. It didn't matter. He'd come. He always came.

The crows that always followed cawed loudly as Callon's beast broke through the trees a few minutes later, large and savage. Fangs that could rip through flesh like a razor through butter, claws that could shred a hide like tissue—there was a time that if I'd seen such a creature, I would've run screaming. Now I waited for him, this beast, this creature who'd never been caged.

On the surface, we looked worlds apart. Callon's beast was raw muscle and power as he towered over me. I was nothing but a scrawny girl with gangly arms, too fragile, too weak, but still standing her ground before him. Deep down, where people couldn't see, I was a savage, like him. That was what my past had shaped me into, something untamed that would bite, claw, and chew my way out of any trap. Deep down, where it really mattered, we were the same.

He bent his head, a low rumble in his throat as he breathed in my scent, his fangs grazing the tender skin of my neck. In a sudden movement, he grabbed me. I didn't fight. I wanted to go with him.

He carried me to a place high above the lodge, into one of the caves of the mountainside. He dropped me into the center of piled furs. There were shadows of other things in here I couldn't make out—a chest, maybe? This was the place he always brought me. The place his beast came when being human was too much.

His chest heaved ragged breaths as he stood in front of the opening of the cave, silhouetted in moonlight. His eyes, a slight shimmer of red and the only thing visible of the face, turned my way.

I burrowed under the furs. He turned back toward the outside as I curled up in a ball, watching him. A gentle snow drifted down outside, but I no longer felt cold. I only felt peace.

My eyes drifted closed. I'd sleep here like I couldn't anywhere else. In the morning, I'd wake in my bed in the main house with no memory of returning.

TWO

Issy stopped beside me with a bowl of sausage and dropped another couple links onto my plate. She gave me a pat on my shoulder and a smile before she went over and put the bowl on the side table. There were many more lined up for the breakfast-goers crowding the great room of the lodge and others in the area that might stop in. Issy liked to cook, liked to feel needed about the place, but she was far from a servant. She cooked when she wanted to cook and would stop when she wanted to as well. She called the shots here, and Callon gladly let her.

We still hadn't spoken about what happened between us, how I'd possibly saved her from death, but she knew. When she'd been dying, she told me she was ready to go. Now that she was firmly among the living, she seemed to have decided she wasn't as ready as she'd thought. Didn't blame her a bit. I wasn't looking to go either. Most people weren't.

Issy walked out of the room, her brown pixie hair

shining like she was in prime health as she gave me a last wave. Tuesday bobbed around Issy as she made her way in. She swerved in between the fifteen or so people, dark curls bouncing around her head with the effort. She dropped into the chair beside me, her plate holding a single egg and one link of bacon.

Her lack of appetite always coincided with the man standing across the room. Koz smiled at her, all boyish charm. A lion's mane of blond hair stuck out wildly, framing a roguish face. I'd seen pictures of musicians from the Glory Days who'd looked like him. Or pirates. Koz would've fit in well with them if he wasn't a beast, but he'd been born to a different pack.

Tuesday nibbled on the end of her bacon strip. If she'd had a different audience, bacon strips would've been shoved in two at a time. She put down the barely eaten meat and wiggled four fingers. That was the code for how many pieces I'd need to smuggle out of here for her after I was done. With as much food as I smuggled, people must've wondered why I was still so thin. Koz would have laughed his ass off if he saw her stuffing her face an hour later.

She tilted her head, not missing an opportunity to flip dark curls from one shoulder to the other. "I saw you running across the lawn last night. I was going to wake Koz. Then I saw Callon running after you," she said softly, before giving me a moue and batting her lashes, because Koz must've glanced our way again.

"Uh huh." There were awkward conversations and then there was this one. I took a sip of tea, trying to dislodge the boulder that was choking me. If there was one person alive that knew me the best, it was Tuesday. But I still wasn't talking about this with her. Why? Because it was weird, even for a girl who could tell you how you'd die, and that said a lot.

"I listened for you but fell asleep before you came back. Where do you two go all night when you disappear? What do you do?"

"Nowhere special, and I sleep. That's all." I kicked her under the table.

When I'd come down for breakfast, I needed my heaviest sweater. The start of winter up north was even colder than it used to be in the village. Now I wanted to start shedding clothes because I was sweating. In another few seconds I was going to be dripping beads off my forehead while everyone else was huddling around the large fireplace in the great room, listening to us, or at least Koz was. All the others were doing a better job of pretending to mind their own business.

She leaned back to get a better view of my face, then moved closer, keeping her voice softer. "You run around the place, he follows you, and then you both sleep. It's weird."

I kicked her again and made jerking motions with my eyes to the others nearby, some of whom were shifters. A beast didn't need you to scream to hear you from across the room. It was really hard to keep a secret around this place, and breakfast was the worst.

I still wasn't certain who could sprout a set of fangs on demand. I could figure it out really fast if I wanted, but I hadn't. When I met a human, I usually saw their death. Not with shifters. I wasn't certain if it was a deficiency in my gift or that most of them would die after I would. Either way, I tried to limit who I got in range of, because I could only handle so many death visions a day, especially the bad ones.

Deaths definitely weren't all equal. Some people died calmly in their beds from some sickness that overtook them. It was best when they were good and wrinkled when it happened, and they had people around, helping to ease the passing. The violent ones were bad. Not my favorites, but sometimes quick. The worst by far were the young ones. It was getting to the point that I avoided children at all costs. Luckily, there weren't too many here, so it had been easy.

"Well? You didn't tell me what you do," Tuesday said, nudging me with her elbow.

"I've told you twenty times already. I sleep."

"You really sleep?" she asked.

"Yes. Really. Do you think I'd lie to you?"

She slumped back into her seat and made a clucking noise with her tongue, as if she'd been promised ice cream only to have the last scoop dropped in the dirt in front of her before she'd gotten a single lick in.

"The whole thing is weird," she said, not being particularly quiet this time around, and a bit crankier. It might've been the hunger pains of eating one strip of bacon when you liked twenty.

I took another look around the room, gauging the interest in us. Continuing the conversation any further without Tuesday saying something mortifying was like trying to walk a greased tightrope without falling. But no one seemed to be paying us much mind. They'd probably been disappointed by the sleep answer.

"I don't know what you want to happen, but it's not." Well, that sentence made no sense whatsoever, and I wasn't going to elaborate on it. Tuesday knew me well enough to know exactly what I meant anyway.

She glanced around, displaying more caution than normal, before turning to me. "Because I've found *it's* nice to have, and I want you to have *it* too."

"*He's* not where I'm going to find *that.*" Callon was good for one thing. Helping me sleep. That was all I wanted from him. A good night's rest.

"Are you going to find it somewhere else, then? There's other people here. In the months we've been here, there must be someone who caught your eye."

"A month and a half, not months. And I will find someone when I'm ready." That probably wouldn't be until I could sleep through the night and wasn't being chased by a homicidal maniac. Tuesday might not have realized it, but I was hauling about two tons of baggage. Most men I'd met liked to travel light.

Tuesday opened her mouth to bombard me with something else but shut it as Callon walked in. He had a thing about him that instantly drew attention, and it had nothing to do with his dark good looks. His presence changed the chemistry of the room somehow. People talked a little softer so they could keep one ear open for what he might be saying across the way. They kept a spot in their peripheral vision aimed on him. I knew because I did it too, and for the love of all that was wild, I had no idea why. It wasn't as if Callon asked every man and woman around to pay such homage to him. At times I would've sworn it annoyed him when people hung on his every move. Most days it seemed as if he'd be happier if everyone disappeared, except for a favored few.

He made his way across the room, accepting greetings with a nonchalance born from years of being in charge, heading toward the food platters lined up along the wall. If he saw me, which I bet he did, he didn't acknowledge it. I returned the favor, because that was how we were. Most of the time I thought we were nothing more than the way our distance during the day portrayed us, two people who didn't particularly like each other but were stuck together. He kept his space, and so did I.

Until the next night I couldn't sleep came. Then I'd try to outrun my demons and would find his beast in the last place I ever expected to, in the sliver of time where I found peace. As much as I sometimes despised the man, I found myself longing for the beast who kept me sane. It was the only time I truly felt safe.

I angled my seat so I wouldn't have to see him, even in the corner of my eye. Tuesday rolled her eyes. I got it. She didn't understand. Neither did I.

Luckily, Koz was giving her a nod. I *knew* that nod. I'd seen him give it to her a hundred times before. It meant he was running out somewhere but he'd be looking for her as soon as he got back. And probably not only looking, but touching and other things as well.

She smiled back. I didn't know if it was because she was excited for all the touching when he returned or if she was about to start shoving food in her face the second he walked out the door.

She didn't waste any time, grabbing half of the eggs off my plate. I always piled my food high for these occasions.

THREE

ZINK WALKED IN THE DOOR BEFORE I'D FINISHED MY eggs and right as Tuesday was really chowing down. There wasn't a pair of eyes in the room that didn't follow his every move, but this was much different than Callon's arrival. Zink looked like he'd walked in from a bloody battle. It didn't show on his clothes or hair or face. It was his eyes that held the heat of war. Zink made a thunder cloud look cheery right now, and it made me feel like a bucket of ice water had been dumped down my spine.

He'd been gone for a few days, and everyone knew why. At least, I suspected they did, since talk tended to leak out about this place like a cracked barrel with a rusted rim. Word was that the strange mud swamps had been migrating. I didn't know how many there were, but I'd seen one once, on our way here to the lodge. I'd never forget it. It had smelled like a lake of rotting corpses and had little rivulets that snaked out from the larger body that followed you—or at least me—as if it had a mind. My memory might've exaggerated it a little, but there was something not natural about the thing, and every hair on your body agreed, standing up and trying to flee the scene.

Zink paused in the middle of the room, looking only at Callon. Callon said nothing as he put his dish down and walked out. Zink followed on his heels.

Tuesday leaned in. "*That* looked bad."

"I know." I sat for a few moments, debating my options. This had to be something to do with the mud lakes. Was it any of my business? Maybe. How many other people had the mud lake tried to follow? I should be in there, just in case.

"I'm going to crash that meeting," I said, sliding my plate over to her. She'd already been eating off it anyway.

"Get all the dirt. All. Buckets of it. 'Enough to serve fifty people mud patties' kind of dirt," she said, taking a link of sausage.

"I will." I walked out of the room casually, as if nothing were amiss. I didn't want anyone trying to crash the meeting with me. That might complicate things.

Callon and Zink were gone when I got to the hall, and I picked up my pace in the direction of Callon's office. I let myself in without knocking. If I gave him warning, he'd tell me to go away. I wouldn't. I was going to hear what was happening, whether he wanted me to or not.

Callon leaned back in his chair. One look and I knew I was going to get the boot.

"Teddy, we're—"

"About to discuss what's happening with those strange mud lakes?" I shut the door behind me, making it clear I wasn't going anywhere. "That stuff tried to follow me, if you'll remember. I think I should be here."

Zink kept his mouth tightly shut, but his eyes were narrowed and doing all the talking for him. Zink wasn't overly fond of me. He hadn't declared his opinion in a drastic way, only the cold stares when he had to look at me, lack of greetings when he couldn't avoid me, and overall distaste of my existence. Your basic, run-of-the-mill *I wish you'd drop dead, but since you haven't, I'll pretend you did*-type deal.

If Zink thought that look was actually going to scare me out of here, he'd forgotten our first meeting when I'd been beaten half to death. I could do a cold shoulder all day long and twice on Sunday. It was a warm greeting compared to what I'd grown up with.

"Teddy." Callon's eyes narrowed. It was clear that a silent *get out* followed my name.

I pretended I didn't hear that last part and walked over to the chair against the wall, making myself comfortable. "I know popular opinion is that I'm fragile. Everyone thinks that I'm on the brink of an emotional breakdown at all times. I'm sure my occasional awkwardness adds to this belief. Well, you're all wrong. Coal is soft, fragile, cheap. It's not until it's under tremendous pressure that it becomes a diamond. Don't underestimate me. I'm a lot tougher than I look, and I can handle whatever is being discussed."

Callon leaned forward. "I'm not asking you to leave because I think you're fragile. I'm telling you to leave because this is none. Of. Your. Business."

Some people might've been insulted. Not me. I hated

when people thought I couldn't handle something. It made me want to punch them. Him wanting to exclude me "just because" merely made me want to scream and fight it out. It was definitely better. I crossed my ankles and leaned back, getting more comfortable.

"Oh, well then, let's switch back to the fact that I have a right to know. If you want me out of this room, you're going to have to drag me out." I gripped the arm of the chair. He'd have to take his furniture too. Let's see how well this went, because I was going to put up one hell of a fight.

Callon stood. "Fine." He took a step toward me.

"I gotta get this out, and it's not going to matter soon anyway," Zink said, pausing our little war.

Callon gave me a last stare before turning to Zink. "That bad?"

Zink nodded, and he indeed appeared like a man that had to unload his burden or crack. "Lake one has moved about fifty miles north."

I didn't know where that put lake one on a map. I looked to Callon. Seeing as he appeared to want to punch something, that probably meant it was too close for comfort.

Callon nodded. "What about lake two?"

"It's getting close to encroaching on Cardach. They're calling them Hell Pits because they make it smell like you're at the gates of hell."

Callon opened a drawer and dragged out a map that had some red markings on it. He leaned forward, resting his knuckles on it. "I need to go see for myself."

"Figured you would. Told them we'd be coming back soon."

"When do we leave?" I asked, getting to my feet.

Callon barely glanced my way. "You're not going..." He leaned his head back. The word "fuck" whispered across the air.

At least that was one fight I hadn't needed to wage. How quickly he forgot he couldn't leave without me.

There would be an aftermath, of course. There always was after a recent reminder that he was stuck with me. It was usually a little chillier between us for a day or so.

"So, when will we be leaving?"

"In a couple of days."

Zink went to leave, muttering, "Fuck," and shaking his head. "Only going to take a fucking year to get there now," he said as he walked out the door.

I got up, following. "Hey, Zink, my legs tend to get tired real easy. Make sure you round up when you're figuring supplies out, okay? That year could easily be two," I said to his back.

This was the exact thing I'd missed most of my life. Open antagonism. No one had ever said how enjoyable it could be.

I was laughing to myself, enjoying the moment, when Callon said, "Teddy, stay. We need to talk."

FOUR

I stopped short so fast that I nearly fell forward. It wasn't because he'd told me to stay. It was what he'd said. *We need to talk?*

I turned, but didn't walk back toward him. I wanted to be close to the exit before I committed to staying in a room and talking.

He walked past me and shut the door I'd left open for my speedy escape. He walked back over and pointed at the chair in front of his desk. "Sit."

He wanted to *talk*. Worse, I was going to need to sit for this conversation? This was not good. Not good at all.

He sat down across from me. His jaw shifted as if he were warming it up. My stomach went into my throat, preparing for a hell of a drop.

"You need to stop leaving the house at night."

Of all the things he could talk about, it was this? We didn't talk about *this*. It was off-limits. What was he doing? My mouth felt like I'd sucked on cotton for an hour and then swallowed it without chewing. I couldn't speak. I couldn't swallow.

In the time since the Magician had attacked, I'd run through the forest more times than I could count. Callon had chased after me every single time. I'd wake the next day and that would be it. We didn't speak about it. Ever.

I didn't *want* to speak about it. I'd thought he didn't either. It was the unwritten rule we'd both silently agreed to. Now here he was, speaking about it and trying to stop it.

The only thing that came to my mind was a resounding no. A no in all capitals that was repeated infinitely. If I gave up my runs, how was I supposed to sleep? The two hours or so I managed between my thrashing? How was a person supposed to survive like that? Absolutely not.

"No." I leveled a gaze at Callon that would've burned a hole through anyone else.

I crossed my arms to hide the rage that was making my hands shake. It was one thing to be mad. It was another to lose control. I was about to do the latter. He was asking me to never sleep again. Did he realize that?

A hint of red tinted Callon's hazel eyes, the beast flaring to life within. He wasn't trying to scare me off. Callon knew better than that. He probably didn't realize how close the beast was to the surface. I knew. I always knew. I waited for it sometimes, wondered how I could bring it out.

Callon the man and I didn't always click. Callon the beast was different. I understood the beast, and the beast understood me. We were alike. Attack first and deal with the aftermath later. Kill, and then count the corpses. Follow your gut at the expense of everything else. Survival was mandatory. Freedom was priceless.

If he were the beast right now, we wouldn't be having this talk. The beast wouldn't cage me. He'd understand what that meant. What it did to one's soul. Captivity wasn't surviving. It was dying a slow and miserable death. If I was willing to live like that, I never would've run from the village.

"No?" Callon asked, as if he'd never heard the word before. Callon leaned back in his office chair. If he locked his jaw any more, I feared it might break in two.

"No." I stared back, eyes narrowed. I'd say it as many times as he needed until it sank in and he stopped asking.

"The Magician attacked you and you're saying no, you won't stop?" Managing to get words out of a jaw made of granite was a true miracle.

"Why is this a problem now but not before?"

"Because it is. I shouldn't have let it go on this long."

Let. Let it go on. *Let, let, let.* The word was a hammer beating into my heart, making it thump until everything in the room was red to me. My fingers dug into my arms from rage.

"You've been *letting* me?"

"Yes. That is what I'm saying, and I can't *let* you do it anymore," he said, emphasizing the word as I had.

Was he trying to make me lose my mind or was this a special gift he had? No wonder we didn't do this talking thing much. We were incompatible at it.

"You don't *let* me do anything. I won't be told where I can go, what I can do, or how I'm supposed to live. I won't be confined to this building during the hours you see fit. I've already lived that life, and I won't do it again. I'll *never* do it again." If the beast were in front of me, this wouldn't be a conversation. He'd be running through the forest with me, relishing in the freedom. It was the man that was my problem.

His jaw twitched again. "Teddy, this isn't the same thing, and you know it."

Easy for him to say. He hadn't been treated like a beaten dog for the majority of his life. Let someone try to cage him and we'd see if he were singing the same tune.

"I'm not an idiot. I know the risks, and it's up to me to protect myself. I won't sit on a bench by the door waiting for someone to say I can go out. Caged is caged. There's no difference." I was the one speaking through my teeth this time. Too bad I couldn't sprout fangs the way he could. A nice, long pair of canines to bare would come in handy. As it was, I nearly growled my words anyway.

He stood and then leaned his hands on the desk as he towered over me. "Don't turn this into a fight. You won't win."

"Ha! We'll see about that. Go ahead, let the beast out and we'll see what happens." I stood, leaning in. "Or are you afraid because he'll side with me?"

Had he learned nothing? Did he think posturing was going to make me run and do his bidding? The only thing that truly scared me was being trapped. He could skip around here all day long in beast form, human form, whatever hybrid form he could come up with. Fighting didn't scare me. Part of me embraced a good fight. It made me feel alive. Nothing would ever be as bad as being trapped.

His eyes flared a stronger shade of red as he leaned back. "In case you aren't aware, we're one and the same."

I scoffed loudly as I tilted my head back. "Hardly. He'd never try to cage me."

"You mean the way you caged me within a certain distance of you? That way?" He tilted his chin down, eyebrows raised, eyes full of accusation.

Bastard. Did he really want to drag this all out as if he were an innocent in it all?

I let out a sigh. "Yes, there might have been some overstepping with a spell and a witch, but you can hardly claim the injured party. Let's not forget that the only reason you ended up stuck with me was because you sent your people to *look* for me. Why? Because there was something to be gained from getting to me first. You're as guilty as I am, and don't forget it. Come to think of it, why do you even care if I go out at night? I can't get that far from here, anyway."

He pointed at me. "Which makes it worse. If someone were to get you pinned down, they could use you to pin me down. I'm not warning you again. Don't wander."

I got up. Even if he'd said nothing else, I would've gotten up because of that pointy finger. When someone pointed at me, I had the overwhelming urge to break their finger. The urge this time was staggering.

He sat down in his chair. "You can go," he said, as I was already leaving.

I wanted to turn around and rip his head from his shoulders.

"Yes, finally something we agree upon. This conversation has been completely exhausted." I walked to the door. If he thought I was going to ask permission every time I walked out of the lodge, he was crazier than I thought.

I turned. The look in his eyes proved he had no such delusions about keeping me in line.

"Don't test me on this," he said as I walked out.

Test? Was that what he thought I'd be doing? That was where he was wrong. I wasn't a child testing anyone. I was a grown woman who wouldn't be living by someone else's permission ever again.

I shook my head but said nothing else. His words and behavior were barely a ripple in the ocean.

FIVE

Tuesday was wagging her foot so fast that it shook my entire bed. "Is it really that big of a deal?"

I'd relayed everything that had happened and she could ask that? I rolled onto my side, to make sure she heard what I was saying. "Tuesday, he's trying to tell me I can't leave the house."

Her eyes moved around as she sorted it out in her head. "But he did have a good point about you trapping him."

If she'd looked directly at me, she would've stopped talking there, but she was too busy in her own thoughts.

"He probably has his reasons." Her hands fluttered a bit.

"Just tell me one thing. When did you become team Callon?"

She might've missed my slack jaw, but my tone got her attention. She turned on her side, unfazed by my facial theatrics. "Do you think it's normal, this thing you guys do? *Ooooor*, maybe there's something more? It seems to me that for two people who don't talk much, you get awfully agitated—"

"Normal? Is that the standard we're trying to live by now? Is it normal to be able to transfer life from one person to another? Or turn from a man to a beast? Normal has no place in my life. What we used to do was fine, and now he's screwing it all up. How am I supposed to sleep? That is what's not normal here. Depriving me of my sleep."

"Does he know that's the only time you sleep well?" she asked, like she were some sort of detective now.

"Tuesday, have you not listened to anything I've said? Of course not. We don't talk."

"But you just did."

"Yes, but I wasn't going to tell him I needed him for anything. That would be insanity." I took a deep breath. I'd battled it out with Callon. I couldn't afford to alienate my only friend here. "Look, I'm not trying to bite your head off, but please don't ask me to stop what I'm doing too. I can't. And Callon better realize it's not happening."

"I'm just wondering if there is some other reason, is all. Why give you a hard time now?"

"I don't know, and he didn't tell me. He threw out a dictate, so he can go to hell for all I care."

TUESDAY MIGHT BE RIGHT. MAYBE CALLON HAD another reason, but I couldn't trust him to tell me if there was. We didn't have a relationship built on trust. Ours was something closer to glued together with tar.

If I stayed in bed, I wasn't going to get much sleep, but I wouldn't be looking for trouble. I had too much trouble as it was. Staying in bed was definitely the safer choice.

But why should he get to tell me what to do? I had to stop listening to Tuesday. She was letting the lovey-dovey stuff with Koz get to her head. Her situation with him was robbing her of all logic, draining all the fight out of her, sucking up her feistiness. I couldn't let it get to me, too. This get-along stuff seemed to be contagious.

I grabbed my sweater and threw on my boots, getting more worked up by the second. Callon was not going to tell me what to do. If I wanted to go out, I was going out. Screw his rules.

By the time I was halfway down the stairs, I saw Callon waiting for me, the light from his office spreading into the hall, catching his profile.

Fine. He could tackle me at the door if he wanted, but this was a war for my freedom.

I kept walking, and he shifted so he was blocking me. I was about to dodge around him.

"There's something you need to see," he said. I looked at his eyes, the telltale sign of his temper. There wasn't a hint of red.

Dammit. Tuesday might've had lovey-dovey head, but she might also be right. There was something else going on.

He walked toward his office, and I followed, like I was walking toward my burial. I already knew about the Hell Pits. There was only one shoe to drop, and I liked that one even less.

He pointed to the seat behind the desk. Then he reached over, opened a drawer, and dropped a piece of paper in front of me, a broken black wax seal flaking onto the desk. There was only one person I could think of who would use a black wax seal.

My eyes went to the paper and then to him. "This is for me?"

It was a stall. I didn't want to touch it and certainly didn't want to read it.

He stood, hands in his pockets, feet shoulder width apart, and nodded once. It was a heavy nod, like his head weighed more answering this question than if he'd been asked if he wanted a second cup of coffee.

I fingered it. "The seal is broken."

"I know. I broke it."

That might've bothered some people, but not me. If it had been a note from Tuesday, I would've cared. The people who were aware I was here were all ones that made the top of my friends list. Even though Callon and my relationship was clouded by distrust and all sorts of mixed-up emotions, he was on my short list of allies—for now. If he wanted to intercept a letter that was probably bringing ill-boding news, he was welcome to break all the seals he wanted. Sometimes our tar bond was tacky and horrible. Sometimes it was warm and gooey. This was one of the latter moments.

"Am I going to want to read this?" I asked, hoping he'd paraphrase so I didn't have to.

"Probably not."

I needed to stop being a ninny, pick the thing up, and read it. I lifted it, trying to not let the tremble in my hand show. It was pointless. The paper shook like a reed of grass in a hurricane.

I read it. Then I read it again, and it still didn't make sense. I read it a third time, hoping it would click.

"He wants a truce?" I continued staring at the note, as if the letters would rearrange themselves. Nothing about this made sense.

"That's what he *wrote*." Callon's emphasis made his meaning clear. Words, especially hastily written ones, meant nothing.

"When did this come?" How long had he known and how mad should I be? Although I didn't feel anything but fear right now.

"We got word he's been sighted not far from here. This came by pigeon yesterday."

"Why didn't you tell me he was around?"

"So you could toss and turn some more? I didn't see the point."

I wanted to be angry. I should've been furious, except I'd known the Magician was out there. If Callon had told me, I wouldn't have even had the twenty minutes of sleep I got here and there. If it had been Tuesday, I might've done the same. There were things I didn't tell her to save her the grief. Things that weighed on me so heavily that I was afraid I'd drown in a puddle one day.

I hadn't wanted to know. If I had, I would've questioned him earlier today when he told me not to leave the lodge. I hadn't.

"Don't hold back on me again," I said, because even if I didn't want to know, I had to. That was what surviving was about. Knowing things, especially when those things could kill you.

He gave a half shrug, which guaranteed me nothing. There was no surprise there. Our tar had switched back to tacky and irritating.

I read the letter again.

"You don't believe this, do you?" I had almost killed the Magician. If I'd gotten close once, I might be able to finish the job next time. But why so vague? Why not write that he was going back to Newco and he was finished with me? If he wanted a truce, we didn't need to see each other again, ever. Why ask for a meeting?

Callon stretched his arms forward, rolling his shoulders while he cracked his neck to the side, trying to limber up muscles that wanted to stay tense and brawl. Except the enemy wasn't here to attack. I hoped, anyway. Problem was that he was out there somewhere and I was still on his agenda.

"It's a trap. If he was intent on letting you part ways, why insist on a meeting?" Callon said.

That wasn't the answer I'd been hoping for. If I said something was too salty, he'd reach for the shaker. If I said I was cold, he'd put out the fire. Why was it that the one time I wanted him to disagree with me, we were on the same page?

The letter dropped from my loose grasp, cracking the last piece of black wax from it and shedding crumbs on the desk. My heart sank as Callon's thoughts aligned with mine perfectly. When the Magician had taken off, and then stayed gone, it had left all sorts of room to wonder and imagine, like maybe he'd been too afraid to come back. That I wasn't worth pursuing.

The longer he'd stayed away, the more time I'd had to bolster my delusions. It would've been kinder to have come back the day after, or even a week later. Instead I'd gotten to live here for days and weeks on end, with a sliver of hope that had grown wider and thicker, making me think maybe I'd find a measure of freedom and peace.

"You can't be surprised by this." Callon had taken a seat on the desk and been studying my face while I'd been buried in my thoughts, letting my guard down.

I leaned back, shamed by my own naïveté. If anyone knew how dark the hearts of men could be, it was me. I'd lived with two souls whose hearts would've made a new moon jealous.

"No, surprise isn't what I'm feeling." Stupid was closer to the right label. Or how about utterly dejected, as if I'd wrapped up all my hopes and dreams into a box that was called the lodge, and had even tied it with a big bow that had fangs, and now it was being lit on fire? Yeah, that summed it up.

I ran my hands through my hair and then fisted them. "Just curious, why are you so sure?"

I shouldn't have asked. It rang of desperation. That question stank like a man who'd been on the brink of dying for two days.

Callon didn't look at me with pity. I wasn't sure he had that emotion in his repertoire. He either got annoyed that you fucked up, pissed if your fuck-up cost him some-how, or livid if you kept fucking up. Even when you were in a situation that was beyond all hope, he still looked at you like *it's fucked up, but figure out a way to fix it, because it's your problem*. Pity didn't enter his vocabulary. So when he was looking at me now, I knew his look was closer to *how could you be so stupid? Stupidity like that is going to cause a fuck-up*.

Some people might've gotten annoyed by the wall of stone he sometimes appeared to be, the craggy harshness of his psyche. I didn't. It was one of the few things I liked about him. I didn't need, nor want, someone's pity. And when I asked a question about how he knew, he'd give me a straight answer, my feelings be damned. Because even when I'd been a scarred and beaten mess, he hadn't pulled his punches. He'd treated me like an equal.

"I'm sure he won't let this go because the Magician rules Newco and everyone is aware he bought you from Baryn. Even if he wanted to walk away from you, he can't. People would know you bested him. He'd look weak. It would be inviting an uprising, especially since word is there isn't a man or woman in Newco that wants to be there. He can't *afford* to walk away from you."

Bought. It was hard to hear anything past that word. It stuck in my craw like a glob of sap in my hair. Maybe it was for the best we were to meet again. I'd almost killed the Magician the first time I met him. Surely I'd be better at it the second time around. Maybe the nightmares would stop when he was dead.

Callon stood and walked the length of the office as he said, "In truth, he's probably debating on whether or not to keep you alive at all. You came too close to killing him. My guess is he wants you dead more than anything."

Talk about a great bedtime story. Just what I needed

to hear when I couldn't sleep. Why we were in sync at the very time I wanted him to disagree was a testament to how my luck was running these days.

Koz walked in without knocking, as if he'd been summoned here as well. Hess and Zink followed seconds afterward.

Zink picked up the note but only gave it a passing glance, as if he'd already read it.

"So, the Magician wants a meeting," Zink said, before passing the letter along. One by one, they read it for what I was sure was the second time. Koz's forehead wrinkled, sadness in his eyes. He was the softy of the group. He'd been the one to break me out of the village in the first place. Hess was silent, but I knew he was concerned because it was logical. No one looked any happier than I was feeling, even Zink, who barely tolerated me.

It was probably because my problems were Callon's problems. Even if they wanted to hand me over, they couldn't, not unless they were sure the Magician would kill me. Although Zink looked like he could think of one good solution, and it probably ended with me limp on the ground.

Koz dropped the letter onto the desk and then wiped his hands on the back of his pants, as if he'd touched some sort of muck. "What if we meet him with a fake Teddy?"

"We can't leave her behind, remember? She goes where I go." Callon couldn't speak on that subject without sounding like he'd spotted a guy who'd sucker-punched him a year ago.

Sometimes I wanted to tell him to punch me back so we could move past it. Then I remembered that his hands weren't so clean either and lost the desire to make amends. After all, it wasn't like they'd simply stumbled across my village. They'd heard whispers and come looking.

How Tuesday thought our relationship was ever going to be anything more than hate—well, maybe not hate, but *strong* dislike—was beyond me. I used him for sleep; that was it. She had to stop reading all the romance books around this place and staring at Koz with gaga eyes. It was clouding her judgment.

"He wants to meet with me. I'd say whoever you brought, he'd still figure out it was a decoy. To be honest, I'm thinking we don't need one, you know, considering..." I waved a hand. Telling people you could suck up a life and shift it over to someone else was too creepy to say aloud. Point was that everyone knew I had the best chance of killing the Magician, especially as he'd immobilized everyone else the last time we'd met. Beasts might think they were the top of the food chain, but only because they weren't used to having someone like me around. There'd been a new link added way up high.

Callon was shaking his head and walking toward me. "No. You're not getting anywhere near him."

"How's that supposed to work? I know you're concerned about being vulnerable, but I can't kill him if I don't get near him." Covering his own ass again. Sometimes I was surprised he wasn't the one who wanted to kill me. It would solve all his problems.

"Then you're not going to be the one to kill him," Callon said.

"How else will it happen?"

When Callon said nothing, I looked at Hess and Koz, who had expressions of doubt. I was the best shot, and we all knew it except for Callon. At least I wasn't the only one in the dark. It was nice to have company over here in the shadows of confusion. I was normally bumping into chairs and furniture all alone.

I didn't bother looking at Zink. He'd disagree because it was me. He'd swear that pigs could fly to spite me.

"You all agree with her?" Callon asked.

Even Zink was nodding. Well, look at that. Maybe pigs *could* fly.

"Because they know it's the right choice," I said.

"It's not their choice," Callon said without so much as a hitch, in that tone he liked to use. It was the laying-down-the-law type, and I didn't care for it one iota. If he thought he was the law, then I was the worst criminal known to man.

"You're right. It's not their choice. It's mine."

"You're tied to me. I'm the one who can get trapped if something goes wrong. I get to choose."

I glanced over at Koz and Hess but knew I'd lost all support. They wouldn't go against Callon. If beasts were like wolves, Callon was the leader of the pack, and they all fell in line. My only hope was Zink. He might not be alpha, but he was most likely to nip back if he were feeling his oats.

One quick look in his direction and his stare into nowhere disabused me of that notion.

Callon was staring at nothing but me, with a *did you really think you'd be able to manage a coup?* look.

"It was worth a shot." I gave him a halfhearted shrug and a face to match.

His lips twitched. If he laughed, I'd punch him for sure. I didn't know what he thought was funny. That I'd failed or that I'd been delusional enough to try.

Either way, it was going to be tough doing things my way when I was surrounded by them.

"Fine. We'll do it your way, but I don't want to drag this out. I want it over with, one way or another."

"We could do it close to Cardach," Hess said. "The Magician will think it's neutral turf, but we'll have the edge of Cardach's spies in the area and a safe place to hole up overnight."

Callon nodded. "It's a good call. I don't want the Magician anywhere near here. I'll send a pigeon telling him we'll meet him in a few days." Callon glanced at me, as if to check if that worked.

"Fine." I shrugged, doubting he'd change it if it didn't. "When do we leave?"

"Tomorrow. It'll take us a day or so to get there."

A few days. That was all I had left before the nightmare might become a reality.

SIX

"I'm never talking to Koz again," Tuesday said, arms crossed and mouth stern. She sat on the bed, watching as I threw a shirt into my bag.

"It's not his fault. It was Callon's call that you didn't come. He wants to keep the traveling party lean." It was all true. Callon had insisted, and I'd never been happier about him being bossy in my life. Koz might've kept quiet as well, not that I'd tell.

"Koz should've argued with him. Instead he tells me how right Callon is."

"He's just worried about you." I knew the feeling well. The one thing I feared worse than my death was Tuesday dying alongside me, or worse, in my place.

I slung the bag onto my back. I didn't have that many things but I wouldn't need much. I'd be coming back, I'd be dead, or the Magician would have me and I'd kill myself. Either way, it was pointless to over-pack.

Tuesday stood and moved in between me and the door. "What about the snow? Koz said he could feel a storm coming. Is it smart to leave now? Maybe you should insist on a postponement."

Her eyes were desperate. She looked the way I felt, except I was burying it deep where no one would see. I couldn't show it. If I did, she'd push harder, and then I might give in.

"I need to get this over with. I have to close the door on this so I can get on with my life." I wrapped an arm around her. "I'll do whatever I have to and make it back."

I felt her head nodding before I pulled back. Then I headed toward the door, only stopping when I realized she wasn't right behind me.

She was still in the middle of my room, head dropped.

"Aren't you coming downstairs? Don't let Koz leave without saying goodbye."

"What if it's the last time I'll see him?" She looked up, a watery sheen coating her eyes and beginning to pool.

"It won't be." I didn't think it would be, but then again, none of us had any guarantees. "But you don't want to have regrets, just in case."

"Teddy," Callon yelled from below.

Tuesday didn't move. I left her with a nod, hoping this wouldn't be the last goodbye and that she'd see Koz again. I made my way downstairs to the waiting guys. Koz looked beyond me, to the empty space where Tuesday should've been.

"She's having trouble handling it," I said softly as I came close to him.

"Sure. I get it." He nodded, as if he did, but then he kept watching for her anyway.

Callon opened the door. "Let's get going."

We all made our way to the door but Koz, who was still looking up.

There was a sudden flurry of footsteps, and I turned to see Tuesday running down the steps. She leapt off the last few and flung herself at Koz. He caught her midair, and she wrapped her legs around him.

"He'll catch up," Callon said.

MY CHEEKS BURNED WITH COLD AS THE WIND whipped my hair about. The smell of pine trees was everywhere, duller in the cold, but I could still smell it. I loved being out here, with nothing holding me back, no walls or chains. I could run forever if I wanted. I'd have to drag Callon along with me, but still, it could happen.

I glanced at Callon's back. Sometimes I felt bad I'd trapped him. It burned him bad. I could understand that. One of these days, if he didn't piss me off for more than a few hours, I might give him a sincere, drawn-out apology. Since he was so adept at pissing me off, it would most likely take a while. When this day did come, he better have an apology ready to lob back at me.

I was still eyeing up his back when he slowed and threw down his bag. The other guys did the same at almost the exact moment. Callon nodded and then took off as the guys began unpacking things. Had I missed some secret conversation, even as I'd been right in the center of them?

"Where's Callon going? We're stopping?" The sun still had a good hour or so before setting.

"There's a storm coming," Koz explained. "We want to get a shelter set up."

Zink turned toward me for the first time since we'd been walking. "And some of us are more fragile than—"

"There's a storm coming, and no one, not even I, want to travel through it," Koz said, eyeing Zink.

Zink narrowed his eyes. There might've been a snarl, but he went back to whatever he was planning on.

Within thirty minutes, our group was running like a well-oiled machine. Hess was spinning skewered meat over the fire as I poked it and kept a steady flow of wood feeding it. Koz and Zink finished setting up tents that looked like they came from a different world, with shiny, bright fabrics in pink, green, and purple. I wasn't surprised. There were all sorts of weird things leftover from the Glory Years at the lodge. Sometimes it felt like we lived in a time capsule.

The colors didn't bother me as much as the fact there were only three tents and five of us. Only one person would get to sleep alone.

Koz walked back to the fire and pointed to the purple tent. "That's the tent for you and Callon if you want to throw your bag inside it."

I was going to be forced to sleep next to Callon. He was out in the wilderness somewhere, probably being all beastly, and then he was going to come back and settle down next to me. I wanted to jump up and down and skip around the fire, yodel to the sky and do a jig. Even knowing that the Magician was looming somewhere nearby didn't spoil the moment—after all, he was right in front of me every time I closed my eyes. That was part of the problem.

Callon walked back into camp, his eyes still glowing. It wasn't the beast, but it was close, as I'd hoped. He walked over to Hess, who handed him a skewer of meat, and then passed one to me, and the other guys as well.

My legs were itching to dance and my vocal cords wanted to sing. Of course, I wouldn't do any of that. I'd sit there and chew the meat calmly. I couldn't act too excited or people might get the wrong impression and think I liked him or something. What if Callon got the wrong impression? That would never do. That meant I accepted the horrible way he talked and bossed me around, and I absolutely did not. Plus, he was such an arrogant ass, believing he was the wronged one—if he thought I was getting soft, he'd want some lengthy apology now. The only apology he'd get was "I'm so sorry you came to the village to try to use me first. Whoops, I guess I got the better of you."

I chewed, keeping a long face as I stared over at the tent. "It's going to be a tight squeeze in there." I made a little hissing noise, my breath escaping through my teeth. It added a nice touch of misery. Needed to really fill out the scene, after all.

Callon ignored me. The guys didn't say much, but they were listening intently. Couldn't blame them. What else were they going to do with themselves right now? I was the best show available when you were sitting around the fire right before a snowstorm.

Callon finished chewing on his dinner before he said, "I can sleep outside. I do it all the time."

Then he smiled. The fucker knew.

"I couldn't make you sleep out here. It's cold and it's going to snow."

"Cold doesn't bother me," he said, popping the last bit of meat into his mouth.

"I'll sleep out here, then." No way would he let me do that. He didn't want me to leave the lodge alone. Would he really let me sleep in the middle of nowhere?

"I insist you take the tent." Callon tossed his finished skewer onto the fire.

Zink sighed. "This is the stupidest conversation I've ever heard. You know she doesn't want to sleep outside."

"Shut up. We have nothing else to do, unless you want to listen to the damn crows all night," Koz said, of course having to bring up the crows that seemed to always flock around me.

"Fine. I'll take the tent," I said, throwing daggers with my eyes at Zink. Pain in the ass. I liked it better when he pretended he couldn't hear me.

We sat around, the guys talking about how they were going to repair this or that at the lodge. By the time a couple of flakes fell, I was happy to get into the tent alone. Nothing else to do, and being snowed on wasn't high on my list.

An hour later and I was shivering. I grabbed my bag, pulling out the extra clothes I'd packed. I piled them on top of me for whatever warmth I could get from them.

Ten minutes later, Callon climbed into the tent. He knelt in front of me and opened his jacket, as if he were going to undress.

"What are you doing?" I asked, all too calmly, considering he was about to strip. I should've been screaming, not staring intently and waiting.

"Your teeth hammering into each other while you're shivering is hard to sleep through."

He left his jacket on as he unbuttoned his shirt until that was hanging open too. I waited to see if he'd go for his pants. He didn't. He settled down on the ground beside me and tugged me into his chest, sharing the heat that effortlessly radiated from him.

"Thanks." I didn't try to fight him or pull back. I was too stunned to do anything, because when he'd entered the tent, for a moment, I'd thought he'd come for an entirely different reason.

I wasn't stunned because I'd been scared. I was stunned because as I lay there now, the only thing I felt was disappointment.

There'd been a time in my life when I'd never wanted to look upon another man, be near one, have them touch me. Now, I was swallowed up in disappointment so thick an ax wouldn't have been able to chop through it.

How had this happened? When had I started wanting him like that? And why? Why the fuck did I want Callon and how did I make it stop?

SEVEN

I woke up from the best sleep that anyone could have. It was as if I couldn't have crammed one more second of sleep out of my body if I'd tried. Sleeping next to Callon was like having a fireplace beside you that cranked out heat and sprouted fangs. I sat up and stretched out my arms, muscles singing with the invigoration of being fully fueled. It was made that much better by Callon having already vacated the tent. I didn't have to worry about stepping over his body while trying to ignore him at the same time.

I made my way out of the tent, smiled at Koz, who was drinking coffee, and headed toward the sound of running water.

"She's on the move," Koz said to someone unseen.

The sun was shining, there were birds chirping, and my sleep tank was full. Today was going so well that I didn't mind when Callon fell in behind me as I made my way to the stream.

I dropped my bag at the edge of the water. "Giving

you fair warning: I need to wash, and I'm not getting my shirt and jacket wet. Watch on if you must." *Watch on*? What was with the words coming out of my mouth? Was I insane? I was keeping my back to him. It wasn't as if I'd sent him an engraved invitation.

I shed my jacket and shirt, and then peeked over my shoulder. His back was to me. I'd told him he could watch and he was looking the other way. I went back to my business, not annoyed that he had no interest. I definitely wasn't annoyed. I *refused* to be annoyed. I didn't need him to want me too. Nope. Whatever I felt last night was idiocy and shouldn't be encouraged to take root.

Callon cleared his throat. "When we get there, we need to tell them you're with me."

"What do you mean tell them? I *am* with you." I splashed water over my face then shivered with the cold.

"He means 'with' as in a man-and-wife-type deal," Zink said.

I was grabbing my shirt as I heard a growl behind me.

"I'm not looking at her," Zink said under his breath.

"You can fill those after she's done," Callon replied.

Which was right now. My shirt was sticking to me, but I was dressed, putting on my jacket as I turned around. Zink was walking away with water canteens.

"It's fine. I'm done." I pulled my jacket closer and started back to the camp. Callon stayed behind with Zink. Koz and Hess were pulling pieces of meat off a stick.

They held it out to me, and I grabbed a chunk.

"Why do I—"

"Have to pretend you're with Callon?" Hess said.

"These people don't believe in females traveling on their own. If they do find one alone, they consider them fair game."

Their hearing could be so irritating. Not just a mild chafing of the skin type, more like someone was pricking you with a pointy needle in the same spot for days.

"Fair game? I don't think so." Let them try to game me and see what happened. It'd be a fair outcome, too.

Koz dropped his head. "We need these people right now. We get information about who is passing through the area. We don't comment on their beliefs."

Hess seemed to have lost interest in the conversation. His head was tilted in the direction of the stream when he started laughing. Koz chimed in almost instantly.

"What's so funny?" I asked.

"Nothing," Hess said.

Koz shrugged.

THE PLACE DIDN'T HAVE A WALL SO MUCH AS A RING of stakes, twenty feet high and all pointing outward. Obviously, they were meant to keep people out, but even more so, beasts. Did they think the creatures were so stupid as to impale themselves?

I glanced at Callon as we approached. "I'm guessing they don't know their allies very well?"

"That would be a misstep on their part," he replied, smiling as he looked ahead.

A spot in the spiked wall swung open as we approached.

"You need to pretend to be civil even if you don't like them. Can you do that?" Callon asked.

"Little late to ask, isn't it?" I kept walking. I'd been stuck to Baryn's side for years as visitors came and went. I knew how to fake it with the best of them. I'd seen hundreds of people fake it.

There were buildings scattered about, a combination of salvaged structures from the Glory Years combined with newer constructions of all wood. A large brick building was in the center, anchoring the village.

People were moving about in the late afternoon sun, slowing down to take a peek at us. First they'd look at Callon, then they'd shift their gazes to the other guys. Eventually, their eyes would settle on me and stay there. They didn't know what I could do, but it didn't matter. I *looked* different. My hair was unnaturally blond, as if some of the deaths I'd seen had worn off on me and bleached it to a ghostly color. I might've stared at me too. It was understandable, but there was one thing I hated almost as much as being trapped. It was being seen.

I slowed my pace, using Callon's large frame as a partial block from prying eyes. Zink stepped closer, crowding me in on the other side. I couldn't imagine he was doing it to be nice. He probably wanted to make sure I went where I was supposed to.

The stares switched gears as a huge beast of a man walked forward. He wore a long fur vest, but his arms were exposed. A black beard hung a foot long. Most of the visible skin on him was covered with black line tattoos, as if his entire body had been sketched upon, including his bald head.

"Rex," Callon said, reaching a hand out to him.

"Callon," Rex said, returning his greeting.

There weren't many men that matched Callon's size, but Rex was eye to eye with him. The poor guy had the swagger of someone who thought he could best any man he met. He probably thought he had a shot at besting Callon, just like he thought the beasts would impale themselves on his wooden stakes.

"You know my men," Callon said. There were some more hellos and nods of acknowledgement.

I kept as much distance as I could, trying to stay far enough away to keep from triggering a vision. That wasn't going to be, as Callon turned around, wrapped his arm around my waist, and towed me forward into death-vision range.

I braced myself for the man's death, locking down my features and blanking out my expression.

He was lying on the ground, an ax sticking out of his skull, blood seeping around it, his eyes dull, his mouth slack. His beard had gone partially grey.

Not the worst death ever. It looked quick. And he appeared to have quite a few years ahead of him before death came calling.

"This is my woman, Teddy," Callon said.

Rex looked me over but didn't address me. He turned back to Callon. "She's handsome. Let me know if you ever tire of her."

"I don't see that happening." Callon gave my waist a squeeze.

Rex shrugged it off.

I hated the guy. I hadn't crawled through mud and

escaped hell to be treated like cattle. Then again, I had survived hell. Did I really care if this man thought he was above me? Callon used him for information. Right now, we needed that more than I needed to kick him in the gut. Rex was probably doing me a favor. Speaking to him might've been painful.

Callon tugged me backward. A hand on the back of my jacket pulled me the rest of the way until I was beside Koz. I gave him a narrowed eye, making it clear that I knew the Magician wasn't the only reason Koz hadn't wanted Tuesday to come.

He smiled and threw his hands up.

So much for shaming him. It was hard to continue trying when it had been a smart move on Koz's part. Tuesday was worse at holding her tongue than anyone, and the affliction had only been getting worse now that she lived somewhere she felt safe.

"We have another visitor here. Dax arrived just an hour earlier and will be joining us for dinner," Rex said.

"What a nice surprise," Callon said.

I'd heard that name in passing before, and more than once. The only surprise here was how good a liar Callon was.

"My wife Zaza will show you to your rooms. I'll let you get cleaned up before the feast tonight." Rex waved his hand forward, and a woman who'd been lingering some ways behind stepped forward.

"Thank you," Callon said, nodding toward Rex.

Zaza had sleek black hair that fell to her waist and soft almond eyes that looked kind. I liked her immediately, and it sucked that she'd die in childbirth, her skin pale enough to make me wonder if death was already creeping up on her. From the slight rounding of her belly, and the youth of her face in my vision, it wouldn't be long before her time came.

"Come this way," she said. She smiled shyly, but my brain couldn't stop transposing the agony from the vision over her happy expression. I'd have to warn her somehow before I left, if I could think of a way. Although was it something that could be avoided? Whatever medical technology they'd had during the Glory Years had almost completely disappeared.

Zaza weaved us through some buildings and then pointed to two small cottages built of stone, which couldn't have had more than a single room each.

"Your men will stay in that one," she said, pointing to her left.

Hess, Zink, and Koz didn't waste any time ditching us to go to their place.

She moved forward to the next small house. "You and your woman can stay in this one." She paused in front of me. "If you'll permit me, I'll lend you something to wear to dinner?"

She was still smiling but made a point of looking at my legs, which were currently encased in my favorite leathers. They were a tad filthy, but I was planning on cleaning up before dinner. She didn't think I'd show up dirty, did she? Or maybe that wasn't the problem. I glanced around at the other women walking around and realized not a single one had pants on. Oh, this was just rich. I wasn't *allowed* to wear pants to dinner.

Callon "accidentally" bumped into me. I let out a

sigh. Bigger problems. I had much bigger issues than what I wore to dinner.

"I'd be grateful, thank you," I said, my voice not sounding like my own as I mimicked the tones I'd heard so often when visitors would grovel to Baryn.

"Of course." She nodded and walked away.

The second she was out of earshot, I turned to Callon. "Why didn't you warn me?"

"Would it have made a difference?"

"No, but I like to know what I'm walking into. I spent my life not knowing what was going to come at me so when I *can* know, I *want* to know."

"Hate to break it to you, but you never know what's coming at you. Doesn't matter where or who you are. That's life."

"But you did know this one, so in the future, if you know, tell me."

"Fine. In the future, I will tell you every minutia," he said, but he'd stopped looking at me. His attention had shifted to across the way.

A dark-haired man approached. He was a beast. Now that I'd lived with several, I'd never be fooled by one again. There was a smoothness to their movements, like they'd never fall or stumble. A depth to their stare, as if they saw so much more than the man walking beside them. Everything screamed *predator*. It was amazing they passed as human at all. No wonder I felt safer beside Callon.

The man stopped in front of us, and I was proven correct. Couldn't pick up a death vision on him.

"Glad to see you, Dax." Callon reached out and gave

the man a half hug. That half hug was more than I'd seen him give anyone else, ever. I didn't think he liked anyone enough to do that.

"It's been too long." Dax's eyes finally shifted to me but didn't linger the way some did. I liked anyone who didn't stare. That was a top quality in my book.

"Teddy, this is Dax."

Dax gave me a slight smile and a nod, which I returned. That was it. He didn't try to touch me or reach out his hand. I liked him even more.

"Glad you got my message in time," Callon said softly.

"Glad you sent it. You're doing me a favor. It might be our only shot."

Callon nodded. "How many you bring?"

"Another ten a few miles south of here. If we can't get this done with fifteen of us, we're not getting it done. How'd you manage to get a meeting? He's very elusive."

Callon was looking off to the side when he said, "We'll talk more after dinner. We've got company coming, and I don't trust anyone in this camp."

"If you did, you'd be an idiot." Dax nodded in our direction before walking away.

There was a large tub on wheels being dragged in our direction by a man, steaming water sloshing as it went. Two women followed behind it, both with hands full of clothing.

The man nodded as he rolled the tub past us and into the building we were staying in.

"I think that's for you," Callon said, as the women followed him, smiling at us as they passed.

"What? Why are they bringing that? I don't need it."
I followed them into the room, which had a large, opulent
bed in the center covered in jewel-toned fabrics and fur
pelts. On another day, I might've run over and leapt into
the center of it. Today I didn't care, because there were
people here I feared were going to try to bathe me.

The man who'd been pulling the tub left, and the
women were laying things out on the bed. Without
saying a word, they walked back to me and pulled my
jacket off.

"What are you doing?" I asked, trying to yank my
arms away from them, but too late.

"Helping you with your bath," the older one said.

"I don't need help. I don't need that, either," I said,
pointing to the tub. "I'll go to the nearest stream."

"Women aren't permitted to bathe at the stream.
They might be seen." The two women, both a bit
matronly, ignored me as they tugged at the hem of my
shirt.

Callon had his bag slung over his shoulder. "I'm
going to the stream. I'll be back shortly."

I wanted to argue, but my shirt was about to get
ripped from me, making it difficult.

EIGHT

I WAS SITTING ON THE BED IN A DRESS MADE OF panels of leather, held together with cords on the sides. That wouldn't have been so bad if there wasn't enough slack that they gaped a palm wide from shoulder to ankle on each side. Every curve I had was on display. As it was, I was afraid to raise my arms because of the sides of my breasts.

I'd gladly taken the shoes. With leather all the way up and over my knee, at least my calves would be warm.

When the door opened and Callon walked in, I had to force my chin up. I'd fought with him to treat me as an equal, and now I was trussed up like a stuffed chicken. The only thing that made it not as painful was that he seemed to be having a hard time looking at me. He probably wanted to laugh, and I didn't blame him. If Tuesday was in this getup, I would've been howling until my stomach cramped.

Callon, on the other hand, was still dressed in his sweater and leathers.

"Why didn't you get a ridiculous outfit? How come you can go like that and I have to dress like this? Do they not know it's cold out there?"

"This is what most of the men around here wear." He dropped his bag on a table near the door and rifled through it like he was overdue for inventory and we didn't have major issues afoot.

The more he didn't want to look at how bad my ensemble was, the more I wanted to show him. He was going to have to see sense here. There was a limit to getting along, and I'd reached mine. I would've put my clothes back on already, but they'd stolen them while I was bathing, with some bull about cleaning everything.

"Do you see me?" I got up from the bed, standing so he'd have to look at me once he turned around.

"They keep it warm in the main house, and it's only dinner," he said, still not looking at me.

"So you think the spectacle they're making of me is good?" I said. "I look ridiculous. I don't look like a killer. I look like a doll or something." I tracked him across the room. "Callon, look at me!"

He turned, and I lifted my arms, showing him how I was falling out of the sides.

He froze, taking me in from my shoulders all the way down to the boots.

His eyes flared red. "Where are your clothes?"

"They took them." Good. He finally got it.

A bell chimed in the distance, signaling that it was time for the feast in the main building.

Callon reached for the black jacket he wore, dropped it over my shoulders, and then pulled it closed. "If anyone asks why you're wearing that, tell them I told you to."

The jacket dropped nearly to my knees. I shoved my hands through the arm holes and rolled up the sleeves. He wasn't going to hear any complaints from me.

———

FROM THE OUTSIDE, THE MAIN BRICK BUILDING OF Cardach looked like it originated in the Glory Years. Inside was a completely different scene. There was only a single room with the same brick walls showing; everything else had been gutted. There were three long trestle tables that formed a U. A fire burned in the center, venting through a large hole in the roof.

The fire kept the place warm enough that I would've shed Callon's jacket under normal circumstances. Rex's wives, all *five* of them, were dressed similarly as they sat in a line to his left. Callon was to Rex's right, and I'd been shoved in between Callon and Dax. Koz, Hess, and Zink were farther down one of the side tables, which may or may not have indicated their value in Rex's eyes.

Young men came around, filling the bowls and plates that were in front of us while I leaned back out of vision range, thankful for the extra-wide tables.

Callon and I only had one plate and bowl in front of us. There were stews of some sort, one soupier and in the bowl. The other was more of a blob that oozed. Neither looked very good, but the smell made me salivate. But were they mine or his? Considering my earlier treatment, I wasn't sure they even fed women around here.

Callon was turned, speaking to Rex. "No other sightings?"

I couldn't hear what Rex said over the din of chatter and eating, and I wasn't hungry enough to interrupt.

"Partners share a plate," Dax said from my other side, pointing to the food in front of us.

I looked about the group and saw several other couples sharing. "Thanks."

Callon was still busy talking to Rex, so I slid the plate, which was closest to me, over and began devouring it with the single spoon provided. It was as good as it smelled. I finished half the plate before switching to the bowl.

The only thing threatening to ruin my appetite was the way Dax's eyes were burning my skin as he pretended to not look at me. I'd thought he wasn't a starer, but I'd been fooled. I had a long history with the no-look starer, people who pretended to be gazing at everything else when the only thing they were actually watching was you. He'd probably counted every misplaced hair on my head by now while he pretended to be amused by the fire dancers who'd begun performing.

I wished I could feign such interest in the dancers. Circus acts didn't do it for me, and the memories that came along with them made it hard to pretend otherwise. They reminded me of Baryn. He'd always been looking for off-the-beaten-path amusements. The sicker and twisted, the better, even if Baryn had to contribute to get them down to his standards. It was ingrained in me to fear that one of the dancers would trip and be badly burned because of an ill-placed item.

"How long have you been with Callon?" Dax asked, jerking me roughly from memories that had begun to swallow me whole.

"Just a while," I said, keeping it sparse and depriving the conversation of any oxygen so it might die a quick death. I shifted my chair slightly closer to Callon.

"He didn't mention you specifically in any of his messages. I was merely curious," Dax said, now trans-fixed on the way I held my fork.

"You'd have to ask him about that." I put the fork down and replaced it with the tankard of ale in front of Callon.

"Do you always do that?" Dax asked.

"What?" Was I eating weird or something?

His eyes narrowed and he leaned closer, pointing at my lips. "That. You roll your bottom lip in and bite it when you're unsure."

I stopped biting instantly. I leaned back the same distance he'd just leaned forward.

"No, I don't." Did I do that all the time? I had no idea. I'd never noticed. Better question, why did *he* notice? Why was he paying such close attention to me? In a room with thirty or forty people, there had to be someone more interesting who wanted to participate in conversation.

"Am I making you uncomfortable?" Dax asked, drop-ping all pretense of eating or looking anywhere else.

Callon tensed on the other side of me, as if nerves were a cold you could catch.

"Of course not." The last thing I'd admit to the person trying to unsettle me was that he was succeeding.

I might not have seen or done that many things in life, but I had a stellar education on being at a disadvantage.

"Your mannerisms remind me of someone." His gaze locked on me; he wasn't even trying to pretend he was distracted by the entertainers anymore.

"Thank you for the dinner, Rex, but we've had a long trip," Callon said. There was a rough timbre to his voice, like roughened nerves had chafed his vocal cords.

Guess he wasn't enjoying the dinner either. I was about to jump up, insisting "my man" needed me to attend him like the good little woman I really wasn't. Callon grabbed my hand before I had to bother. He pulled me up with him as Rex was nodding his goodbye.

"Of course," Rex said.

Callon had already looped his arm around my waist, pulling me close, as he nodded to some of the other people in the room. He steered us away from the table without a glance at Dax.

"Are you all right?" he asked as we put some distance between the feast and us.

"I'm fine. Are you?" I asked. I thought I'd had a bad dinner. What had Rex said to trigger the beast?

"Yes," he said through clenched teeth, not looking at me. The question might as well have been "Are you planning on killing someone tonight?" with the way he answered.

We made it back to the room, the fire already tended to, my cleaned leathers lying on the bed. Relieved to have one worry off my mind, I turned to study Callon. I took in the hard lines, the tendon that ran down his neck and seemed to merge into the ridge that made up his shoulders. I backed away until we were on opposite sides of the room.

His chest rose and fell a few times before the tension softened a little.

I took a step forward, waffled, and took a half step back. It had nothing to do with fear and everything to do with control. He was teetering on the edge of it, and I knew how that felt, how badly you sometimes needed space in those moments. The thing that bothered me most was that I didn't know why he was like this.

"Are you all right?" I asked.

"Yes."

He might be now, but he definitely wasn't a few minutes ago. Still, it had gotten me out of that dining hall. I should let it rest and be grateful.

My fingers played with the edge of his coat I still wore. "Did he say something about the Magician? Does he know something about the meeting tomorrow?"

Callon's gaze went to my hands. "No. It was a personal matter. Not important."

I let the subject drop. I wasn't delusional enough to think we were at a place where I could press the issue. Personal confessions would not be on the menu. Most days, we barely talked.

Callon's frame went rigid again. A second later, there was a knock at the door.

Callon walked over and answered, "Not a good time."

"I didn't mean to upset Teddy at dinner. She did something that reminded me of Dal, and it caught me off guard." Dax's gaze shot over Callon's shoulder to me for the briefest moment.

"Not right—"

"Who's Dal?" I asked.

Callon looked over at me, his hand still on the door, ready to shut it in Dax's face. I didn't know what had set Callon off, or why I'd gotten so uptight either, but I knew we needed this man tomorrow. Callon couldn't drive him away, not now, even if I wanted him to.

Truth was that I didn't want Callon to drive him away. All Dax had done was ask me a couple of questions, and I'd gotten my back up. I'd walked into the feast like a warrior walked into battle, waiting for an attack. When I hadn't gotten one, I'd imagined it. I might've lost the visible scars of my abuse, but the real ones were still carved into my soul and always would be. That didn't mean I'd let them rule the rest of my life if I could help it. The Dax guy had ten more beasts hiding in the woods for the confrontation tomorrow. I wasn't letting him go anywhere until things were normal between us again.

"She's my wife," Dax said. He loved her. It was in the way his voice softened when he spoke of her.

I'd let my unease at the feast heighten my reactions, but I'd been right about this guy. There was an honesty in his face, his voice.

I took a few steps toward the pair of men, both of them watching every step I took.

"I'm sorry if I was short with you. You didn't do anything wrong. I'm on edge." I wrapped Callon's jacket a little more firmly around me.

Dax nodded. "Understandable."

Callon moved his shoulder a little more toward me.

"Truce?" I asked, and then held my hand out to Dax. It was the first time I'd willingly touched a stranger since I could remember.

"Of course," he said, as he grasped my hand.

I glanced at Callon, his eyes a nice, calm hazel. He opened the door a few inches wider. "Come in."

Dax walked in slowly, as if I were a spooked horse that might stampede away.

"You never told me how you managed this meeting," Dax said, looking from Callon to me. "I saw the way you tried to steer clear of people at the feast. You've got Plaguer blood, don't you?" His eyes shot to my hand.

Although they had all but phased out that marking by the time I was born, I knew what he was looking for. A scarred P burned onto the top of my right hand that would indicate I'd survived the Bloody Death. The practice of marking Plaguers had originated back in Newco, long before I was born. If someone managed to survive the Bloody Death, which was almost never, and they weren't killed by those around them who feared a contagion, the kindest outcome was to be scarred with the letter P.

You were an outcast for the rest of your days, if you weren't rounded up into an asylum-type jail. I didn't know what my mother had gone through, but it had been known she was a Plaguer when she sold me. People didn't normally announce that, so she might've had the mark. Although I'd been sold for whatever magic I'd prove to have, so maybe she did announce it.

"No, I'm not. My mother was. Her magic passed down to me."

Dax's eyes narrowed. "A lot of Plaguers I've met have trouble bearing children. We don't have much information. I didn't know that the talents passed down in that way."

"As opposed to another way?" I asked, catching the unsaid alternative.

"As opposed to *our* way," Callon said.

It took a minute before what they were both saying clicked. And once it did, it didn't lock down tightly.

I turned to Callon. "Wait, beasts are born to Plaguers?"

"As far as we know," Callon said.

Dax scratched his chin. "The sex of the person must alter the way it expresses."

It made as much sense as putting an apple in a bowl beside a pear, but suddenly I felt like I belonged, because we were all fruit. It was a connection when I was used to having none. A link to a shared past. Like, maybe, just maybe, I'd been meant to end up with these people? The same thing that had changed me had changed them. In a completely different way, but it bonded us somehow.

Callon walked to the door and opened it before Koz had to knock.

"Heard there was a meeting going on?" Koz joked as he entered. Hess and Zink came in behind him. I nodded at the guys, even smiling as Zink passed me.

Zink's gaze skimmed over me, as if he was about to ignore the smile directed at him, but he couldn't seem to get past it.

"What?" he asked, as if he suspected I'd stuffed his socks with leeches or something equally heinous.

"Nothing." I continued to smile. Of all the people, Zink was the last beast I'd explain my reasons to. Still, he was my people, so even if I disliked him a lot, I was going to make an effort henceforth to be cordial. Until I couldn't stand it, anyway.

Zink sneered and made his way to where Koz was scribbling on a paper he'd brought, discussing war plans for tomorrow. I barely heard him. I had one thought on my mind: what were Dax's stakes in the game ahead? It was the only way to know how easily he'd fold or how hard he'd hold his ground when we met the Magician tomorrow. Had the Magician killed someone he loved? Was he here for vengeance or for sport?

I inched my way over to Dax's side, determined to get some answers. I didn't get a chance. He lobbed a doozy at me first, and in the process stopped all other conversations in the room.

"You're the one the Magician has been looking for, aren't you?" Dax asked.

Callon's eyes blazed, and there was an immediate friction in the room. I reached a hand out toward Callon, laying it on his forearm.

I'd regrouped. I could handle this. We both had questions and both deserved answers.

"Tell me first why you're willing to get in this fight," I said.

Dax smiled slightly. "I have no secrets, at least not among friends. The Magician runs Newco. If he'd stay there, I'd leave well enough alone. But he's not. He's been slowly expanding south, and he doesn't plan on stopping until he makes it down the southeastern coast, where my home is, where my wife sleeps at night. This is my fight too. If I can take him out now, it'll be easier than dealing with his troops later."

Again, it came back to his wife. It was why I believed him.

"And if we do kill the Magician, what about the person who takes his place?" I asked. Chopping off the head of this snake would solve my problem, but another one always grew back.

"The fear of the Magician is what keeps most in line," Dax said. "Once he's gone, his replacement will be too busy trying to keep control of the territory they have to think of expanding."

"We hope, anyway," Callon said, moving to stand behind me but calm again. Callon's moods lately were getting more unpredictable than mine.

Dax was waiting for an answer to his question. He wouldn't ask again, but if we were going into battle together, I was going to have to trust him. He'd probably hear tomorrow anyway, right?

"I'm the one he's after," I said. Callon's hand moved to my shoulder.

Dax didn't miss it either, glancing there before he said, "I've heard rumors of what you can do. I was wondering how we were going to kill him once we got him."

"I can and I will, given the chance," I said. "I'd rather not get into specifics, but it's true. I have an odd relationship with the living and the dead."

Dax laughed. "You know, you looked a little meek before, but I might've misjudged you. You certainly don't shy away from blood, and that's not an insult."

"I'm going through a bit of split personality at the moment. I'm fairly certain the person who's winning is the one who'll rip the Magician's head from his body without hesitation."

The room laughed. I wasn't sure why that was so funny, but it was better than the tension of a few moments ago.

"Tomorrow, hang back until I give the signal," Callon said. "If we can get a clear shot at him, we take him down. Teddy will finish him off."

Dax nodded. "Can't wait. We'll be there," he said, before nodding at the rest of the guys and exiting our room.

Koz pocketed his paper and then left with Zink and Hess.

Callon shut the door and turned to me, a finger to his lips. I'd forgotten that there was a new set of ears that could listen in.

Callon stood by the door, as if he were listening to Dax walk away. It was altogether possible, and a bit alarming when you thought about it.

He finally turned his full attention back to me, giving the all-clear sign.

"Do you trust him or not?" I asked. Callon was the one who'd invited Dax, but I couldn't tell one minute from the next whether he trusted the guy or not. I thought we should, but Callon had barely let Dax in the room earlier.

His brow furrowed. "I trust him with my life."

Okey-dokey, then. Callon being hot and cold with the guy wasn't helping my trust issues any. I might be in the same bowl of fruit with them, but I was fresh from the vine and hadn't thoroughly checked out the rest of the pieces for rotten apples yet. I trusted one person, Tuesday, and it would stay that way, even if she weren't fruit, maybe closer to a veggie.

"Koz mentioned we're meeting the Magician near one of those Hell Pits. Do you think Dax will get weird if—"

"If he knew the mud followed you around? I don't know, but it doesn't matter because he's not going to know. When we get there, you're going to steer clear of it." Callon walked to the bed, grabbed a pillow off it, and then stretched out on the rug beside it.

"Glad we're on the same page, then." I walked around him and climbed onto the bed, staying close enough to the edge that I could keep an eye on him in case he tried to leave.

NINE

I should've tied Callon to me with a rope last night. He was gone, and I was about to go crazy. Didn't he know you should at least leave a note? He'd either been abducted, which couldn't be that easy to do, or he'd be back, because his bag was still here. Still, he'd been gone for an hour.

There was a bang at the door before it swung open. Callon walked in and grabbed his bag.

"Are you ready?" he asked, as if I hadn't been sitting there ready for a good twenty minutes.

"Yes," I said, while I squinted and shook my head. Lips pursed, I grabbed my bag and walked from the room. *Are you ready?* That was what he said on possibly the worst morning of my life after he went missing?

Hess, Zink, and Koz were waiting outside. I gave them the friendliest nod I was capable of and continued walking. I was going the right way because there was only one exit out of this place of spikes.

The guys caught up to me easily.

"Why's she all pissed off?" Hess asked.

"It's probably where we're headed," Koz said. "I wouldn't be in a good mood either. Actually, I think it sucks, too."

The meeting with the Magician was only the half of it, but I couldn't complain about Callon out loud. They'd side with him anyway, even if I was right.

Callon overtook me and passed through the gate first, taking the lead. At least I didn't have to break my silence to ask where we were going. I could stew in my own thoughts without having to mind the direction.

And stewing was only the beginning. By the time we'd walked fifteen minutes, my stew was boiling and overcooked. Why had I wanted to get this meeting with the Magician over with so quickly? I should've stalled for time.

After thirty minutes, my stew was burned and leaving a horrible taste in my mouth. I was a complete idiot and was going to die, probably today. The only thing that pulled me from my thoughts was when the unmistakable smell of a Hell Pit hit me like a fist to the nose. The Hell Pit was the easiest landmark with which to coordinate the meeting, but that didn't mean I liked it.

A few more steps and a gap in the trees opened up. Its size took my breath away, which might've been a good thing, considering the smell wasn't getting any better. The strangest part about it: my crows seemed to be flocking around even more than usual.

Hess stepped closer to it. "It's really spread."

"We can't worry about it now," Callon said, and nodded toward a small pasture twenty feet or so away.

He glanced at me. *Stay clear of the mud* was coming through loud and clear.

I didn't need the warning. I wasn't getting anywhere close to that stuff. We didn't want anyone seeing anything funny.

Callon's head went up. "They're coming."

The guys fell in around me, Callon's position and attention giving away their direction.

Fuck. Fuck. Fuck. What if they couldn't pin down the Magician? What if they could and I couldn't kill him? And were we alone? Where was Dax? Was he out there with the other men? He was supposed to be, but I hadn't seen anyone else. Was he late?

Either way, I was going down fighting. At dinner last night I'd lapsed into old habits, backing off scared, as if I had no option but to cower and retreat. I wouldn't again. I wasn't that girl anymore. I refused to be, and I'd remind myself as many times as needed.

I could be as tough as nails, but I still needed them to pin the Magician down. Where was our backup?

"Are the others here?" I whispered.

"They won't be seen until they need to be," Callon said from in front of me.

I wasn't always quick on the draw, but that made sense. If the Magician saw Dax, it was going to be right before he was killed—at least, I hoped so.

"*You* need to stay calm because *I* need to stay calm," Callon said. His voice sounded like someone had gone over his vocal cords with a steel file.

Now I was going to be blamed for him getting uptight? I had enough on my plate with the shit I did do.

I'd opened my mouth to blast him for blaming me for more things when Zink edged in closer.

"Perhaps you could have this argument at another time? They're coming." Zink gave me a stare that called me a liability.

Zink, with all his grumpiness, could come in handy. The Magician was coming. I needed to prioritize and keep my fights in order. First the Magician, then Zink, then Callon.

"How many?" I asked no one in particular.

"I'd say about twenty, but I think they've got more following a bit farther behind," Callon said.

The Magician, plus twenty we could see. Then there were more? The place seemed quiet enough, but this was one crowded forest.

I could kill. I knew that. But kill en masse? It wasn't that I didn't have the stomach for it. From the stories I'd already heard of what this man wanted to do to me, I'd kill every person he sent and not lose an ounce of sleep. But would I be capable of it? I wasn't sure. I'd only killed one man at a time. Then there was the problem of their lives. If I sucked them up like a vacuum, did I have a max capacity? Issy's basket in the kitchen could only hold so many eggs. What if I could only hold a couple of lives at a time? Would they explode out of me if I didn't dump them somewhere?

The sounds of a group walking became loud enough for human ears, and my gut knotted. The moment had come. Do or die, and I wasn't sure I could do either. I might not have the chops to kill him. The Magician might keep me from dying. All I could do was hope

Callon was right, that if we did lose, the Magician would kill me.

The Magician approached, looking like an unassuming middle-aged man, with thinning salt-and-pepper hair and a paunch in the center to go with it. Even his clothes were plain, drab weaves in a grey or brown. I wasn't sure, since not even the color could distinguish itself.

And yet he stirred up fear in all who met him, myself included. The man who'd planned on debilitating me so that there'd never be a chance of escape. Then he would've used me over and over again until I wished for death.

I tried to slow my breathing, which was becoming so loud that you didn't need beast ears to hear. My heart was trying to flee my chest and make a run for it, since its human was too stupid to do the same. Still, I kept my head up and my shoulders straight and tried to put on the best show I could with the parts of me that would respond.

The Magician's mob, for lack of a better word, slowly filed in behind him, all thugs in uniforms. I wondered if he'd upgraded them. Would this group be more loyal, or would they run as fast as the others had once there'd been signs of trouble?

They stopped about thirty feet away. He took a couple steps forward without his group, and then Callon did the same. I thought about following suit. Zink on my right and Hess on my left moved infinitesimal steps closer to me, penning me in more, as if they knew. It was clear they had orders to take me down if I acted on instinct.

If they tried, I'd have to let them. I couldn't kill them. They were on my side of the line, and we were already short on numbers. I also wasn't ready to be tackled to the ground and go down like a sack of potatoes. With no choice left, I fisted my hands and stayed where I was.

"I'm glad we could meet here in peace," the Magician said.

"Sure," Callon responded. Unlike the Magician, who could pull off a fake statement like that, Callon's single-word reply rang false.

"As Teddy's representative, may we speak in private for a moment?" The Magician waved his hand to a spot still neutral but out of earshot. "I think it would be in all of our best interests if we discussed this privately."

Maybe he wanted to offer a deal and didn't want to shame himself in front of his people?

"I want to hear him out," I said softly, hoping Callon would listen, since I knew he'd heard.

Callon moved his head slightly to the side before he said, "Fine."

It took all my control to stand still. I was near vibrating from the need to confront this myself. This was about me and I wasn't going to be invited to the talks? It was almost more galling.

"He wants you. Putting you that close to him would be idiotic," Zink said, with a glance at my tapping foot.

"You better tell me everything being said or I swear I'm following him. If you think you're going to tackle me, I'll suck the life out of you until all you have left is enough to keep breathing. And remember, I'm a novice, so I might not succeed in leaving you even that much." I'd laced my words with venom.

Zink stared back like I was your garden-variety slug. "Chill your horses. I'll tell you what they're saying. No need for the dramatics."

I didn't have time to argue further with Zink. Callon was standing in front of the Magician.

"Well?"

Zink sighed loudly, as if his new duty was already annoying him. "Magician is giving him fake nice to see you bullshit."

The Magician's face turned red.

"Callon told him to—"

"Go fuck himself? I figured that one out on my own," I said.

The Magician coughed a few times before his lips began moving again.

I gave Zink enough time to hear before he relayed it. Telling me made it harder to listen, but it killed me to stand there and not know.

Zink angled his head toward me, his voice softer this time. "He's asking for a partial split of possession of you. Callon told him to fuck off again." Zink laughed a little after that one.

Part time? Was this some weird setup? It didn't make any sense.

I was in the lag of Zink listening again when a glimmer in the distance caught my attention. I narrowed my eyes, trying to focus better and make out what it was in between the feet of the Magician's mob. It would appear and then disappear, a twinkling here and there. If this was a setup, did it include all of us? Had they brought something magical to kill us?

I sucked in a breath. Holy mother of all in the Wilds. It was a stream of mud from the Hells Pit.

Callon's voice rose, but I couldn't drag my eyes from the weaving path of mud as it curved around the Magician's people. No one seemed to be paying it any mind as it crept slowly toward where the Magician stood.

I moved an inch forward for a better angle, and Zink shot me a look intended to get me back in line. What he didn't know about me would fill that Hell Pit in the distance. I gave him a look back and held my ground.

When I didn't move again, Zink turned back to give Callon and the Magician his full attention. I had eyes for the mud alone. What was it doing? If I weren't crazy, I'd say it was heading for the Magician, but that was too weird. Was he going to use it somehow? Were these Hell Pits of his doing? No, that didn't make any sense. We'd chosen this location. So what was going on?

Nothing good. Of that I was sure.

Zink turned my way again, more concerned this time when he realized I wasn't bugging him for a play-by-play. He was slow but he was catching on. There was another threat looming that his big, bad self had missed.

Part of me wanted someone else to see what was happening, even if it were Zink. Not wanting to point, I used my eyes to signal him in the direction of the impending threat. He followed my lead, scanning the area.

His forehead wrinkled and his eyes narrowed. He glanced back at me, a question there, as if he couldn't quite believe what he was seeing either. I nodded. We both watched the stream that could only be an inch wide, maybe not even that, continue to make its way toward the Magician.

Zink made a strange clicking noise that was barely audible above the wind blowing through the trees. Ranks closed in around me by another small degree. I hoped that was precautionary and not because he thought that shit was coming for me.

The weird mud was on the move. Maybe *we* needed to be on the move too. But the more I watched it, the more I didn't think I was its target.

Callon was still arguing with the Magician. All I cared about was watching the winding mud. It took precedence over all else, because I was suddenly realizing there might be a bigger threat among us.

What if it wasn't heading for the Magician? What if it was going for Callon?

I went to move again, and Zink grabbed my hand. "Wait this out," he whispered.

I tugged my hand from his grasp. "Callon."

"He knows. He's watching."

I turned my attention back to the mud, warring with myself whether I should be listening to Zink. Callon continued to talk to the Magician as if nothing were amiss. He *must've* heard the warning.

The mud was almost to where Callon and the Magician stood, so either way, this situation was going to blow up soon.

The mud made it to the Magician and began forming a circle where he stood while Callon continued to speak to him. Callon had to see it now. He was too observant not to. But the Magician was too focused on Callon to realize.

It wasn't until it began to climb the Magician's boots that one of his people finally noticed. I caught sight of one girl nudging the man standing beside her and pointing. More whispers, more pointing. But no one said a word to the oblivious Magician.

The Magician was in the middle of speaking when he looked down. The mud was making its way up his lower legs now, and he must've felt something slithering once it came over the top of his boots.

Callon took a step back, his job done. The Magician tried to lift one leg but couldn't. He tried the other, but he seemed to be glued to the ground.

"What is this?" he asked, his voice rising, as if Callon had laid a trap for him,

"It's not of my making," Callon said. His voice was so cold that the temperature could've dropped another degree as the words carried across the clearing.

The Magician made jerking motions with his legs as he thrashed about with his arms, trying to reach for something to help pull him free. There was nothing to grab. Callon had dropped back out of reach, and none of the Magician's people made any attempt to approach him.

The top half of the Magician turned to smoke, but then sputtered out like wet wood trying to catch flame and failing. He was anchored by the mud climbing up his legs.

"Help me! Cut me free or drag me away from this." He turned at his waist, looking back at his people, as he slowly lost the ability to move his legs at all. "I command you to help me!"

Their response was to back away farther. The more the Magician screamed, the farther they moved.

He spun back to us, the thick scent of desperation warring for prominence over the putrid smell of the Hell Pit.

"Help me! I'll give you anything you want. You can have Newco. Anything," he yelled to Callon.

Callon shook his head and then continued to back away until he was beside us.

Part of me wanted to run from the horror of what was happening. A larger part of me was as glued to the ground as the Magician, watching the mud slowly creep farther up his body. If this stuff was going to kill him, what a vile death to have, and yet such a deserving end.

It climbed up his torso and then moved down his arms. It wound up his neck. He wouldn't have too much longer before it covered his face. Was it planning on suffocating him?

"Help." He kept repeating that plea. For a moment, I almost wanted to. To watch someone die like this was almost too much. But how did you fight against a thing you didn't understand? I wouldn't get close enough to risk my own life for his, even to give him a quick end. It didn't seem as if anyone else was willing to either.

The mud began to cover his face, and he stopped screaming, keeping his lips sealed as he tried to block it from getting inside his mouth. It didn't matter. It crept up his face, into his nostrils, his ears, over his eyes. The mud swallowed him whole until the only thing left was a vague outline of his shape.

I'd barely kept my breathing in check when the mud seemed to shift, morphing around his body until it seemed to form a hand. A hand that was pointing in our direction.

As if orchestrated, everyone there, the Magician's people and us, realized this was the moment to run.

I took off. Koz sprinted past me. Callon fell in beside me, and a pair of hands threw me onto his back, where I clung for dear life. Hess and Zink took up the rear.

A low rumble grew, shaking the earth and echoing through the trees. The rumble turned into a deafening growl. No one looked back.

TEN

WE DIDN'T STOP FOR A GOOD HOUR OF RUNNING. IT wasn't a leisurely jog, either. It was fast and unrelenting. If it had been up to me, we would've still been going. I wasn't sure if a place existed far enough away from what we'd seen today.

Now we stood here in silence, our tents and bags all abandoned when we'd taken off for dear life. I looked about our group and saw varying degrees of the same shock and horror I was feeling. Had that really happened? We had started the day prepared for a battle against the Magician and his people. Instead we witnessed the end to one monster, only to give rise to an even greater terror. What was that shit? Whatever it was, it wasn't mud.

There was one question I could get answered. I turned to Zink. "How did you know it was going for the Magician?"

Zink took a chug from his water bottle, one of the

only things he'd kept. "It snuck up on him like a predator would, stalking, staying as small as possible until the last moment, when it struck," he said, the shock robbing him of his normal bitterness toward me.

Hess was shaking his head. "Whatever that is, it's not mud. That's for damn sure."

"Well, at least the Magician is no longer a problem. That's something, right?" I asked, afraid to peek over at Callon, who was remaining uncomfortably quiet. I could guess why. I'd hoped it was my imagination or paranoia that had made me think it was leaning toward us, toward me. But all the hope in the world wasn't going to change the fact that I had been its next target. Callon knew it too.

When we ran, its howl had churned my blood and curdled it right on the spot. Callon was realizing he wasn't stuck with the girl the Magician wanted anymore. He was stuck with the girl that monstrosity wanted. For a while there, I'd thought our wrong deeds had been some-what balanced. That thing had just put a boulder on my side of the scale.

"I'd rather deal with the Magician," Zink said, all the bitterness crashing back a thousand-fold.

Hess turned to me. "Did you see what that thing did? The way it leaned in our direction?"

It wasn't a coincidence that he directed that question to me. He'd seen it too. We all had.

"It was pointing at her," Zink said, staring at me.

Koz glanced my way, remaining quiet, more pity than condemnation in his eyes.

Hess cleared his throat, as if he weren't sure what else he should be saying at this moment.

Callon, who'd been lingering a little farther away, walked back to the center of our group. "We don't know if it was pointing at her."

Zink didn't argue, but I knew what he was thinking. We were all thinking it. The mud from one of the Hell Pits had followed me before. There was a high likelihood it was me it was pointing at. There was an old saying that if something quacked like a duck, it was a duck. Well, this thing was quacking like all its feathers were being plucked beside a spit and a roaring fire.

There was rustling in the trees that didn't make anyone jump except me. Callon gave me a shake of his head, as if to say it was all right. Sure enough, Dax stepped into the clearing a few seconds later.

He stopped and looked around, all of us with matching wide eyes and varying degrees of gaping jaws still.

He shook his head before he finally spoke. "I've seen some shit in my life, but nothing like that." He shook his head again, as if that might settle something in his brain and make this puzzle fall into place.

"Where are your guys?" Callon asked.

"Heading home. I told them I'd catch up." Dax was a man that didn't appear to rattle easy, but as he ran a hand over his hair, I'd say he'd been shaken up like a rattlesnake's tail right before a strike.

"Do you know what the fuck that was?" Hess asked.

Dax scratched a shaded jaw. I wasn't sure if it was always darkened, he was coming off a few rough days, or it was just another mark of the beast. They seemed to sprout hair faster than human men. "I have a little knowledge of where they might've started. I'm willing to share if you've the stomach for it." Dax was looking at me as he made his last remark.

"You'd be amazed by the things I can stomach. Don't hold back," I said. I had more of a vested interest than anyone here.

Dax smiled, but it was fleeting and gone before he began talking. "Have you ever seen people that have a black mist around them? That's how they look to Plaguers, and since you have the gift of vision, you might be able to see it too. They're called Dark Walkers."

"No." The term Dark Walkers chimed in some distant memory, settled in somewhere between the old stories of beasts eating babies and winged demons that came out at night and stole virgins. I'd never thought they were real, but I was now certain it was going to be the case.

"Long story short, there were two ancient races that had a conflict of interest. When they warred, one race cursed the other so that they couldn't walk in the light anymore. The only way they could survive was to wear the skins of people who had a certain natural magic in them. The easiest way to find these people was to weed them out with a disease. That disease was the Bloody Death. The people, as I'm sure you're guessing, came to be known as Plaguers.

"The Dark Walkers would clothe themselves with the skins of these Plaguers, but the magic would only keep the skins alive and fresh for so long until they'd need another one. When the skins they wore went bad, they'd 'shed' them. I have reason to believe that these Hell Pits originated from the places that the Dark Walkers shed their skins."

"How sure are you about this?" Callon asked.

I was glad he could still talk. I was on overload. My brain couldn't handle much more after finding out these creatures destroyed an entire civilization so that they could rob a select few people of their skins. Billions of people dead so they could harvest flesh. At least it made sense why they smelled like pits of rotting bodies. I'd bragged about what I could stomach, and Dax had certainly taken me at my word.

The only thing that kept me standing there listening was fear that if I fainted now, no one would ever want to give me the truth again. If every time you heard an unpleasant truth, you dropped to the floor and played possum, people would leave you out of the loop. I knew because I'd do it too. Life was too short to be waving around smelling salts all day. I couldn't afford to be left out of the loop this time.

That didn't mean I wouldn't mind a chair. I'd kill for one, but I stayed standing, pretending I was made of iron, even as I caught Callon's glance that made me think my color might have lost a shade or two and my bones resembled something closer to glass.

Dax's head was shaking again as he was staring off into the distance. "As far as what happened? I'm guessing some of the Dark Walkers' powers shed along with the skins, blending with the Plaguer magic. I believe something that wasn't planned has mutated in these areas." He shrugged and threw up a hand. "But it's all just guesses."

None of us said anything for a few seconds, because

when you talked about mud pits from hell that were really dark magic shifting into a monster, well, it could rob you for words if you really gave it some deep thought.

Dax shrugged again, a mental hands up in the air. "At least we don't have to deal with the Magician anymore."

Finally someone else saw the teeny-tiny silver lining here besides me. I knew I'd liked this guy for a reason.

Dax turned his full attention to me. "Any idea why it was interested in you?"

"We don't know what it was pointing at," Callon said, jumping in before I had an opportunity to answer. On very rare occasions, his controlling nature had an upside. Although I didn't think sticking to denial was helping right now. The shit had pointed at me. It yelled in agony when I left. We were way past denial and definitely into the bargaining stage.

Dax switched his attention to Callon, looking a little like Zink had a few moments ago. "It was pointing right at her."

"It might've been pointing at all of us," Callon said, taking a step toward Dax.

Oh, for fuck's sake. Callon had to give it up. If I didn't believe the bullshit, and I was the one with the most to gain from sticking my head in the sand, nobody else was going to go along with it.

"I don't know why it wants me," I told Dax, destroying Callon's pretense. That weird mud was coming for me and there was no point in denying it. It might as well have said my name. Who knows, maybe that growl we'd heard was mud-speak for *"I'm coming for you, Teddy."*

Callon didn't say a word, but his expression charred me where I stood. I tried to shoot flames out of my eyes back at him. Mine must have sizzled out on the voyage, because he seemed unfazed.

Dax looked pointedly at Callon. "I'll keep what happened under wraps, but there were a lot of witnesses. That thing wanted her and we all saw it. Look, if you can make the trip out to the farm, I think you should come see Bitters. He might be able to help."

"Bitters is still alive?" Callon asked, finally breaking off his stare of death aimed at me.

Bitters? I knew that name. I'd heard him mentioned before. Wasn't that the guy who made up weird riddles?

What was that thing the witch Hecate had told us he'd said? *When the dark trickery rises, the beast must dance among the shadows of death. As the world shudders with wounds unhealed, the reckoning will come at the cost of souls.* Yeah, still made no bloody sense.

"That wizard will outlive us all," Dax said. "He might be old and crazy, but he knows a few things. If that shit wanted me or one of my people, I'd be looking for answers anywhere I could get them."

"You're a lot closer to Newco. Is that a good idea?" Koz asked.

Dax turned to Koz. "There might be some who don't believe the Magician is truly gone and want to curry favor. My guess? Once they believe it's final, you won't hear from them again. They won't want to follow in his footsteps."

"Is it final?" I asked. Yes, the Magician had gotten swallowed by the Hell Pit, but that didn't mean he was definitely dead, did it? I had learned very well that death was a blurrier line than most believed. Like, some real grey shit that wasn't anywhere near as dependable as people gave it credit for.

Dax turned back to me. "I had the luxury of hanging back another couple minutes, since I wasn't in the direct line of fire. I'd say that was about as final as you get. The mud collapsed back into itself and then puddled on the ground. There was no trace of a body left in its place, or one that would revive, at any rate. I'd bet my life that he's gone for good."

What a relief that would've been if a thing dubbed a Hell Pit hadn't replaced him.

"I'm going to head out. I'll send word if anything changes near me." Dax's eyes darted toward me before he took off.

Callon turned back to us. "We keep this quiet at the lodge until we know more. I don't want mass hysteria that a lake of mud moving in our direction is capable of killing people." Callon looked about our small group for nods.

Zink and Hess went along with the request quickly. Koz and I looked at each other, with the same obvious conflict of interest. Callon would have to settle for quiet-ish. There was no way I wasn't telling Tuesday about this. It was too serious by far.

Koz and I cracked at the same time, both of us saying, "I'm going to have to—"

"Tell Tuesday," I said, finishing for us both.

Callon was scowling. Koz straightened his shoulders, but there was a little bowing in his spine. His forehead wrinkled up like a newborn baby as he prepared to with-stand the wrath.

As soon as Callon shook his head a couple times, it was obvious he was going to cave. "If she says a word, it's on you two."

Tuesday wasn't so hot with secrets. I'd have to avoid her until Koz got to her first. Then I'd reap the benefits of being able to talk it over with her without the burden of keeping her quiet. Win-win for me, and I needed a win in a bad way right now.

———

THE TRIP BACK TO THE LODGE WASN'T ANYWHERE AS leisurely as the trip there had been. We barely stopped. When I was too tired to walk, Callon carried me on his back. When I was going too slow, Callon carried me on his back. When I begged to stop for a minute, Callon ignored me and carried me on his back. You'd think a piggyback wouldn't be so bad until you couldn't feel anything south of your kneecaps.

There was no talking or jesting to break up the misery, either. It was straight suffering. The tension had been bad before, but not like this. On the way there, we'd known our enemy and knew we might be able to defeat him. What was coming now was a complete enigma. How did you fight this?

But that wasn't the worst of it. I could feel Callon's muscles bunched underneath me, and they hadn't relaxed once. It had been like holding on to a stone the entire trip back, and it wasn't the strain of carrying me.

When we finally got to the edge of our territory and he stopped, I was ready and waiting. There was a fight brewing. I slid to the ground and then grabbed a tree, cursing and stamping my feet, praying the feeling would come back soon.

"We'll meet you at the house," Callon said to the guys.

Oh, there was definitely a fight brewing. If I'd known why, it would've helped me prepare, but as always, there were so many things it could be.

The guys barely nodded before they took off like there were burning coals beneath their feet. I was left to burn in Callon's gaze. He waited for them to get out of earshot, which prolonged the anticipation and made me wonder if there was anything secret at the lodge, or were there always a set of ears listening?

He tilted his head slightly in the direction of home before he turned toward me.

"Why did you tell Dax the Hell Pit was coming for you after I'd denied it? Did you not think I had a reason?" The tone, the angle of his head, even the way he ran his hand through his hair before resting his palm on the back of his neck—it all screamed *brawl*. I was ready.

He wanted to tell me where to go, and now he thought he was going to tell me what to say? And to what end? The jig was up. Everyone there knew. There would be no hiding it.

"He already knew. There was no point in denying it. It was obvious to every single person there."

"I stood there and denied it to everyone, and you

couldn't keep your mouth shut to save your own ass." His eyes flamed red.

I was exhausted and here he was, dangling the beast like a red candy apple in front of a kid with a sweet tooth. If he shifted, maybe he'd take me up to that cave? Man, I could really use a good sleep, and I was doomed without him. I'd just added another monster to the horde waiting for me to shut my eyes at night.

Maybe I could push Callon over the edge? There had to be a way. What would do it?

I stepped closer, crowding him. "That was your friend, your ally. If I can't be honest with him, maybe I shouldn't trust your judgment? Do you even know what you're doing?" I'd wanted to set him off, but that might have been a little more dynamite than I needed.

His eyes narrowed, as if he were warring between killing me and asking me if I'd lost my mind. I was asking myself the very same thing.

But if I pushed even harder, would it make him shift? Most people would call me insane, absolutely fucking bonkers for trying to lure the beast out. Those same people also slept when they crawled into a bed. Nothing was scarier than fighting for another night of sleep, and the beast was right there, right below the surface, and ready to give me what I needed.

"What? Did you not hear me?" I moved forward and slapped both of my hands against his chest.

His eyes flared; his skin burned under his shirt. I could feel a rumble in his chest.

He turned and was gone.

Dammit. That wasn't what was supposed to happen. He was supposed to take me *with* him. Now not only would I not get sleep, I had to walk the rest of the way to the lodge on my own.

Fuck!

ELEVEN

By breakfast, it was clear that Koz had run straight to Tuesday and spilled everything. There was a permanent crease on her forehead while she ate like a bird. This time, her lack of appetite might have been genuine. It seemed breakfast was to be an awkward affair, with a lot of chewing but not a lot of talking. Tuesday and the guys, the only people I really talked to other than Issy, all sat zombie-like, stewing in their dark thoughts. I hadn't seen Callon since he'd taken off last night.

I was imagining they were thinking much like I was. We knew these Hell Pits were slowly moving closer to here and weren't *that* far from our borders. That had been disturbing enough. Watching what one could do to the Magician? It was hard not to gasp from the memory alone. Add in that the thing had basically called me out? I didn't think I'd be getting sleep for a year, and I was already walking around like a zombie.

Callon appeared at the entrance to the great room about twenty minutes after I'd been sitting and eating silently beside Tuesday. He tilted his head toward the other room, making a point of giving me a direct invitational stare.

Shit. I ate the last piece of sausage off my plate before lagging behind, letting the guys beat me there. The topic of the day was far from my list of things I wanted to discuss. Another minute of respite was appreciated as I tried to wrap my mind around it. Tuesday lagged even farther behind as we fought for last place. Considering she wasn't invited to this meeting, I let her win/lose the race.

Callon was already seated by the time I walked in. He glanced up before he immediately shifted his gaze to Tuesday, following behind me.

He looked away, and I could hear the exhale before the slight shake of his head.

Tuesday couldn't read him as well and missed the signs of resignation.

"It's hardly right to exclude me." She walked past with her chin up and proceeded to take a seat next to Koz along the wall.

With a small smile, he gave her thigh a pat. It was hard to tell if it was condescending or encouraging, but being short on pats myself, I would've taken either variety.

Meanwhile, I found the farthest free wall space to lean against while Callon and I shot daggers at each other across the room. We had so many issues at this point that I wasn't sure who was mad about what anymore. It was like rummaging through a garbage heap. Was he still mad because he was stuck with me? Because I'd admitted the mud was following me to Dax when I'd known he was trying to keep a lid on it? Or that I'd tried to force the beast to come out while we were fighting? There were so many pieces of toxic debris between us that it wasn't worth worrying about which one it was anymore. I just had to dodge the fallout.

My answering anger had lots of fuel too, not that he'd want to hear about my side of things. At least I knew what I was most mad about. Before we'd gotten to the village, when Callon had crawled into that tent, I'd wanted him to undress and have his way with me. That was a Tuesday term I'd never quite understood until now, but whoa, was it accurate. I'd wanted him to rip my clothes off and then do all the things Tuesday kept telling me about.

Wanting him was the best reason to be pissed off, and it didn't matter if it made sense or not. I was fuming.

Callon leaned back in his chair, his eyes narrowed on me, as if he could sense my dark turn of thoughts.

I squinted back at him. *Nothing to see here. Keep it moving.*

He didn't keep anything moving. He kept staring. My breathing increased, because I was mad. Real mad. Furiously mad.

Zink broke our eye contact as he passed between us and then took a seat on the edge of Callon's desk. "There must be a way to contain it."

I let shuttered eyes slip back to Callon. He was leaning to the side, looking at Zink, but saying nothing.

What was that supposed to mean? Did Callon agree it could be stopped or not? He wasn't allowed to be silent.

I'd tell him if I was talking to him. If Zink was the only one who was going to speak, we were in worse shape than I'd imagined.

"We don't know how many there are and we can't be sure they're going to keep coming toward us," Koz said.

Nope. We'd been better off when it had only been Zink talking. We already knew the Hell Pits were migrating toward us. If Koz wasn't among the very few people I still liked, I would've been rolling my eyes and making exaggerated sighs in his direction.

The entire room looked at him, even Tuesday, and it wasn't her normal adoring face. It wasn't the skeptical look *I* was giving him. But it was a strong departure from the celestial for sure.

I could see Callon swallow before he spoke. "We know there's one fairly close that's been moving this way. That's enough to be a problem, and we can't simply hope it stops after what we saw."

Boom. The room grew quiet again.

I waited.

I looked around.

I waited some more.

No one was picking up the reins.

As much as I'd wanted to fall into the cracks and pretend I wasn't here, the thing was coming for me. I couldn't afford even the tiniest crack if this was the way it was going. I needed to get this situation moving in the right direction, away from me, or it would be my ass swallowed by the mud next time.

We didn't have time to sit around and ponder for another couple of days, which might turn to weeks, which might turn to a Teddy-shaped pile of mud. Callon had never struck me as a man of no action, but he didn't seem to be stepping up to the plate. I'd have to save my own ass, and everyone else's in the process.

I pushed off the wall. "We need to build a barrier around the one closest to us. It might not stop it, but maybe we can slow it down."

I looked around the room, trying to ignore Callon. No one seemed overly enthused.

"That thing turned into a monster," Hess said. "Should we really be getting close to it again?"

He had a good point, but maybe not a valid one. "It's never acted like that before. Even as it approached the Magician, it was slow. I think that was an isolated event, as if it drew out some of the Magician's magic. And we wouldn't go to that one. We go to the one closer."

"What'll contain it?" Tuesday asked, trying to make sure her voice was heard in this meeting.

"We use me to lure it and we find out what it can't breach. There's going to be something, whether it be fire or acid or stone. Nothing is invincible. There's always a weakness." I looked about the room, and there was less resistance this time, only nods. Yeah, I'd thought that was a good point too.

When no one else picked up the baton by chiming in, I realized I was going to have to continue leading this meeting, this thing, this possibly doomed mission. When had I become a leader? I'd not signed up for this, and the whole thing grated, but I continued past the chafe.

"We don't have a lot of time to figure it out, not after what we saw," I said. "These Hell Pits, whatever they are, they're much worse than we feared. I say we head out to the closest one tomorrow, armed with supplies. Anything you can think of that might work. And I mean *anything*— bring an old, stinky sock if you think it'll repel it. We go, and then we go again, and keep going until we find something that stops it." I'd paced up and down the room twice when I realized I'd pretty much given them a war cry. I was getting fairly decent facial responses, but they kept looking.

It needed a solid ending. I didn't want to be a leader, but they were waiting for a closer. "We're going to kick this fucker's ass." Boom. There was my ending and as good as I had. Which wasn't that great, but seemed to do the trick for some.

Tuesday was smiling, as if she were about to raise her fist in the air and cheer me on. Koz was patting Tuesday's leg again as he smiled at me. Hess was nodding. That wasn't too bad. Zink shrugged. It was something, especially from him.

I wasn't going to look at Callon because I didn't need his approval or encouragement. If I looked, it meant I wanted it, which I did not. The guys might need his approval, but I was not part of his pack. I didn't even want to be in the same fruit bowl anymore. I shouldn't even be leading this debacle. I had no leadership skills.

Then my eyes flicked to him for a fraction of a second. He gave me a shrug. What the hell was a shrug? I'd done a lot better than a shrug. He should keep his stupid shrug to himself.

"We'll start out at first light tomorrow," Callon said, standing. "Zink, organize and send people out to any of the other Hell Pits within fifty miles of here. I want to know what other ones are shifting, and I want as accurate a location as they can get."

"On it," Zink said, getting up and leaving the office.

Hess moved toward the door. "I'm going to start gathering supplies."

"We'll help." Tuesday stood, grabbing Koz's hand and tugging him along with her.

Tuesday paused by the door with a look, telling me to find her later.

I was the last one to leave. I moved toward the door, not sure why I'd dallied at all.

"You did well," Callon said as I walked past him.

I stopped, looked his way, and shrugged.

I went to leave the room and then slowed my steps. Had he just forced me into taking the lead? Nah. Why would he do that? This was Callon I was thinking about. He didn't hand over the reins for anything, not even cooking his sausage.

But he had. I turned back to him. "Why did you want me to lead this meeting? What was the point of that?"

He leaned back. "I don't know what you're talking about."

Well, that was a bald-faced lie if I'd ever heard.

"Are you mad because of last night? Is that what this is about? Slow torture?" I kept a close eye on his eyes, watching for a flash of red. There was nothing, not even a glimmer.

"Not at all."

I walked out. He could keep his secrets.

TWELVE

I STARED AT THE SHELVES IN THE CELLAR: DRIED meat, potatoes, different-colored stuff in jars, some other root-looking things I couldn't name. Nothing struck me with inspiration for the Hell Pit, but I didn't want anything left behind.

The clatter of someone making a mad rush down the stairs had me turning in that direction.

"I've been looking all over for you," Tuesday said.

She locked her hand down on my wrist and began tugging me out of the cellar.

"Is it important? I'm still looking for stuff to bring."

"We can't carry all the stuff we already have ready." She continued to drag me along after her.

I let her because it was Tuesday. Anyone else and I'd have told them to get the hell off me.

"Where are we going?"

"I don't want to tell you. I want you to *see* it." Tuesday pulled my arm forward until it was locked under hers so tight that there was no chance of escape.

We pushed through the door into the kitchen where Issy was having her late tea. She had tea three times a day, like clockwork. Breakfast, afternoon, and right before dusk.

"Teddy, do you want to have a snack? I've got one last jar of strawberry preserves," Issy said as Tuesday dragged me through the kitchen.

"I'm good. Thanks anyway," I said.

Tuesday paused by the back door, thrusting my coat at me. I barely had time to put it on before she was pushing me outside.

"How come she's so much nicer to you than me? Do you think I did something to piss her off?" Tuesday asked as she took the lead, since I had no idea where we were going.

"You didn't do anything to piss her off. I did something to make her like me with the whole lifesaving thing. I'm new to this, but it does come with some benefits."

"Yeah, I'd give you the last preserves too. Has she asked you about it?" She was huffing a little as we began hiking uphill.

"Luckily, no, because I definitely don't want to talk about it. It's creepy. *I'm* creepy." I looked about the trees as we kept climbing. There was nothing up here. "Where are we going?"

"Somewhere spectacular that isn't so far that we'll have an issue with your Callon problem." She was pushing through trees and barely squeezing through.

Were those wind chimes? "Where's that tinkling noise coming from?"

"You mean the water?"

"No. That chiming sound. Don't you hear it?"

"No. Come on, hurry up."

I didn't move right away, trying to hear it again, but it faded into the sound of water. "We have a stream closer to the lodge. Why are we climbing all the way up here to get water?"

"Just come on," she said, walking until we hit a clearing with a lot of rocks and a small pond.

She stripped off her jacket and dropped it to the ground. Her boots were kicked off next, then her pants dropped.

"Are you nuts? It's going to be freezing."

She pulled her shirt off. "It's a hot spring. It's fantastic," Tuesday said as she jumped in. "Come on. This'll help you sleep tonight."

She was right. Steam rose from the surface of the water in lazy spirals. I stripped out of my clothes and jumped in with her, my entire body unwinding as the warm water surrounded it.

"This is amazing." I leaned my head back on a rock as I let the water suck all the tension from my limbs.

Tuesday stretched out her legs. "I know. Koz brought me here last night after he told me about the Hell Pits." She leaned her head back and then smiled. "It really limbered us up," she said, and then giggled.

An image of Callon climbing in here with me popped into my mind. Only Callon would try to hijack my daydreams too. Maybe I needed to get it out of my system. If being around him helped me sleep, maybe sex with him would cure me for a week?

"How did you end up getting together with Koz?

Like, how *exactly* did it happen? What did you do or what did he do?" I dipped a little deeper into the spring, letting the water take the blame for my flushed skin.

"You mean the nitty-gritty play-by-play?" Her look started with a squinty eye that corrupted the rest of her face until she was beaming at me with a toothy grin.

"Yeah." I ducked my head under the water for a couple of seconds. Her face hadn't changed when I came back up for air.

"Why? What are you thinking about? I know it's not Koz and me."

I leaned my head back, taking in the place one more time. "We're pretty far away from the lodge, right?" Even beast ears wouldn't be able to hear up here.

"It's safe. Spill." Tuesday stared at me like I was about to tell her all the secrets of the universe. The pressure was almost too much, considering there was nothing to spill.

"There's nothing to tell." I was wishing like hell I hadn't started this.

Tuesday rolled her hand and her eyes at the same time. "I know there's something. Spill already."

The crease between her brows said she wasn't going to drop this.

"When we went out to meet the Magician, we stayed in tents the first night. I thought Callon was going to sleep outside. When he came in the tent and started to take off his jacket, there was a moment that I thought he was going to try to fuck me. Or at least kiss me." The memory of him kneeling over me as he undressed, and then doing *nothing* else, made me bitter even now.

She leaned closer. "Did you freak out?"

I shook my head quickly. "No. That's the thing. If you had asked me before it happened, I would've told you I had no interest." I wouldn't have been lying. Baryn had ruined that for me, or so I'd thought. Years of Baryn being his twisted self had created scars you couldn't see. The idea of a man touching me had revolted me before now.

I wasn't sure what had happened or why I'd switched on with Callon. I barely tolerated him most days. And yet I wanted him.

I ducked my head under the water again before I broke the surface and said, "I might've been a little disappointed."

"So you're admitting you like him?"

I pushed off the rock, wading around the hot spring. "No, I'm doing nothing of the sort. I *don't* like him. I'd even go as far as saying I hate him most of the time. He's controlling and pushy and just..." I raised one hand and made a growling sound, because the words to describe how much I wanted to rip Callon apart had not yet been invented.

Tuesday leaned back, watching me as she shook her head. "Most people don't want to sleep with a person they hate. That's an awful lot of emotion in one direction. You know, feelings can overlap. Hate can layer over love and make a person all sorts of confused."

"I may not be in touch with my feelings all the time, but I'm not in love." Burying emotions had been one of the ways I'd survived. But to suggest love? She was crazy. Disdain? Dislike? There were plenty of fitting words for the kinds of feelings I had.

Suddenly, it hit me. It made sense why I wanted him.

"You know why it had to be him? He's too cold to care if I use him and I don't want entanglements. I don't want love. I want to test the waters, you know? Have some kind of normal experience with a man I don't have to worry about being with. Like, maybe sex with Callon can be a reset? He'll wash away the other memories like spring rain over dirty skin, and then I can move on."

The gleam in Tuesday's eyes died with my words, and the corners of her mouth finally found anchors strong enough to weigh them down.

Just when you thought you knew someone, they threw you for a loop. Sometimes Tuesday could confuse the hell out of me.

"What now? I thought you wanted me to get together with him?" I asked.

She gripped one of the stones that formed the pool and tilted her head slightly to the side. She said in the quietest voice, "Teddy, you're not dirty."

I laughed. "Of course I'm not. I'm in water."

She didn't laugh with me. "I'm serious, Teddy."

"I know. I *know*," I said, trying to move the subject along.

She was shaking her head slightly. "I'm not sure you do."

"I *do* know. Can we move past this? I don't want to think on the village anymore, or Baryn. I want to move on, and Callon might be helpful in that area. So, are you going to help me?" I asked, knowing her answer would be yes. It was always yes. She'd help me, whether I liked how or not, sometimes whether I wanted her to or not. She was Tuesday.

She waded in the water, nodding. "Okay, so let's make a game plan. I'm sure we can get him in bed with you. Sex? Easy-peasy. Getting an 'I love you' is the hard part." She stared off for a second. "I should know. Koz has said everything else, how I'm beautiful and smart and funny and oh so wonderful. Just not *that*." She raised her hands as if she were choking an invisible man.

He'd say it to her eventually because he did. I saw it in the way he looked at her. I was also positive because if he didn't, I was going to beat him to a pulp and threaten to suck the life from him.

"You two haven't been together that long, but it'll happen," I assured her. I was the last person in the world who should be giving advice in these matters. I knew little of love in general and nothing of the romantic kind. But this conversation had little to do with knowledge and everything to do with gut and knowing I'd be around to make sure she heard the words she needed to be happy.

Tuesday turned her eyes back to me. "You really think so?"

"Yes, I do." Clearly my lack of experience didn't seem to devalue my opinion in Tuesday's mind. Although if a toad could talk and tell her the same, she'd probably listen. As long as the message was right, she didn't care who delivered it.

"Well, luckily we don't have to cross that hurdle with you. All you want is easy stuff," she said.

"Are you sure?" Nothing about Callon had been easy yet.

"Oh my wilds, yes. If he were with someone else it might be different, but the single ones always seem to be looking for a place to stick it in."

My face scrunched. "That sounds horrible."

"Don't worry. This is a good thing." She shrugged and smiled.

THIRTEEN

It had taken us two hours to get here, and now all I was supposed to do was stand in one spot. That was it. I'd gone from leader of this expedition to a big, fat boulder with a moldy northern side.

"I can do more than this."

"Yes, you can. You can move farther back if needed. You don't get any closer to it. You don't cross this point." Callon pointed to the ground while he watched my face to make sure I was paying adequate attention. Not only was I paying attention, everyone here was too. Zink, Hess, and Koz were standing closer to the Hell Pit but kept glancing over.

Tuesday was only a few feet away and didn't bother with the pretense of having an interest in anything else. She stared at us like she was examining a piece of evidence.

Of course I was paying attention. How could I not when he was mentally bludgeoning me with his bossiness, and right in my face? Sometimes I wondered if I were actually free, or had I merely upgraded to a more attractive jailer? He was *definitely* better looking than my last captor. There was even something intriguing with the way his brow quirked up sometimes.

His eyes narrowed a hair, as if he could sense my interest. Shit. Could he? Dammit.

I needed to put out "pissed off." Go back to pure anger. I couldn't show my hand here in the middle of the field next to the smelly Hell Pit. This was not the right moment.

"Can I ask a question?" I crossed my arms and gave him a glare that should've warned him what was coming.

"Yes," he said, sounding less stubborn and more curious.

"Do you imagine I'll run over there and dive into it? I'm not sure what would happen without your wise directions. I must say, I *do* have the urge."

His eyes narrowed. "Unfortunately, left to your own devices, I'm not sure you wouldn't go leap in."

Why did I want to sleep with him?

That was right. To wipe my history clean. I needed someone exactly like him, an arrogant ass that wouldn't care if I used him as long as he got something out of it too. He was perfect for the task.

"You know, I wonder if diving into that smelly sludge might be a blessing in disguise? It might be less painful than this." I kept my tone logical and calm, as if I were seriously debating it.

"I didn't chain us together. You did. You chose to be here." He smiled, as if he'd trumped my high card.

"Really? You want to go there again? Because the

only reason I could chain you is you dumped the chain right in my lap while you were hunting for opportunities." I was insane. I could never sleep with this man, ever. Fuck cleansing. I'd die filthy and be fine with it. He was lucky I didn't drag him over to that Hell Pit and kick him in.

"Callon, it's on the move," Hess called. He was standing near the danger zone with Zink and Koz, thirty feet or so from me.

"Not. A. Step." Callon pointed at the ground by my feet.

"I already said. I. Wouldn't."

Callon left me with a parting glare.

"Let's try the fire first," he said to the guys as they cleared a path in front of the mud. They had every concoction we'd brought lined up. There was gasoline, which was expensive as hell to trade for. Sugar, which might have been more expensive, but I wasn't exactly sure, since I'd never traded for either. There was plain water. Wax. Vinegar. We'd even brought honey, because if it could help fight a sore throat, it was worth a shot. If we had some, we'd brought some.

And now I couldn't participate. I was made to sit here like a stone.

Tuesday moved closer to me now that we were left alone. When we all set out this morning, I'd been glad to have her along. The wide smile on her face was making me rethink my initial reaction.

"What?" I asked, knowing I was rolling the dice by uttering a question whose answer could be overheard and prove mortifying. At the same time, the guys seemed more intent on starting a fire than what we were talking about.

"Nothing, really." Her smile widened, proving the opposite. It took about three seconds before she explained anyway. "You guys are cute, is all."

And there it was.

"Cute? All we do is fight. What is cute about that?" I kept a keen eye on the scene below. Koz's head turned a hair toward us and then stayed in that position. Callon appeared to be consumed in the experiments, but if Koz was listening, Callon was too.

I gave Tuesday a tap and pointed to the guys. I mouthed, *Don't say anything crazy.*

"There's nothing else to say. You bicker. It's cute. I find bickering cute. It's not a crime, and I'm allowed to think it's cute. I won't stop, either, so don't try to make me." She crossed her arms.

I was about to do exactly that, make her stop, when there was a sizzling noise. The smell, which had already been bad, grew worse as I saw the tips of flames rise. I got up on my toes, straining to see. I put my hand on Tuesday's shoulder so I could balance a little higher.

"Get off, I'm trying to see too," she said, trying to shrug off my grip.

I let go and dropped down flatfooted.

"Then go see for both of us. I'm the one stuck this far away." Damned if it wasn't killing me, too. I should be over there, experimenting. Half of the things we'd brought were because I'd thought of them, and here I was relegated to the kiddie corner, doomed to watch as a bystander. It wasn't like the stuff moved that fast. I could outrun it if needed—probably. If the Magician hadn't been singularly focused on Callon, he could've avoided the disaster too.

"You think it's safe?" she asked, not nearly as gung-ho to get into the thick of it as she should've been.

"You don't have to get that close. Just closer than me so you can see. Go down, see what's happening, and report back. I want to make sure they don't screw this up somehow." I gave her a little push toward them.

All four heads turned to me, proving they were a bunch of eavesdroppers. It was hard to remember that they could hear everything, everywhere, *all the fucking time.* Exhausting. Only word for it.

"I was exaggerating," I yelled down to them. "It's not like I don't know you all listen to everything."

After a small pause, they mostly went back to what they were doing. Callon shook his head.

"Go," I said to Tuesday, giving her another little shove.

Tuesday made her way closer as I waited. She tried to lean in close and get a better view when Koz's attention shifted to her. That was when things went to hell. She shifted her stance into something all sorts of weird. Koz couldn't possibly believe she'd normally stand with her foot bent at that angle. It looked like something was wrong with her knee, as if it were out of its socket. If she flipped her hair again, she was going to fracture her neck. She was supposed to be watching the Hell Pit for me, and now look at her.

Koz smiled. Dumbass. How long was this fake period going to last between them where they acted all gaga toward each other? I felt like I was getting sugar sick just looking at them. Hopefully they'd start acting like normal human beings soon, because it was nearly intolerable.

Was that why Callon and I didn't get along? Did he think I should act all weird like Tuesday? Would that get me smiles and pats of encouragement?

Callon glanced my way, probably checking to make sure I was following his "no movement" instructions. I didn't smile. I might've moved my leg inward, the way Tuesday had, and my hair might've needed a flip because it was in my face. And if I looked like I was mimicking Tuesday's behavior, it was purely for experimental reasons.

Callon didn't smile. He narrowed his eyes instead, as if the sun were right behind me and hurting them.

Whatever. Tuesday's weirdness must only work on nice guys. Callon was who he was, a miserable man, a curmudgeon, and we were bound to fight. There would be no pretending in our immediate future, and not in the far-off distance either, if I had to bet on it. I went back to ignoring him and checked Tuesday's status. Not only was she still flirting, she'd lured Koz farther away from the Hell Pit, diminishing our manpower.

I gave up, grabbed my bag, and found a spot on the ground that didn't have snow. I shoved the bag behind my head and ignored the chill that tried to seep through my jacket as I flipped open the book I'd brought.

I'd borrowed it from the stash at the lodge a week ago, before all the madness had ensued. It was a story written before the end of the Glory Years, when there were still places that printed books en masse. When they'd been cleaning the lodge, they'd found a bunch of books stored in trunks that had survived.

I'd never read an entire book before. They hadn't been plentiful at the village, and the people who did have them hadn't been willing to lend them. Issy had suggested it the other day and said it might relax me, as if I were uptight or something. She also mentioned it was fun. They'd done a lot of fun things back before the world had gone to hell. Maybe those sticks they used to go downhill fast were fun too. I might have to try them if this worked out. Either way, the book would save me from running down there and asking what they were doing.

AN ARM WRAPPED AROUND MY WAIST, AND MY FEET were dangling as Callon walked twenty feet away before dropping me to the ground. "Thirty feet. We moved. You were supposed to move. That's all I asked you to do. You saw what happened to the Magician." His eyebrows nearly connected as he glowered at me.

"I fell asleep. I didn't do it on purpose." I wasn't sure how I'd even drifted off, except that Callon was near. He seemed to be my only ticket to Lullaby Land.

Was that red I saw tinting the edges of his irises? It might be hard to utilize here, though. Where would he drag me to get in some more napping time? We didn't have a cave nearby. Still, it was worth exploring for future use.

"Are you mad?" I asked.

His eyes grew redder. "You know, sometimes I miss the days when you were afraid of me. What happened to them?"

I shrugged. He shook his head and walked off.

It was a valid question. When had I lost my fear of him? He was probably the most dangerous man I'd ever met, yet I didn't fear him at all. He'd just hauled me across the field and I hadn't flinched.

Tuesday made her way to me, throwing a thumb in Callon's direction. "He's completely overreacting. It wasn't *that* big of a deal. Someone else would've noticed before it got any closer to you."

Callon walked around as if he'd heard nothing, but Zink threw a glare our way.

"No, he might've been right," I whispered to Tuesday. "I could've ended up swallowed. I can't expect everyone to watch out for me."

Zink's expression softened. He'd heard me. Damn he was annoying.

I watched as the guys went back to work. There seemed to be a lot of cursing and scowls. They were moving slower than they had earlier this morning, and the bags we'd brought were spread around the ground, deflated.

"Did they make any progress?" I asked Tuesday, not liking the scene in front of me.

She sat on a sunny patch of ground. "Nope. Nothing seems to be doing anything. It smothers the fire, runs right through the gas, the honey. It defies gravity and crawls over anything they put in front of it."

I took a seat next to her, resting my arms on my legs. "Does anything seem to slow it down?" I asked.

"Barely."

"Do you hear that?" I asked. The stupid chiming sounds had come back.

"What?

I wiggled a finger over my ear.

"Your ear hurt?" Tuesday asked.

"No. I just keep hearing noises. I think there's something wrong with my ear."

"Put some vinegar in it when we get back to the lodge."

"Yeah, I will." The last thing I needed was for my hearing to go on top of everything else.

Our shoulders slumped farther, along with our moods, as the sun continued to sink. Zink was cursing with every new try. Koz was quieter, his smiles in our direction forced. Callon was staring at the mud with a quiet intentness as Hess and him talked. We hadn't just hit a wall—we'd run into it full force and slammed hard.

The sun was only a couple of hours from setting when Callon said, "We're leaving in five. Get your stuff together."

But Callon didn't turn to leave. He knelt down and did something near the mud. He straightened and then moved farther away, where they'd set up a fire.

He was spinning something over the flame while his back was to me. When he finally turned, I realized what was in Callon's hand. He had a jar of the stuff. It looked like he'd sealed the top with wax, but that didn't matter much to me. He was bringing it back with us.

Distance be damned—I marched over to him.

He met me halfway. "Do you not listen?" With a hand on my back, he began pushing me to a safe distance.

I sped up so I could get clear of his hand and turn on him. "You're taking that with us?"

"Nothing we've tried is working. I need a sample."

"We can bring more stuff here." I didn't know what was left to bring, but I'd find something.

"We might have to go in search of answers. It takes us all day to get here. We need this. I'm bringing it back," he said, as he walked over to pack his bag, bringing the jar with him.

———

WE'D BEEN WALKING FOR AN HOUR AND HAD another hour left to go, but that wasn't the problem. Knowing we didn't have an easy way to stop the Hell Pit made the trip back to the lodge seem even longer. Zink and Koz were leading the group. Tuesday and I took our time following. Mostly I was trying to walk as slowly as possible so I could hear Callon and Hess talking behind us.

Callon talked to different guys for different reasons. Zink was wartime. Koz seemed to be everyday shooting the shit. Hess was his logic sounding board. I'd only caught a few words, but each one was about the Hell Pit.

"You're going to have to tell them," Hess said to Callon.

Tuesday's eyes shot to me. I appreciated her alarm on my behalf, but there wasn't much to do about it. Not only that, but I agreed with Hess. Maybe it was because I'd lived my life in the dark for so many years, never knowing what my fate would be. The people at the lodge deserved to know. I wasn't looking forward to that moment, but still.

"After today, there might not be a choice in the matter," Hess continued. "The sooner they know, the better. It'll give everyone a chance to find somewhere else to go. That stuff is headed here as long as—"

"We don't know that for sure."

Callon had cut him off, but I didn't need to hear the rest. *As long as she's there.* Hess was right. It might not be absolute, but it was looking like a safe bet that the stuff wanted to get close to me for whatever reason. Callon could say whatever he wanted, but even the sample in the jar was trying to get to me.

I'd been watching it since we'd started back. When Callon had sealed it and put it down for a minute, it shifted to where I was. When I'd moved around, it had moved with me. Now, as he walked with it in his hand, it was again trying to climb the side of the glass toward me.

Tuesday bumped me, smiling, trying to pull me from my morose thoughts.

I smiled back, pretending I was fine. It was easier than saying, *He's right, about everything.*

Tuesday already knew that anyway.

FOURTEEN

Initially, I'd been too tired to realize people were staring at me. Then I thought it was because I'd been late for breakfast. That had been more than a half an hour ago, and they were still staring. Some filtered in as others left. Some peeked quickly, while others gave a full-blown visual interrogation. Some of the looks were confused. Some were hostile. One thing was very clear: between last night and this morning, everyone knew the Hell Pit was heading here and that it might have something to do with me.

Considering that, the full array of reactions were understandable. If the Hell Pit was heading here, it might steal their home. The confusion was even more justified. Who the fuck had a swamp after them?

It was ruining my meal for sure. The scrambled eggs I usually loved felt like chickens trying to poke their way out of my gut. I finished up my food, cursing Tuesday for sleeping in and making me eat alone under full examination. I nodded to a few people on my way out and went to go find the source of my current predicament.

His office was empty, and the jar was easy enough to find in his cabinet. I placed it on his desk and the games began.

———

AFTER ABOUT AN HOUR, IT WAS CLEAR THAT IT didn't matter where I sat in Callon's office, whether it was by the window, behind the desk, or across the room—the stuff moved until it was as near to me as it could get. I was starting to think I could hang like a bat from the rafters and the mud would shift in the jar until it was piled up onto the underside of the lid.

I picked it up, shook it again, and put it back on the desk. The stuff slithered around, doing its thing again.

My life used to be controlled by Baryn. When he died, I still wasn't completely free. The Magician had stepped up to the plate. That problem had been solved, only to be trumped by whatever dark magic these Hell Pits were. It got to be that I wanted to throw my hands in the air. Some insane part of me that was tired of living life under the sword wanted to break the seal, drop the goop into my palm, and see what would happen. Take my best shot and see where the chips fell.

Luckily, I was only a little crazy. Maybe in a few weeks of worrying about yet another threat, if I lasted that long, I'd be mostly crazy and wouldn't care what the stuff did to me. I'd want this whole thing over, one way or another.

Or more likely, I'd still be me and want to torch the stuff again. Stupid mud, thinking it could steal the only home I'd had. We'd see who'd win this war.

The door opened and Callon walked in. He looked at where I sat, staring at the sealed jar in front of me.

"Is this going to become a habit?"

"Perhaps." I rotated the jar once more. This mud, this sludge, this darkness, did it never tire? Wouldn't it eventually stop moving? It was cut off from everything. The wax around the seal cut off its air. It didn't have water or food, and yet it still continued on.

Callon walked over and plucked the jar from the desk in front of me. He put it inside the cabinet and shut the door, then rested his hand on it.

"Do I need to lock this?"

I wasn't sure if he was busting my chops or serious. Either way, it was the same answer. I didn't need to watch it anymore. "No. I'm done for the day."

He crossed his arms, leaning a shoulder against the wall. "Issy said you've been in here for an hour."

I shrugged. "Must've lost track of time." Actually, I *had* lost track, as the future had rolled out in front of me and I'd buried myself in its murky bleakness. How did you kill something you couldn't put a name to? There had to be a way, but it was hard to find.

He took a seat on the desk in front of me, and I let my head loll back, waiting for whatever lecture or commandment he had now. It was as if he made them up for fun in his free time. *How can I torture Teddy today? What will get under her skin?* While I tried to sleep to no avail, he probably stayed awake thinking up fun ways to screw with me.

"Yes?" I asked, with no lack of attitude piled into that short word.

"We'll figure something out," he said.

"Easy words, but not so easy to do."

He was talking to me like we were friends. He hated me almost every other day of the week. I alternated and returned the favor on his days off.

I didn't know where this pep talk was coming from, but the Magician had been eaten by this stuff. The Magician, who had run Newco, who had almost bested all of us, had been destroyed by the Hell Pit with barely a fight. This was no time to be cavalier.

"What about that Bitters man? The wizard? Maybe he can help?"

I leaned my head back farther, looking at the ceiling so I didn't have to look at him. I wasn't ready to share all my motives yet. Bitters might not know what to do about the Hell Pits. But if Bitters knew as much as Dax alluded to, he might be able to break the spell the witch had used to tie Callon to me.

Did I want to leave here? No. Not a cell in my body relished the thought of leaving this place. Leaving the beast meant I'd never sleep again. But I probably wouldn't have a choice. I couldn't let the Hell Pit destroy this place, and someone would probably kill me before it got to that point anyway. They'd have to.

"Not yet," Callon said.

What? I jerked my gaze to him. "Then when? We've got a bit of a time crunch here, don't you think?"

His expression hardened. "I'm not traipsing halfway across the continent until I've exhausted all possibilities."

"I'm pretty sure we did that yesterday." I could barely form more words. That look on his face meant he was immovable. I'd seen it before, too many times.

"One day is far from exhausted," he said. He might as well have a shovel in his hand, digging further in as we spoke.

"If you don't want to go, point me in the right direction and I'll..." *Fuck!* I couldn't go myself. This really did suck. I was used to our tie being a benefit, not a liability.

"Sucks, doesn't it?" Callon asked, smirking.

Glad it lifted his mood. He wasn't the one with the lake of sludge after him. Would he keep me stuck here until it was too late?

"It wants me. What happens if it never stops coming for me? Will you let this lodge be swallowed up or kill me instead?"

"We'll find a solution."

We. Of course he'd put it like that. He couldn't get away from me. It had to be *we.* And if he could kick me out right now? Where would the *we* be then? It would be dust. He'd. Kick. Me. Out. I knew it in my gut because it was what I'd do. It was the only sane move. And if he couldn't kick me out? He should kill me. My life wasn't worth the destruction of this place and all the lives it provided for. That was the bottom line.

"There's no 'we' in this room. There's you and me and this place. To be honest, this lodge is worth more than both of our lives. There aren't that many good places left in this world. I can't let this place fall."

In a world as barbaric as ours, it was too precious a commodity to be wiped out. I knew what happened to people under bad rulers, how people shifted their psyches around to survive, rationalized what they had to do until they were the "helpless" and their sins weren't their own. I couldn't let the only decent place I'd ever known of fall.

"We won't," he said, persisting with the "we."

Between the encroaching threat of destruction, that *we* was one too many to stomach. "There is no we. We aren't a team. If you weren't stuck with me, I would've been kicked out of here weeks ago, and *we* both know it."

"I'm so glad you know my mind better than I do." His shoulders, once relaxed, straightened. His stare that had been almost friendly was now nearly feral, with a hint of red.

Red was becoming my favorite color. I got up and walked around the desk, getting closer to the beast that was simmering right under the surface.

"Teddy, I don't know what you're thinking lately, but you need to back off."

I kept walking toward him. "What if I don't want to? Why do you keep him chained up all the time? Are you afraid of him? I'm not. I say let him out."

I hadn't realized I was pressing my palms against his chest until he wrapped his hands around my wrists and pulled them off, holding them in between us.

"You little idiot. You know nothing."

"I wish that were true." I already knew more than I ever wanted of men. If I could bleach my brain of some of the things I'd lived through, I'd chug a gallon of the stuff right then. If I could torch away the memories, I'd gladly stand upon scorched earth. But I couldn't.

I flexed my hands in his grip, moving slightly closer in spite of it. There was something deep within him that soothed some wild part of me. He was pulling back, but I could see the look in his eyes as they grazed my neck, my mouth.

He wanted me.

I wanted his beast. It was a fair trade.

"What's a little mutual using between enemies?" I said, leaning in.

He shook his head and pushed me away from him before turning and leaving.

What the hell just happened? Tuesday said he'd jump at the chance. So why was I staring at his back as he walked away?

FIFTEEN

I walked into my room, kicked off my shoes, and didn't move any farther. My once-beautiful white cover was bunched into a shredded mess in the middle of my bed, yellow stains splattered all over it. At least one person with a very full bladder was pissed, literally, that they might have to leave their homes because of me.

"Teddy?"

I ran to the door, blocking Tuesday before she walked in. I couldn't afford for her to go on the warpath. Then Koz would join forces to help her—at least, I'd hope. This whole place could end up divided over a prank because someone was in a bad mood. The worst part was that they had a right to be.

The doorknob in one hand, I filled the rest of the opening.

"What are you doing? Why are you blocking the door?" She was looking over my shoulder, but I knew she couldn't get a clear shot of the blanket from her angle.

"No, I'm not."

"What's going on in there?" She ducked lower, trying to peer around the bend of my waist.

"Nothing." I shifted in front of her.

"You know your nose twitches when you lie, right?"

Actually, I hadn't. I put my fingers to my face, without even thinking about it, all but confirming what she'd said. Everybody has their dull days when the brain doesn't want to work that well, but this was a doozy.

She pushed into me until we fell together in a lump on the floor. She was up and past me, scanning the room like a dog on a scent. She stopped in the same spot I had. "What the—"

"Don't freak out. I don't want to make this into a bigger thing than it is. They've heard about the Hell Pits, and a few of them aren't happy." I grabbed the bag I used for laundry and rolled the ruined blanket up, shoving it inside.

Tuesday took a step closer. "Washing isn't going to fix that."

"I'm not washing it. I'm going to bury it, but I don't want anyone to see it."

"Why are we keeping it a secret?" Tuesday asked, watching me stuff the last of the blanket inside the sack while trying not to touch any of the wet parts.

"Because I don't want to encourage others." Where had she been all those years? People had a herd mentality. Once they saw this, they might all pile on. That was the way it always went. You would've thought she hadn't grown up in the same village as me.

"You think they'd gang up?"

"Yes. That's what people do, but that's not going to

happen because we aren't going to make a thing of it."
Holy smokes, had she never paid any attention?

"Are you really sure we aren't going to do that?"
Tuesday dropped onto the bed like a giant that was told
she wasn't going to be allowed to eat the villagers.

"Yes. Really sure, maybe the surest I've ever been."

Her mouth turned down and she walked from my
room, muttering something about being a killjoy.

I grabbed my bag, made sure the hall was clear, and
then dodged down the stairs and outside. There was
always a fire heap ready to go farther down the lawn
about twenty feet from the lodge. There were still embers
burning in the pit as I tossed the blanket on the pit. The
fire sprang to life with the new fuel. Five minutes later,
the last identifiable remnants of the cover burned away as
the crows came to land on branches nearby, cawing.

I looked up at them on their perches. "Do you guys
have nothing better to do than watch me?"

They cawed in response, and it sounded like heck-
ling. I turned and made my way into the kitchen. Issy was
peeling potatoes at the counter.

One of the girls, Frenchie, was there helping her, plus
a guy named Tommy. Neither of them gave me more
than a passing glance. Probably not the culprits.

"Issy, do you know where I could get another blanket?" I didn't whisper. I spoke just softly enough that it
wouldn't carry, but loud enough that it didn't seem like I
was trying to keep a secret.

"Sure. What happened to yours?"

"I get really cold sometimes."

"Oh," she said, nodding, as if it all made sense. "I

forgot you're in Callon's old room. It's got the best view, but you pay for it at night. Didn't bother him none, but you don't have enough meat on those bones to manage too well."

She put her knife down so she could poke at my stomach and give my hips a squeeze, all the while appearing to be adding up how many more calories I might need a day.

She picked up her knife and went back to the potatoes. "Too skinny, and you don't eat enough at dinner. I'm making my special creamy potatoes tonight. I'll put aside a special batch for you."

I could feel the other sets of eyes in the kitchen on me now. As if they didn't already have enough reasons to hate me. If I got special catering, the gang ready to torch me would grow from a little snowball to an avalanche.

"You don't need to do that. I eat plenty at dinner. I promise."

"All right," she said, but I saw a glint that told me there'd be a large bowl set aside for me anyway. "Oh, the blanket. In your hallway, third door down is a closet. There's a pile in there. Take whatever you need, and I'll make sure there's some extra logs for your room later."

Frenchie narrowed her eyes. I narrowed mine back.

"Thanks, Issy."

She smiled and patted my shoulder, but there was something deeper brewing in her eyes. Sooner or later she might try to talk about what happened. I could sense it hovering in between us lately, even more so the last couple of days. I got out of there before things got awkward.

"You had no right." Callon's voice echoed in the hallway.

He wasn't the type to raise his voice. He'd get angry plenty, but you knew it from his tone, his eyes, not how far his words carried.

Hmmm. Curious. Who had crossed the line? Make a right, go up the stairs, and go get a blanket from the closet? Or make a left into the alcove and retie my boot? I made a left. I wasn't sure why I bothered debating that one. I might be living here now, but that didn't mean I'd be here in a week. All he needed was one strong witch or wizard and I'd be out on my ass. I couldn't afford to not listen.

"They asked," Zink said. "They had a right to know."

And now I knew who'd spilled the beans on me. He hadn't wasted much time at all getting the story out. It was so obvious now that I thought about it.

"When the time was right. Not when you—"

The door shut with a loud thud. It didn't matter. I'd heard enough. I'd been in agreement that the people here should know what was coming, but I guessed a heads-up would've been nice. Maybe a chance to tell them myself, explain things a little, let them know I'd try to leave. That I wouldn't intentionally rob them of their home.

Now it was out there, but not in an open way I could address. It was filtering through all the nooks and crannies of this place, being whispered about when no one was around. The truth of it had been bad enough, but now it was probably being twisted as it traveled its lurking path.

They were going to hate me—not that it mattered. I'd been shunned before. I'd live. There were worse things.

I found the third door like Issy said. The second I opened it, I heard the murmur of voices. I drew a mental map of this place and realized I was right over his office. I didn't bother debating this time; I moved as quietly as I could, shutting the door without the sound carrying. The closet was filled with supplies, but huge, as I navigated my way toward the voices.

"You need to get rid of her. You know this," Zink said.

"And *you* know I can't," Callon responded, his voice a near growl. No one sounded any happier than when I'd heard them downstairs. That included me, since I might've gotten a splinter in my earlobe from pressing it against the old wooden floor.

"You could if you find a strong enough witch or wizard. Bitters might be able to do it."

Zink thought it too. I had to get there.

"Bitters is hundreds of miles away. He might be dead before I get there," Callon said.

The room went silent for a few seconds before Zink said softly, "Then there are other ways."

Well, at least I knew who'd be the first to come for me. Zink was above pissing on covers but not above taking me out, if that was what had to be done.

More silence.

"Are you suggesting..." Callon didn't finish the question. He didn't need to. I wasn't in the room and *I* knew what Zink was suggesting.

"We might not have a choice." Zink's words were

chilling in their accuracy. It sucked when you agreed with the henchman who wanted to kill you.

"Nothing touches her unless I say so. That better be clear, because I will *not* let that slide."

There was a long pause. It sucked not to have eyes in the room.

"You'd choose her over me?"

"It's not a choice that needs to be made yet," Callon said.

"Yet." My life might be hanging on by a "yet." I would've felt a lot better with a "never." But "yet" was better than *go have at it.*

"Are you in love with her? You said it meant nothing, but you—"

Callon cut him off before he could finish his thought. "Try to not be more of a paranoid ass than normal."

Was Zink out his mind? Why would he ask such a thing? Callon hated me. And what meant nothing? What was he talking about? This was almost worse than hearing nothing. I had more questions than before.

"Then what is it? It's something, because you're risking an awful lot for her."

"I don't kill innocents." There was a finality to Callon's voice that gave some comfort.

"She can steal the life out of someone. That doesn't feel so *innocent* to me," Zink said, his voice growing louder.

"She was able to save someone close to us because of that same gift. She's hardly the devil." Callon's voice was growing softer. I'd barely heard him this time. *Now* he was mad.

So saving Issy was now coming around to save me. He felt indebted to me. How had I not guessed? And fuck, why did I hate that? What did it matter why he was sparing me if I was alive?

"If she stays here—"

"This conversation is over." The way Callon said it, it was clear things were going to escalate if Zink pushed it further.

I held my breath as all sounds stopped. I imagined them staring each other down, but that was only a guess.

I heard some shuffling around. The door slammed.

I wasn't sure if I was relieved or terrified by the precious perch my life wobbled upon. I'd known it would come to this, but hearing someone discussing your death was still a chilling affair. I lay there, cheek still pressed to the floor while it all sank in. I didn't move from the closet for a long while.

SIXTEEN

I ate more potatoes than I wanted under the watchful eyes of Issy. She wasn't the only one keeping tabs on me. I could feel the eyes of others when I wasn't looking. Some of the people who lived in the smaller building around the lodge had decided to filter in tonight as well, popping in and sizing me up before leaving. They could look all they wanted. This was old hat to me. Easier, in fact, because I wasn't chained to a pole. I had a full plate of food as I sat beside Tuesday.

Zink was down at the other end of the table, throwing red-hot glares my way. The two of us were going to have a little chat, but I'd do it after I ate another five potatoes and made Issy happy. Then we'd brawl. Right now, though, he was making it hard to chew through my own anger, and I had to eat.

Callon was across the room, staring at Zink. He shot a warning stare in Zink's direction and then gave a parting word to Hess. Hess gave him a nod and then went back to eating. All in all, dinner was a pretty hostile affair. It was a good thing I'd had serious training in this type of environment.

"What's going on?" Tuesday asked for the fifth time. Maybe sixth? I'd lost count.

I gave another shake of my head, but she was being stubborn today. Koz walked in, late for dinner. His eyes shot to us on one side of the table and then to Zink. He looked at Hess, who was standing up eating in the corner as he tried to steer clear of getting in the middle.

Koz's gaze then shot back to me, but I didn't see any surprise. He'd heard the fight too. He hadn't needed to press his ear to wood. He probably heard them arguing a few rooms over.

I rolled my eyes in Tuesday's direction, hoping he'd understand my plea for help. Tuesday was definitely gearing up to ask me what was wrong again. I'd shared almost everything with Tuesday for years, but this one was tough. If I told her Zink was ready to kill me, it would divide the house, maybe the guys. If it got ugly enough and sides were drawn, what happened if Callon sided with Zink in the end? Would Koz side with Tuesday, or would it cost her him and her new home? And to what end? So she could be chased across the continent with me? Never setting down roots? Robbed of all her dreams because she was loyal? Fuck no. I wouldn't do it to her.

Koz walked over, slid into the seat beside Tuesday, and wrapped his arm around her shoulders. He pulled her in for a kiss. "I missed you today."

Koz might be doing me a favor, but none of that affection was fake. I wouldn't be the reason she lost it, either. It wasn't long before he was tugging her from the room. She gave me a last look, saying she'd be finding me later for interrogation. I smiled back, pretending there was no need.

The few stragglers left emptied out and we were down to three: Hess, Zink, and me.

I watched Zink finish his plate and head out of the room. I finished up quickly and followed him. Hess pushed off the wall as I did, and I put a hand out to stop him.

"Trust me, I don't need a babysitter."

Hess looked down at my hand and then nodded, leaning back against the wall. "Didn't think you did."

Zink made his way upstairs to the end of the hall and out the door, where there was a deck that overlooked the property. I followed.

Zink was leaning on the railing, back to me. The cold didn't exist as rage burned my flesh and boiled my blood. I could kill him right now. I knew it in my gut. I wouldn't, but I could.

He didn't bother turning as he said, "You've clomped your way after me. You have something to say?" He looked over his shoulder with a smirk. "Unless you're too scared?"

"You think I'm afraid of you? You think you're special because you've got a pair of fangs?" I walked up to him until we were less than a foot apart. "Go ahead, get all beastly on me. Let's see who makes it off this deck."

He snorted. "You've got some balls on you. I'll give you that."

"You had no right to tell anyone about the Hell Pits.

That was *my* story to tell." I pointed but stopped short of shoving him the way I wanted. I was so angry that I feared I really would kill him if I touched him, and we hadn't come to that point, *yet*.

"And would you have told?"

"You really think I'm the scum of the earth, don't you? But you don't know me."

"What I think is you don't belong here. You're a liability and a taker. You bound yourself to Callon and locked us all up with him. They deserved the truth. So excuse me if I don't give a fuck if you thought you should be the one to tell the people *I've* been living and surviving with for years." Zink thumped a fist against his chest.

"And you didn't waste a second telling them, did you? No, you wanted to be the one, and you didn't care how bad I might look or how Callon might be portrayed either." What the hell? I was so angry that I was even defending Callon if it meant attacking Zink.

"I wouldn't do anything to hurt—"

"I don't want to hear it. You keep on believing your truth and I'll do the same. If I have to stay out here and discuss it with you for another second, we're going to really find out who won't make it out alive."

I gave him my back, daring him to try something as I walked inside.

Callon was in the hallway, leaning on the wall. Great. Now he'd want to lay into me and tell me what an ass I was.

"What? Would you like to have words with me now?

Would you like to tell me how wrong I am?" I asked, knowing he'd heard every word.

He straightened up and shrugged. "Not at all. Thought you handled that fairly well," he said, and then turned and walked away from me.

I walked down the stairs as quietly as I could, avoiding the centers that always made them creak louder. The place was dark except for the lamp I carried as I crossed the hall and made my way into Callon's office.

I opened the top cabinet door and lifted the lamp. There it was, slithering toward me already. How was a normal person supposed to sleep knowing this stuff was here? And for me? Who wasn't anywhere near normal? It was an impossibility.

Callon might not want me to leave the lodge at night, but I didn't have a choice if I wanted to get sleep. He'd left me none.

He couldn't know until I was at least a good mile away. After all, I didn't want the man. I needed the beast. That was the only way I'd get a few hours of sleep tonight. At this point, there wasn't much I wouldn't do to get some, either.

I blew out the lamp, leaving it on the desk before tiptoeing out of the office and across the hall barefoot. My shoes dangled from my fingers. I'd don them as soon as I was outside.

There was a creak, and I froze, listening to nothing but my own breathing for a minute. Even that might've been too loud, but there wasn't much to be done about it. I slowly twisted the handle, holding it open until I grabbed the opposite side, then slowly released it, trying to keep it from clicking home loud enough for someone to hear. I wasn't giving him too much credit, either; the things he heard would make a ladybug blush red.

A shape moved on the horizon, a dark silhouette against the snowy pines. I could've stood there all night and watched Callon. He had a glide to his walk that was so graceful it couldn't be human. Although I would've preferred to watch another time. I'd had plans for tonight.

"Going for a walk?" Callon asked as he strode toward me. His head shifted down an inch.

Had he been waiting for me? Had he known? "Am I not allowed to get some air?" I asked with feigned nonchalance.

"You're not going for a run tonight. Inside." He walked to the door and held it open.

I didn't budge. "The Magician is dead. The Hell Pits are still hours away. It doesn't matter if I go for a late-night walk anymore."

"His people aren't dead." He angled his head toward the door.

"They will be if they touch me." I looked out at the pines.

"Inside."

The threat was clear. Go inside or he'd make me go inside. Damn if he'd miss an opportunity to manhandle me. If it had gotten me the beast, I wouldn't have cared. And not just a taste of the beast, because he was right there under the surface, but full-blown fur, fangs, and the scariest thing this side of the ocean. Scary to everyone else, that was. To me? It was like going to sleep with the best security blanket ever crafted. That was how I'd get some sleep tonight. Not this human shit.

I measured the distance, wondering if I could make it to the tree line. How far ahead would I need to get before the beast would take over the chase?

"You won't make it two feet."

God, sometimes I hated him. I wasn't even sure why I hated him so much, but I did. He made something inside me want to turn feral and scratch his eyes out.

Tuesday could say whatever she wanted about how feelings overlapped, but she wasn't the one experiencing pure rage at his high-handed ways right now. No, this wasn't anything good. This was pure, undiluted hate of a purity not yet experienced by most of humankind. The sickest part was that was why I could sleep with him. There wouldn't be any hard feelings if things didn't work out, because no one would be looking past that moment.

I turned and walked back inside. He followed my every step, intent on giving me an escort back to my room. He opened the door and then stepped aside.

I walked in and stood there, looking at the bed with the mussed covers. The clock on the table showed how many hours I had left before the sun came up and the ruse of trying to sleep would finally end.

"What's wrong with you? Why do I smell fear on you?" he asked, and I could hear a timbre that almost sounded like the beast trying to break free of the man's bonds. It was the hint of the beast that drove my answer. The beast was loyal to me—he wasn't Callon, calculating and resentful that he was tied to me. The beast understood me the same as I understood it.

"I need to run. It's the only way I can sleep." That wasn't the full picture, but it was true enough.

Callon took a step toward me. "The Magician is dead. Baryn is dead. You're in a house surrounded by shifters that could rip most things apart with their teeth. You're safe."

He turned and walked toward the door, taking any chance of the beast coming out with him. I wanted to let him go. I was tired of this game. But one look at the bed wrenched my fears from me. "They're not dead—not for me, at least. When I fall asleep, they're all there waiting."

He stopped walking. I watched his back as he stood still for a few moments, as if he were being pulled in two directions. He turned partway toward me. "If you need me to stay, I'll stay."

"I don't *need* you. I *need*…" It didn't matter. I crossed my arms and looked away from him. "Just go."

Thinking of another night of those dreams felt like I had Baryn's hands wrapped around my throat, stealing my ability to breathe.

"You need the beast," he said.

I didn't confirm nor deny. It didn't matter. I wasn't getting the beast tonight, and nothing else would do at the moment.

He walked toward me.

I stepped away.

"It's close by," he said, his voice even rougher.

I turned, forgetting my annoyance in the face of my

need. When I looked at him this time, I could see the red shading his eyes.

"I'll stay." He made a slight motion toward the bed.

I should do as he asked and not push the matter, be happy for whatever I could get. Except what good would it really do me if I was waiting for him to leave as soon as I fell asleep? Then I'd be tossing and turning all night—again. When he was the beast, I knew he'd stay all night.

"What?" he asked, growing more agitated.

"Nothing." I shrugged.

"Teddy."

Did it really matter anymore? He already knew every embarrassing, horrible thing about me. What was a little desperation to top things off? "How long do you think you'll stay, exactly? Just so I know and don't get startled when you rise."

"How the fuck did I end up here?" He was shaking his head.

He wrapped an arm around my waist, hoisted me up, and walked to the bed. He picked me up when he was the beast too. Did this mean he was going to change? Was there still hope?

He dropped onto the bed with me. "I'll stay until morning. Get under the covers," he barked.

I would've preferred a growl, full fur, and fangs, but we were getting closer. I couldn't complain. It was obvious he didn't want to be here. I might've seen lust in his eyes earlier, but there wasn't any like along with it.

I kicked off my shoes and pulled the covers over me. He pulled off his shirt and tossed it to the chair. I looked at the clock and did the math. Not ideal. I'd be a couple hours short of what I needed to really catch up, but I could work with it.

He settled into the bed and, with an arm around my waist, dragged my back against his front. That was new. He was right. The beast was close to the surface. I couldn't imagine it was Callon who wanted me close. I thought I had to go running through the woods to get this, but it seemed other things triggered him almost as well. It wasn't perfect, but then again, this was pretty comfy. Now if I could figure out what I'd done to get it...

His breathing evened out behind me.

"You have such good control." *Except at certain times.* "What makes you shift, exactly? Do you just choose, or does it come on suddenly?" *Tell me all your secrets.*

"Your fear makes it hard to stay human."

Hmmm. That was interesting, and he gave it up easily enough. It wouldn't do me much good. I wasn't going to intentionally scare the shit out of myself. That would be counterintuitive to what I was trying to achieve —a nice, calming sleep. Still, it was a start.

"Why is that?" I shifted away from him just enough to turn over and face him. Him admitting that another's fear made it hard for him to stay human sparked a lot of questions. It must've been a predator-type thing. Like dogs or something? I'd keep that comparison to myself. The dog reference wouldn't be flattering at all, and I was going for answers, not chasing him out.

He let out a long, annoyed sigh. "It makes me want to kill something."

I knew I was right to like the beast. "Does it always want to kill things?"

"No. Sometimes it wants to do *other* things."

Other things? I couldn't imagine it sitting around and reading a book. Oooh. It liked to kill and it liked to fuck. How *very* interesting. Now we were really getting somewhere.

"If the beast likes to kill and fuck, how come you don't?"

"I can't go around randomly killing people."

"I'm not talking about killing people. How come you don't fuck?" I had a feeling he knew I'd not been asking him why he didn't go on a killing spree.

"Who says I don't?" His offhand answer wasn't what I wanted to hear.

"Who is it that you're fucking?" He was *my* beast. We had a thing. It wasn't a normal thing, but there was some weird sort of ownership. I'd trapped him, after all. They should trap their own beast. It was a lot of work and grief, and now I was supposed to share?

"No one at the moment. Go to sleep."

He did want to fuck. This was perfect. We could use each other, and maybe I could get him in my bed every night and sleep too.

"I don't have anything for you to kill, but maybe you should fuck me? You're stuck with me anyway at the moment. I mean, it's convenient in that way, right? We could mutually use each other." My confidence was picking up. I'd presented him with a logical reason why we should share a bed for more than sleep. According to what Tuesday said about single guys, Callon would be jumping all over my offer.

"You use a lot of people that way?" The slight growl to his voice didn't remind me of the beast this time, but something was off.

"Are you afraid because of the death thing? Is that why you don't want to sleep with me? It's okay. We can discuss it. I'm not personally offended. I'm curious, is all."

"Can you *please* go to sleep?"

That sounded nearly painful, and I was fairly certain Callon had never used that P-word ever before. "Does that mean you don't want—"

"Go. To. Sleep." He pulled my head down and planted it to his chest, so even if I did talk, it would be muffled.

That hadn't worked out so well. I'd talk to Tuesday and regroup tomorrow.

SEVENTEEN

THE LODGE WAS LOUD IN THE MORNINGS, BUT I sensed the absence of certain voices before I set foot in the great room for breakfast.

Callon had been gone when I woke up, and now he wasn't here either. Neither were Zink, Hess, or Koz. The mountain of food on Tuesday's plate told me they wouldn't be returning anytime soon.

I grabbed some eggs and bacon, my plate looking modest compared to hers, and dropped into the seat beside her.

"Where are they? Why are they missing?" I asked.

"They went to experiment with some of the sludge," she said with a full mouth of eggs, right before she shoved a piece of sausage in.

"How?" Callon couldn't get that far without me.

She struggled to swallow a large mouthful before answering. "He sent Koz to fetch some more samples and bring them back to the farthest spot Callon could go without you."

He was experimenting without me? I was supposed to be the leader of these expeditions. It wasn't like he didn't have the chance to tell me as he was rolling out of bed this morning. I stabbed a big chunk of eggs, but the mush didn't fight back, making it wholly unsatisfying. Should've gone with sausage. At least it would've felt like I was breaking skin.

"You can slaughter those eggs, but I think he was trying to let you sleep," she said around a piece of bacon.

"Whose side are you on?"

"Sorry. You're absolutely right that you should've been included. He should've woken you before he left at dawn. That was. *So. Incredibly. Wrong.*" She shook her head.

"Thank you," I said, not caring that I'd had to prompt her back to my side. As long as she was there now, I wasn't going to split hairs.

I looked about the breakfast room. Only a couple of stragglers left: some guy named Tommy, who did repairs and was quick with a smile, and Frenchie, who never smiled at all. Both lived in the surrounding cottages, outside the lodge. I wished they'd get a move on. This was definitely not a conversation that needed to be over-heard. It was bad enough I had to have it.

"They're all gone?" I asked.

"Yes. Why? What happened? Is this about that weird tension last night?" She was curious enough to put down her fork for a minute.

"There was no tension last night. I offered that thing to *you know who* last night. He pretty much ignored me."

Her lips parted and her eyes got squinty. Her gaze

shifted down, staying there for a second before coming back to me. "We're talking about *the* thing? And nothing?"

"Yes, *the* thing. I thought you said I only needed to present myself for the taking? That it would be a done deal?"

She curled her lips in and chewed on them. "You must not have presented yourself correctly."

"I did what you said. He wasn't taking. He didn't want to take. There was no appetite for this meal." I'd laid it all out. Couldn't have made it plainer if I'd stripped down in front of him.

"No," she said, wagging her finger and finally looking confident about something. "He wants you. I can see it. You must have done something wrong. You messed up somehow."

"I put myself out there like a sacrificial lamb. You said it was easy." This was not my fault, no matter how she tried to twist it.

"Did you look dead? That's not good. They like to think you want them really bad."

"I did not look dead. I offered and he didn't want me." If we didn't have company in the room, I might've yelled. As it was, I had to whisper violently in her direction. She was totally trying to pin this failure on me.

She turned away from her plate. "It normally is. I need a play-by-play of exactly how it went down so I can pinpoint where you went wrong."

Had she not heard me? "I gave you a play-by-play. I asked if he wanted to have sex and he ignored me."

She rolled her eyes, as if I were the problem. "But

how? Did you touch him? Did you lick your lips and bat your lashes? Maybe get a hair flip going?" Tuesday enacted all of these movements as she asked, as if I needed visual cues and the words weren't enough for my feeble brain to take in.

It didn't matter. It was a no all around. "No, no, and no. You said it was easy, so I went with the most direct approach. I didn't bother with all that fluff. I asked him outright and he ignored me."

She shook her head and then slipped a hand over her forehead. "Well, there's your problem. That's almost as bad as lying there dead. You need to warm them up first."

I waved a finger at her. "You didn't say anything about warming him up."

She shrugged. "Because a lot of times it's not needed. Clearly he needs a warmup."

I didn't respond as I sat back in my chair, staring at her.

"What?" she said, with no lack of defensiveness on her part.

I made a clicking sound with my tongue. "You have no clue what you're doing, do you?" I crossed my arms and shook my head. "None."

"I've never had this problem," she said, then went back to shoving sausage in her mouth two at a time so she didn't have to answer any more questions.

"I'm going before I kill you," I told her.

She said something in response, but I couldn't make it out while she was chewing.

I left Tuesday to her chewing and made my way into the kitchen, knowing today was a busy day. Issy had to can the last of the sweet potatoes before they went bad. If I couldn't go stare at sludge that wanted to swallow me up and burp me out like a bad meal, I might as well help somewhere, even if it was a futile chore. Who knew—maybe the sludge would like a taste of sweet potatoes as it devoured this place.

There were four of them bustling around the kitchen. Two guys I'd seen in passing who were safe as far as death visions went. One would die of an infection, but not for a while. Tommy would die from what appeared to be a heart attack of some sort, but long after his bones wouldn't straighten out and he'd lost all his hair.

Then there was Frenchie. Her blond curls would be white when she bled out. I wasn't sure how she ended up with her ankle chopped off by an axe, but it didn't end well.

"Issy, I'm free today. What can I do to help?"

Issy looked up from where she was dragging a rag across a filled jar, getting ready to seal the opening with the hot wax. Normally Issy would tell me she had everything under control. Today, she scanned the kitchen for what else needed to be finished.

"Can you take over Frenchie's spot so she can start the evening stew?" she asked, while picking up a filled crate of jars. "I've got to move some crates around downstairs and make more room."

"Got it." When I'd been at the village, and they had given me chores before things got really bad, I hadn't been allowed around the food. No matter that I was a second-generation Plaguer; contagion of the Bloody Death still lingered in some minds.

She smiled and left, assuming I'd know what to do when it came to canning. She headed down the cellar, and I didn't say a word. She was already running crazy, and how hard could it be?

"What do you need me to do? Where should I pitch in?" I turned to Frenchie, trying to appear friendly, even though I didn't particularly care for the young woman. It wasn't that she'd done anything wrong to me. It was this tingling in my gut when she looked my way, like I'd swallowed a worm. Still, I was here to help.

She wiped her hands on her apron as she picked up a knife and started chopping up potatoes. She waved toward the center counter behind her and said, "I was about to start some more water to boiling. We need to sterilize the rest of the jars. You could start there."

I walked over to the large cast iron pot she'd waved at, getting ready to bring it to the large fireplace that was rigged with hooks and poles across it. I picked it up and dropped it with a hiss, splashing hot water onto my arms to go with the burning hands.

Frenchie turned around. "Oh my, are you all right? I meant that pot," she said, pointing to another one on the other side. "Let me see your hands."

I saw the smirk on her face. She'd known what pot I was going to pick up.

"I'm fine. No harm done." I smiled even as the stinging pain of the burn throbbed up my arm. I had a better inkling on how she might end up with an axe chopping off her ankle. Only curious thing now was why it took so long.

"Of course. You can't possibly be burned, right? Don't you heal people?" She smiled.

I'd thought her distaste for me might've come from the Hell Pit heading this way. Now I was wondering if it came from a different direction, maybe being able to save Issy?

"Only if I suck the life out of someone first. You willing to donate a little?" I asked, holding out a scalding hand. I let the silence drag out for a second before I laughed and waved it at her. "Only kidding with you."

A lie for a lie. She hadn't meant to point me in the direction of the hot pot, and I didn't want to suck some life out of her. I turned and, with a pep in my step, went to the pot with cold water, determined to ignore her for the rest of the day. It worked out well, since she couldn't stay far enough away from me now.

By the time we were done, it was still light out, but none of the guys had come back yet.

I walked outside, wanting to hunt them down but forcing myself to go to a different destination.

MY HEAD BROKE THE SURFACE OF THE WATER, AND I saw Callon's feet by the side of the hot spring, a tinge of red in his eyes.

"I couldn't find you."

"I was here." After hours in the kitchen beside Frenchie, I'd needed an outlet that didn't include punching her in the face. This was the best I could come up with.

He might've looked human, but the beast still raged within. The beast, his strength but also his weakness, at least when it came to me. I was sure of it now. Something about me called to that side of him, and I wasn't sorry for it. It called to me as well.

I lifted myself out of the pool, the t-shirt I'd been swimming in clinging to me.

His gaze didn't drop from my face, but I saw the red grow stronger. He'd ignored me when I offered myself, but I wasn't a complete innocent. I knew desire when I saw it. I grabbed my pants and tugged them on. If he was going to pretend he didn't want me, I wasn't going to keep putting myself out there. I'd pretend too. In the end, we were both liars, and life moved on.

"What's wrong with your arms?" he asked, still looking at my face. Clearly he'd taken in the rest of me.

"I was helping out with the canning and splashed a little water. How'd it go today? Did you find anything that worked?" I tugged on my coat, pulling my wet hair out of the back.

"Not well. That's why I'm here. We're leaving for Dax's in the morning. Only us. I want the guys here to keep working on it while we're gone."

Just like that, Frenchie didn't matter anymore. Callon's and my little game of pretend was wiped from my mind. Everything became real. I hugged myself, pretending my wet skin was what gave me a chill when it was Callon's words. We'd hit a brick wall and there was no more denying it.

One of four things was going to happen next. The guys would figure out a way to stop the Hell Pits, which was unlikely. Bitters would know something that would help, which was equally unlikely. Bitters could break the Death Spell that joined Callon and I—possible, but again, unlikely.

Or someone was going to try to kill me. Highly probable.

He'd said "only us." Was he afraid Koz would balk at what had to be done? Would it be only Callon returning?

EIGHTEEN

"Don't do it. You're crazy." Tuesday was hovering over me as I threw my few items into the bag.

I turned, putting my finger to my lips. Callon and the guys were outside making an awful racket, but that didn't mean they couldn't somehow hear anyway.

"You're going to get me caught," I whispered.

"Trying to get Bitters to undo it is crazy," she said, but in a much softer tone that even the freaks of nature downstairs probably wouldn't hear. "First off, you don't know this wizard or what he's about. He could trick you and do something bad instead. Second, why would you do that? What if they give up trying to stop the Hell Pits and figure it's easier to kick you out instead? Well? Then what?"

And if Bitters can't break it, they kill me instead. But those words wouldn't leave my lips. I'd rather not make it back here than cost her the life she had now. Koz was a good man. He wasn't a killer. She'd be happy with him. He'd eventually tell her he loved her, they'd have furry little babies, and life would go on. She'd fought for me too many times. This wasn't her war.

I tied the string on my bag and tossed it over my shoulder before turning back to her. "If they kick me then that's their choice. I don't have a right to ruin their home."

Tuesday hugged me so tightly that it was as if part of her feared I'd be dead by tomorrow. Great. That made two of us.

He'd said he didn't kill innocents. I was going to cling to that, too. And if it were bullshit, I wouldn't go down without a fight. If one of us wasn't making it back here, it wasn't a sure thing it was me. I had some skills now. Hadn't used them much, but I might be starting soon.

"I gotta go. He's waiting." I pulled out of her hug.

"You better come back." Her demand started out strong but ended on a quiver.

"Don't have anywhere better to go," I said, laughing a little. It was all nerves, though.

Callon was talking to Koz in the hall when I walked down the stairs toward the front door. They stopped speaking before I hit the bottom stair. Could they have made it more obvious? I hated when people talked crap about you and then you had to guess what horrible things they'd said. It would be better if they told you. The stuff that ran through my mind was always the worst-case scenario. Like had Koz just asked Callon where he was going to bury my body? Asked him to be kind and make it quick? Had Callon been gracious enough to say he'd wait to kill me until after Bitters failed?

"Ready?" Callon asked, his stoic expression giving no clues to what their discussion had been about.

I nodded, my mouth too dry to speak.

He walked to the door and opened it. A big metal thing with a bench and handles was waiting outside. I'd seen things like it that had wheels attached. This machine had weird ski-looking things underneath.

I wasn't worried until I saw his bag and another already tied down on the back.

"What is this?" He better not want me to climb on that thing.

"A snowmobile." He walked toward it and then sat on it. Worse, he looked at me as if I were going to climb on behind him. "We're taking it part of the way."

Callon wasn't going to kill me miles from here. He was going to kill me a few hundred feet from here with that machine in a "tragic accident."

"You want me to get on that thing?"

"I don't like wasting what gas we have, but you're too slow and we've got too far to go. This will be more comfortable."

His words were like flies buzzing around my head that I wanted to swat away.

Hell Pits. Bitters. Hadn't I told Tuesday how important it was that I meet this Bitters guy? If I didn't, I'd be dead before the month was out, and not because of sludge. They'd have no choice. Someone would do it, probably while I slept.

If this was how it had to happen, then so be it. *Walk forward. Walk forward, damn it. Climb on the back of the metal monstrosity like you didn't have a fear in the world and do what you have to do.*

"We're losing light," Callon said.

With a deep breath, I forced myself forward and climbed on the back of the thing.

When it sprang to life, I jumped, wrapping my arms around Callon's waist. I might've shrieked a bit when we took off, but I'd gotten on.

I'D NEVER THOUGHT OF MYSELF AS BEING STUPID, but it took me longer than needed to realize we weren't stopping for anything as silly as sleeping or eating. This revelation should've hit me when he'd handed me some dried meat before we got on the bike after our last call of nature. It hadn't. I didn't catch on until the sun settled in for the evening but we didn't. I'd given up on stretching my legs, and my back felt like I'd been stoned, but I'd tolerated it because Callon obviously felt a pressing need to get to Dax's as fast as possible.

When he stopped suddenly without me requesting it, my breathing hitched, my pulse raced, and my hands shook. And now here we were, stopping in the middle of some strange hills for no apparent reason. This was it. He was going to kill me.

"Get off. I've got to switch us out."

I jumped off the metal monster and then took a few more steps backward for good measure. I tried not to take it personally. He didn't have a choice. He couldn't get rid of me, and I was the draw for the Hell Pits. It was me or his home. Me or his people. It wasn't personal, right? But couldn't he at least wait to see if Bitters could help? Didn't I deserve that?

Fuck him. This was personal. He drove the thing into a hole in the hill as I shook out my arms and cracked my neck. I was as ready as I was going to be, and I wouldn't go down without a fight.

He walked back out of the hole in the hill with another metal machine, this one with tires and our bags already strapped to the back.

He walked it closer.

I jumped back. "That's all? You just wanted to switch out the bike?"

"What did you think we were stopping for?" he said, eyes intent.

He knew what I was thinking. He had to. It wasn't a crazy thought.

"If you're going to try to kill me, then let's get on with this. May the best person win."

He rolled the bike a few feet toward me. "Get on the bike, Teddy. I don't have time for this."

I waved my hand toward the bike. "Why? So you can kill me farther away? Or after Bitters can't help? It's going to happen. You're going to have to kill me, so let's get this over with. Give it your best shot." I reached out so if he charged me, I'd hopefully have time to kill him first.

Fuck. I was going to have to kill him. Now my eyes were burning as if I were going to cry. What kind of ninny was I? This wasn't the behavior of a survivor.

"I'm not going to kill you now. I'm not going to kill you if Bitters can't help with the Hell Pits, because I don't want to. Can you get on the bike now?"

"How am I supposed to believe that? It makes no sense. That's not a good reason." Lots of people didn't want to do things. What kind of stupid logic was that? I didn't want to kill him, but if he came for me, I would.

"It's all I have, so get on the bike. We're wasting time."

I looked at him, then the bike, then the woods. It wasn't as if I could get away from him. We were stuck together unless one of us died.

"Your hands are capable of sucking the life out of me while I willingly let you wrap your arms around me. If you think I'm going to kill you, go ahead and take me out first. Otherwise, we need to be moving." He climbed onto the bike and waited.

I didn't move. Could he be that stupid? Or that trusting? I would kill him if I had to. Did he not believe it? I would. I could do it under the right circumstances.

"Any day now," he said, his back to me.

How stupid was he? You didn't turn your back on your adversary. He was going to get himself killed one of these days.

Or was it his inner beast who was giving me his back? Callon might not like me, but it wasn't that simple, was it? I walked over and climbed on the back, feeling a bit more confident.

"It's the beast, isn't it? He won't let you kill me, will he?" I asked, already knowing the answer.

"You're gloating like I've been bested. *I'm* the beast; the beast is me. We. Are. The Same. Fucking. Person."

"You say that, but I'm not so sure."

The bike roared, ending the conversation.

NINETEEN

The bike slowed. I lifted my cheek from Callon's back, wondering if we were doing another switch or if the bike needed to drink more stuff. It needed to drink more than I did.

I knew it was neither of those when I saw the gate we were approaching late in the morning. A man pulled it open. As we turned the bend, he nodded to Callon. He took a longer look at me as we passed. Strangers weren't a good thing in the Wilds, especially if you had something worth fighting for, and they definitely did.

They called it a farm, but I'd thought that was a nickname. It wasn't. This was a *real* farm. It looked like it had been plucked right out of a picture from the Glory Years, back before the world had gone to shit. There were fields with cows, big black and white spotted things roaming around, and fluffy-looking sheep. There were chickens squawking and pecking in front of a large yellow house that had a wide front porch with chairs and a swing.

Beyond the house there were smaller buildings scattered around. One was big and red. Other ones looked like smaller houses, like the smattering of cottages that were around the lodge, but not as hardy looking, like they didn't need to withstand the same elements.

There were quite a few people going about their business, carrying baskets and working the land. *Too* many people. I'd have to try to keep my distance, or I was in for a long and torturous day.

The front door of the main house swung open as the bike roared its way toward it. A woman about my age stepped out onto the porch, her hair so blazing red in the sun that it made all the other colors around seem dull. Dax followed behind her, stepping too close to her to make the woman anyone but Dal, his wife.

Callon pulled the bike up, and I climbed off before he turned it off. I straightened up a little slower than I had a few hours ago, which had been slower than the time before.

Dal and Dax walked to the edge of the porch toward us. I took a peek at the scar on the top of her hand. There wasn't a P visible, but the placement was telling.

She paused out of my range of death vision. It wasn't out of courtesy to me. It was most likely *her* range as well. She smiled at Callon, before her eyes, the color of spring grass on a sunny day, met mine. "Teddy?"

"Yes. Dal?"

She smiled and nodded. "Perhaps we shouldn't get too close? I can see certain things from your past, usually the worst."

Wow, she *had* been stopping for me. I'd never even considered warning people of my visions.

"If you're game, so am I. I've got nothing to hide."

Callon stepped in front of me. "Maybe Dal has a point."

I jerked my head in his direction. Why would he care? Was he embarrassed by me? Why else would he stop us? Was it too much to be tied to the girl who'd been abused for years? An embarrassment that he couldn't escape? He was a beast, after all. He didn't have the same vulnerabilities. He was probably disgusted by my weakness.

That was *his* right. Also *his* problem. I stepped around him, but not before I gave him a look that could've scorched the earth he stood upon.

Dal immediately took a step back. "Callon might be right. It can be an intrusion."

I took another step toward her. "I don't have any secrets. And as to what I see, which I'm sure Dax has told you, I can share it if you'd like, or not. That's your choice."

She nodded and closed the gap between us. Nothing. I couldn't see her death, and my shoulders relaxed. There'd be nothing to tell if she asked, and I hadn't realized until that second how badly I didn't want to tell Dax when his wife would die.

As to what she saw, that was a different story.

I still struggled with keeping my emotions off my face when I read a death, but she was a pro. Callon had said she was older than she looked, and he must've been right.

There were no gasps of horror, and my past could easily elicit some.

I was also adept at what to look for. I knew the signs of seeing the worst and having to hold it in. I wondered which horrible vision she'd seen. Was it one of the vicious beatings, or the day Maura died? If you asked me which memory was the worst, there wouldn't have been a second thought. When one of the only people who'd ever shown you kindness or love in your life disappeared, there was no worse agony.

Her eyes flickered away but then came back to meet mine. I could hear Callon's steps on the wood planks as he stopped beside me, his hand landing on the small of my back as if that was where it belonged.

"Did you see my death?" Dal asked.

"No. I'm not sure why, but that happens occasionally. I can't see theirs, either," I said, motioning between Dax and Callon.

There was a look that passed between Dax and Dal that made me think they might've known *exactly* why I hadn't. They didn't offer an explanation.

"Would you like to know what I saw?" Dal asked.

"No. Whatever it was, I've already survived it." I didn't need to relive it. Didn't need to have a conversation about it, either.

She smiled, as if she understood all too well. If I hadn't known she was a Plaguer, and all that came with it, I would've doubted the empathy I saw in her expression. That scar on her hand told me this woman had been through some of her own hard times. She must've survived one of those asylums that used to exist in Newco. That was where most Plaguers used to be sent. If she had, what she'd seen in my past wouldn't be that much worse. Who knew—I might've had it easier.

"Why don't you come in? You've got to be tired. The lodge is a long way from here." She smiled again, like it was easy for her, a thing she did all the time without thought. If she did have a dark history, she'd moved beyond it. She'd cleansed it from her psyche somehow. It didn't haunt her at night, stomping all over her soul in the dark, stealing her dreams when she finally collapsed in exhaustion.

I'd gone a lifetime believing my soul would be scarred forever. Her smile gave me hope.

"Come on," she said, walking into the house.

The inside was even better than the outside had led me to believe. There were colorful woven rugs over wide-planked wood floors. Furniture that was worn enough to cradle you was placed in front of a fire that would warm you on a chilly night. There were blankets folded to curl up under and pillows to prop up your head.

"If you're here, I'm guessing you haven't had any luck with the Hell Pits?" Dax asked.

"Unfortunately not," Callon said.

"Dax, let them get settled first." Dal laid a hand on Dax's chest. "Bitters won't be back until tomorrow, and we can talk after they have a moment. We've got one bedroom open upstairs for Teddy, and I can put you in one of the cabins, Callon."

I'd gone from a strong, confident woman with hope,

who didn't care what anyone knew about her past, to feeling my entire body seize up, wanting to wrap myself around Callon's leg if he tried to leave.

Breathe, for fuck's sake. It wasn't like he'd be far. He'd be a stone's throw from here. I could probably look out the window and see him at night. This wasn't an issue.

My lungs refused to work. I had to at least pretend to breathe so I didn't look a fool. The way they were eyeing me made me believe they were catching on anyway.

Callon's hand landed on my lower back again. "We don't want to put anyone out. We can share. It's not a problem," Callon said, his hand sucking all the tension out of my muscles as he spoke.

"Are you sure you'll be comfortable—"

"Dal, let them be. That's how they want it," Dax said.

"Oh, okay. Do you want to go up now and take a nap before dinner?" Dal asked.

I was already halfway to the door when I answered, "That would be great. Let me just go get my bag."

Callon followed me outside. I made it to the bike, ignoring the occasional looks from people farther away, all wondering who the newcomer was.

I was fiddling with the knot when Callon moved my hands aside to do it. I would've been able to do it easily if my insides didn't feel like they'd been tossed in a barrel and rolled downhill. I wasn't sure if I was angry at Callon for being ashamed of me or thankful he'd saved me from humiliating myself. Or was I pissed at myself for caring about either? That was the problem with burying your emotions for most of your life. When you had strong ones, it was hard to determine where they were coming from.

I stepped closer and watched as he undid the knots, debating whether to say something about what he had done. It bubbled up anyway. "Why did you try to block Dal from seeing my memories? Are you ashamed of me?"

His eyes flicked toward the house and back, letting me know that we might not have the privacy I thought.

I didn't care. For me, this conversation didn't need it. If he had something to say, he could say it aloud for the world. My past was horrible and an all-around mess, but it was my mess. It was me, where I came from and who I was.

He grabbed the bags and took a step back toward the house. I grabbed his arm, refusing to let him walk away that easily.

"I'm not ashamed of who I am or what I've been through. My life was agony, but I survived it. I was forged in the fires of hell, but I'm still standing."

"I'm not embarrassed of you," he said, in a whisper that somehow seemed like a scream. "What I think is that it's personal. You should share what you want to share, not because someone can tinker around in your head."

"I don't believe you."

He scoffed. "What a surprise. I'd be insulted, but you don't believe anyone, do you?"

He went to walk away again, and I got in front of him. "Why should I? Because everyone is so trustworthy? As if they aren't having conversations about how life would be easier with me dead?"

"Maybe because I'm the one saving your ass all the

time? What about that? Is that a good enough reason?" He didn't bother whispering this time. I was fairly certain he'd given up caring who heard.

He tossed our bags on the porch and walked away from the house.

TWENTY

Everything about the place was homey. From the curtains in the bedroom I was in to the way the wood banister was worn to a patina. I loved how the stairs dipped in the center from so many footsteps as I made my way downstairs toward the smell of food.

The house was empty except for sounds coming from the kitchen as I continued to follow my nose. Dal was pulling a roast out of a wood oven.

"Do you need help?" Dal had mentioned dinner earlier, right? They were going to feed us, hopefully?

"No, all done," she said, placing the big pan on top. "Fudge taught me how to make this a very long time ago," she said, staring at the big hunk of meat with a bit too much emotion.

"Fudge?"

She nodded, a wistful smile on her face. "She's gone, but she was like a mother to us all here. She'd make this dish right around the first frost, when the nights were cold enough that all you wanted to do after sundown was curl up by the fire with people you love. Now I make it. Somehow it feels like a little piece of her is still here with us when I do."

I leaned back against the counter as she scooped juices out of the pan and poured them over the meat. Dal seemed to have an iron will. She might be small, but she was a fighter. It exuded from every short inch of her. She might enjoy making a roast, but I wouldn't let that fool me into thinking she couldn't kick some ass if needed.

"So, you and Dax have this house all to yourselves?"

"Oh no, we're usually packed. You came at an odd time. Bookie—who's like a brother to me—is a digger. You know, someone who likes to dig up old pieces of history? He's out at a site and won't be back for another week or so. Tank went with him to help. He lives here too, and has been with Dax for longer than I can remember. Bitters *also* lives here, but he'll be back tomorrow. He went to go..." She turned to me and shrugged. "Actually, I can't tell you where he went. He disappears without a word, but he's never gone longer than a day."

She moved the roast to a plate and then heaped some creamy potatoes in a bowl beside it, smiling. "Just like Fudge's," she said softly to herself. She walked to the door and waved to someone. "Sit," Dal said, pointing to a chair at the table in the next room.

Dax walked in the back door, looked at the table, and smiled. "Just like Fudge," he said, running his hand over her shoulder.

"First frost." She closed her hand over his briefly before he moved to the seat on her right.

Callon walked in a minute later. I wondered if he'd take the seat the farthest away from me.

He took the empty seat beside me. My lips parted, but then I closed them. He gave me a slight nod. I returned it. We'd have a truce, at least through dinner.

"So how bad is the upheaval in Newco?" Callon asked, as if he were picking up a thread of interrupted conversation.

"Bad enough that they'll be warring amongst themselves for quite a while," Dax said.

"Would you like some bread?" Dal asked. She still had the basket in hand when she continued, "Dax told me about the Hell Pits. Did you bring a sample for Bitters?" She was looking at our bags as she asked, as if she wanted to tear them open.

"We did." Callon dug into his food, making no effort to go fetch the sample, even though it was in his bag sitting right by the door.

Dax barely gave it a second before he said, "I've never examined the stuff up close."

Callon stiffened. "Looks like mud."

Callon didn't want them to see it. He was afraid it was going to follow me around the room like always. I was sure Dax had already told Dal that it pointed at me. This wouldn't be a surprise, and it wasn't something that was avoidable. They'd see it once Bitters got here anyway.

And maybe, this time, it wouldn't follow me. It had a full-blooded Plaguer right here. If it liked me, it might love her. Wouldn't that be wonderful?

I skidded back my chair. "I'll go get it."

Callon stopped eating. "We should wait until Bitters comes."

"Dax already knows, and he clearly tells Dal everything, so she knows too." I stood and walked slowly away from the table, watching Callon for any sudden movements. He leaned back in his chair, watching me. I'd gotten past the first hurdle. Callon wasn't tackling me on my way to the bag.

He wasn't smiling, but neither was I. It wasn't something I was looking forward to, but I'd rather get it over with. And there was a very real chance it would have a new favorite after today.

I opened the bag and unwrapped the cloth that cradled the jar. The sludge was already leaning toward me. Or was it leaning toward where Dal stood behind me?

I picked it up and checked the seal on the lid, which appeared to have an even heavier layer of wax than last time I'd seen it. Still, I kept my hands toward the bottom. Didn't want to encourage it to break free.

I'd never walked with more caution in my life. They were watching me as I returned, the table already cleared in preparation. I placed the sealed jar on the table, near Dal. It hit the wood with the thud of a boulder. If it were attracted to my Plaguer ancestry, surely it would prefer first-generation blood? She had to outrank me with that.

Callon remained seated, an elbow on the armrest. Dal and Dax were out of their seats, bending over to examine the stuff.

"If I hadn't seen the Magician getting eaten up by it, I'd think it was a hoax," Dax said.

Dal reached for the jar and then held it closer to the oil lamp in the center of the table.

"Be careful," Dax said.

"Don't worry. I have no intention of dropping this stuff in my home," she told him, keeping two hands on the bottom of it.

There it was, a pure Plaguer, holding it. I began inching away in a different direction, hoping it wouldn't slither over with me. The farther away from Dal I moved, the more it shifted in my direction. How could this be? It had her! I wanted to take the jar and yell at it.

I'd hoped this was going to go differently, but I was beginning to realize that hope was a useless emotion that set you up for failure. Expecting the worst was a much better way to prepare yourself for reality than all this *ooh, wouldn't it be nice* crap.

Thankfully, I'd almost completely given up on hope. If I hadn't, I might've been more disappointed.

Eyes darted to me. Callon stood and moved closer to Dal and Dax, which conveniently put him in between us.

Dal passed the jar to Dax. He spun it around until all the stuff was furthest away from me. We all watched as it slithered right back toward me.

"What do you think the draw is?" Dal asked, still looking at it.

"I was hoping it was my Plaguer blood, but that doesn't seem to be the case, since you would surely have the stronger draw." I crossed my arms and leaned against the wall, belatedly realizing that I was now mimicking Callon's stance. I crossed an ankle to change it up a little.

"And nothing kills it?" Dax asked.

"Nothing kills it or stops it. It defies gravity to get to her," Callon responded, his hand going to the back of his neck.

"Dax talked to Bitters," Dal said. "He didn't have any ideas, but he's never looked closely at a sample. Hopefully with this he might come up with something." She shot me one of her hopeful smiles.

I wanted to tell her to stuff it. I was done with that crap. Hope wasn't worth a damn. I didn't say it, though, because the bed upstairs might've been the most comfortable thing I'd ever lain on. I'd tell her tomorrow as we were leaving where she could stick her hope, right after I ate some more of her roast for breakfast.

Or maybe I'd say nothing. She seemed nice. I just wish she'd stop with all the good thoughts. I didn't have time for that nonsense.

"Do you know if there's been any change in the Hell Pits near here?" As soon as the question was out of my mouth, a look passed between Dax and Dal that made me wish I were sitting again. What did they know? The longer they took to answer, the worse it was, and it seemed there was a silent debate going on. Maybe it wasn't who would answer but if they'd answer at all.

"What is it?" Callon asked, more impatient than I was for once.

"I was going to mention it later," Dax said.

"When I wasn't around?" I asked.

Dal took a step toward me. "Dax, she has every right to know."

Dax's jaw shifted, sort of the same way Callon's did when he didn't like what he had to say. "There's one several hours from here. I haven't been out to see it in a bit, but I have people keeping me posted. It's been slowly migrating in a northwesterly direction."

Was that bad? What did that mean? I didn't even know where northwesterly was. Callon knew, but he wasn't speaking.

"Can someone please tell me what that means?" I asked, turning to Dal.

Dal stepped even closer. She lifted her hand toward me and then dropped it, as if she'd read some *back off* expression on my face I hadn't been aware of. She clasped her hands together, as if to keep them from touching me.

"The lodge is northwest of here. It's been moving toward you," she said.

TWENTY-ONE

I TURNED OVER SO MANY TIMES THAT MY FEET HAD to fight for freedom from the blanket. The bed was still amazing, but it didn't seem to matter. Callon was missing, and with the newest revelation, there'd be no sleep on the horizon.

How could I sleep when there might be nowhere safe on this earth for me? I thought if I found a way to leave Callon, got away from the lodge, and kept going, I'd find a safe place, somewhere. But if a Hell Pit days away was moving toward me, there might not be anywhere I could go that would remain safe.

This was it. If Bitters couldn't help, I'd be on the run from these things for the rest of my life. I'd be damned to the life of a lonely wanderer because I couldn't condemn anyone else.

It sounded like these things had been around for years. Why did they want me now? Why couldn't they have overtaken the village when I'd been miserable and wishing for death more days than not? What had changed?

Why now? Why? What had changed?

The witch, that day in the tent, when she'd used my magic. I'd never killed anyone before. If I could've saved someone, I would've saved Maura as I held her hand for days as she died. She hadn't *only* used my magic. She'd woken it up somehow. And now? It was going to be the end of me.

I got up, wrapped the blanket around my shoulders, and made my way down to the back porch. I settled onto the bench. Winter here was nothing like the cold I was used to. The trees were barren and there was a chill, but not the bone-deep freeze of up north, or "northwesterly," as I now knew it to be.

I rested my head back on the yellow shingles of the house as I looked beyond the scattered cabins full of sleeping people to the tree line beyond. Was Callon out there running around? Was he planning on coming in sometime tonight, or would he avoid me until forced? I wished I had that option. It was getting that I couldn't sleep without knowing he was nearby, preferably next to me.

I would've rather been at the lodge. Not that this place was bad. It was the opposite, in fact. It was amazing. But I wouldn't be getting too much more time at the lodge. Days were numbered wherever you were. I knew that better than anyone, being constantly reminded of death. But there was something about having that number defined that added a preciousness that didn't exist when time was sprawling out in front of you, seemingly endless.

The back door creaked and boots sounded on the wooden porch. I knew it wasn't Callon before Dax leaned a shoulder on the beam, leaving a healthy gap between us. I wrapped the blanket around my shoulders as a gust of evening air swept over me but uncrossed my legs and lowered my feet to the ground. Dax seemed nice enough, but that meant nothing. Lots of people seemed all sorts of things they weren't until you met them alone with no witnesses about. There was nothing like the dark of night to bring out someone's true shade.

He nodded in my direction. "I didn't mean to startle you. If I'm disturbing you, I can go back in."

I nodded, giving a tentative *we're fine*. Not because we definitely were, but he was currently behaving. Also, this was his porch—and his house. It didn't seem fitting to kick him out when the only thing he'd done so far was be an unfamiliar male.

He turned from me toward the trees, as if he sensed my unease with his stare. I was glad. I preferred having his back to me, even if it were a false sense of security.

"Dal mentioned you've had a bit of a rough go of it," he said.

"You mean like half the population of this fucked-up world? Yes, I guess that's true." I might not be willing to hide my past, but that didn't make it open for discussion.

He looked over his shoulder. "Maybe a little worse than?"

I gave him a faint grunt. He might not look that old,

but he sure spoke like he was. I was having a fine time out here alone, and he was going to drive me back inside.

"Look, I know it's none of my business and I can't quite explain it, but I feel a closeness to you—"

I jumped up from the bench and took a few steps away from the house, my heart pounding, ready to run.

He held up both hands. "I'm sorry. That's not the type of *closeness* I meant. Actually, it couldn't be further from it."

Only the thinnest thread of sanity kept me in my spot. I was overreacting. I knew it. Just being here alone with a man I didn't know, with Callon nowhere around, made me feel vulnerable. It was as if I were back in the village, and everywhere I turned there was a threat. Like I'd forgotten that I could kill with a touch. I was the meanest, baddest thing in the Wilds, and I had to remember that. I didn't need to run anymore. I was the predator. The top of the food chain. If I could stop feeling like the victim and remember it, maybe I wouldn't be about to run through the woods with no shoes and a blanket pulled over my shoulders.

"I'm not afraid of you." I gulped in a few deep breaths and took a step forward, and then another. I was almost back at the bench, and he was keeping a respectable distance.

"You like space. I can respect that," he said, taking another step away as if the awkwardness were his fault.

The better he was, the more my skin burned. "I over-react occasionally, but I'm fine. I'm a lot tougher than I look, and being too trusting is stupid."

"I completely agree."

He needed to stop being so accommodating and shut up or I'd be telling him things I shouldn't. I was already blathering like an idiot.

"Can I give you a piece of advice? You don't need to take it, but just listen."

I shrugged. He could take that however he wanted. I wasn't talking any more, no matter what he said. Who knew what idiocy I'd say next?

"Callon is a hard man. For whatever reason, he's willing to protect you, and he doesn't seem to be looking for anything else. Don't feel like you need to repay that."

"I really don't think this is any of your business." I hadn't planned on talking, but that definitely needed to be said.

"It's not, but I needed to tell you anyway. I'm not blind. I see there's something between you two. You need to understand that, at heart, he's more beast than man. He's got an untamed savage in him, and you need to realize that before you decide to get any deeper."

"Nice way to talk about your friend." He was lucky I didn't have one of those dinner knives with me, or I might've stabbed him with it. Some friend he was.

"This isn't a betrayal. He'd tell you himself." He smiled like I hadn't pretty much called him an asshole.

I stood, anger burning away any fear of getting too close to this man in the middle of the night. "Let me tell you something: he's no more savage than I am."

Dax let out a short, soft laugh. "You know, you really do remind me of my wife. If my daughter had lived, she might've been a little like you."

But I wasn't his daughter. I hadn't had a father who

gave a fuck; I'd had a jailer who tortured me. Sitting here waffling about things that could've been didn't do anyone any good.

I nodded and then walked inside. The cost of fresh air was getting too steep.

———

Callon walked into the bedroom an hour or so later, bringing with him the smell of the forest and all things wild. Red tinted his eyes as the beast clung to him, not ready to be forgotten.

I turned, giving him my back as I burrowed under the covers a little farther. The mattress dipped as he stretched out beside me.

He pulled me to him until my back was to his chest and his arm was around my waist.

I shoved away from him. "I don't need you to—"

He pulled me back to his chest. "I'm not embarrassed of you."

I stopped moving.

"I would never be embarrassed of you," he said.

I nodded, once again afraid to speak for fear of what stupid thing I might say. Or worse, he'd hear my voice crack. What he thought shouldn't matter. I kept telling myself that, hoping I'd believe it soon.

TWENTY-TWO

Callon was already up and gone before I got up. I could hear the din of the full house as I made my way to the stairs. I paused halfway down and peeked over the banister to see a line of people extending from the front to the back. I turned around and walked back up the steps. I didn't like people more than I liked the food. It was too early to be surrounded by this many of them.

I was curled up on the window seat a half an hour later when the door opened. Callon walked in and held out a biscuit with several pieces of bacon shoved in between the two halves. This was something different.

"I wasn't hungry," I said.

"Eat it. You'll need it. Bitters is back. We're going to go talk to him as soon as the house clears out."

I took the biscuit. Was this a Southern thing? Or had they run out of other foods?

"Dal made it for you. She's got a thing for bacon."

I took a bite. The bacon wasn't cold, but it wasn't hot either. She'd made it a bit ago. He hadn't wanted to bring it to me, but now here Callon was, a shoulder leaning against the window, bringing me food, waiting to take me to Bitters to solve my problems.

I wanted to be mad at this man, but the truth was that I didn't know if I had the right anymore. Somehow that made me even angrier, because that was what I did when I was helpless. But I couldn't this time.

I took another bite of my cold bacon sandwich and leaned my head back, watching Callon not watching me. He stared out at the field beyond the window, probably wondering how he'd gotten to this place as well.

"I'm sorry. I shouldn't have gotten mad at you for trying to protect my privacy." That was the hardest sorry I'd ever said. Truth was that I'd only said sorry a handful of times in my life. I hadn't been in a position to cause harm to many people until recently, and if I had, they'd had it coming.

His eyes shifted to mine. "You're a little fucked up. It's okay. I get it."

I didn't say anything, couldn't talk past the lump that had formed, which had nothing to do with the biscuit being dry and the bacon being cold. I hadn't completely believed him yesterday, but I did now. He wasn't embarrassed of me. But I hadn't believed him because *I* was. My past was an embarrassment, and I wore it like a shield, so used to people shunning me that I pushed most of them away first.

I ate the last of my biscuit and bacon in silence.

When Callon turned his head slightly toward the door, it was showtime.

"They're ready for us," he said.

I got up from the seat while he went and took the jarred sample off the dresser.

I paused before the door, taking a few slow breaths. "Even if he can't help with that," I said, pointing at the jar, "he might still be able to remove the spell. At least it won't be your problem then."

I wouldn't have to stay at the lodge, either fearing for my life or waiting for its destruction. Tuesday wouldn't take it well. I'd have to leave like a thief in the middle of the night and leave her a note. She'd follow me otherwise.

Callon flattened his hand on the door. "Bitters can't do that."

"How do you know?" I asked.

"Dax already asked him this morning. He won't deal in death spells."

I should've been more disappointed than I felt. Maybe I would've been if I'd thought Callon was telling me the truth, but I didn't. He seemed too determined to squash it. Why wouldn't he ask Bitters himself? But that didn't make sense either. Why wouldn't Callon want the spell severed?

"That sucks, but I guess we're stuck," I said with a shrug. Bullshitter. We weren't stuck at all. I'd be asking Bitters myself before we left.

Dal was waiting for us downstairs. "Dax is already down there filling Bitters in on some of the details," she said, walking to a door at the underside of the staircase. "Don't mind the smell. It's the special blend of tobacco he likes to smoke. It's safe—ish. Mostly safe? You might get hungry, but no lasting damage."

Dal opened the door and disappeared. I took a last

deep breath of fresh air before I followed her into the haze. Callon was right behind me, but I knew he would be. He always was.

The basement didn't look like it belonged to the rest of the house, and it had nothing to do with the stone walls. The place was piled with scrolls and papers. Books were heaped high in front of and on top of the furniture. Stacks also climbed the walls. The only surface that wasn't totally covered was a bed, and even that had some scrolls scattered upon it.

Dax stood in the far corner of the room beside a man who looked well beyond the grave. Bitters turned with a pep in his step that didn't match the crumpled paper skin.

"So this be the girl?" he asked. His voice sounded younger as well. He walked toward me, taking a puff of the pipe in his hand. A foul-smelling smoke filled the air in between us, adding to the thick haze.

I wasn't sure if it was this place, these people, or me, but this was the second normal human I couldn't get a read on. My hunch was that it was the people. They were too odd, like flipping open a book in a language you didn't know.

Callon moved around me, jar in hand. "This is the reason we're here."

Bitters put his burning pipe down on a stack of papers. Dax quickly picked it back up and put it on a metal plate before the place went up in smoke.

Bitters took the jar in his free hand and gave it a shake. He made a huffing noise. "How am I supposed to tell you like this?"

He cracked the wax seal before anyone could stop him and stuck his nose in the jar.

"That stuff ate a person," Callon reminded him, although I was fairly certain he'd already been warned.

Bitters didn't pull his nose from the jar until after he'd taken a really long sniff. "Smells a little foul, but I wouldn't worry about it."

I watched as the stuff was climbing the side of the jar, looking for an escape.

"It *ate* the Magician," Callon said.

Bitters held up the jar, looking at it again, but without any urgency or alarm. He lowered it. "It'll be okay."

Dax and Dal were hanging back, staying out of the conversation. Couldn't say I blamed them. Dax was the one who'd said to come out here. We'd traveled days and the guy was a nut.

Callon's chest expanded and then slowly deflated before he asked, "Do you know what the stuff is?"

Bitters dipped his finger into the sludge. I took a step back and heard a gasp come from Dal. Then we all stared in horror as he licked the stuff off his finger.

"It's some sort of magic, that's for certain. Can't say as it's good or bad, but then, I guess good and bad depends on which side you're playing for, right?" He laughed, screwed the lid on, and handed the jar back to Callon, who was speechless.

I inched forward, waiting to see if Bitters was going to die. If he was, I couldn't see it. Maybe it had been too little? Maybe he'd die in his sleep? What I did know was that I needed whatever information I could get from this man before he went belly up and I did the same shortly after.

I stepped around Callon, who was partially blocking me. "You might not think that this stuff, which swallowed one of the scariest men I've ever met, is a problem. But it doesn't want you. It wants me. It's trying to get to me, and I need to know why."

"I can see that," Bitters said, motioning to the jar in Callon's hand and the sludge that kept relocating itself toward my position in the room. "Come closer and let's have a look. I'll try to see if I can figure out why."

I glanced at Callon. He ran a hand through his hair, as if to say we had nothing else to try.

Bitters walked to a spot in the corner, the only place that had two chairs that weren't piled high with papers and bottles. They only had a couple of sheets of paper each.

Callon, Dax, and Dal slowly crowded in around us, leaving only enough room to not trip over us.

I sat in the chair opposite Bitters as he looked around until he found a large piece of curved glass.

"I have to say, the moment you stepped into the room, I've wanted to get a good look at you." He brought the glass to his eye and then leaned in close to my face.

"Why is that?" I asked, trying not to lean away from him. I'd asked him for answers. I'd have to sit through his exam.

"You've got an odd glow about you that I can't quite put my finger on. I know I've seen it before, but I can't remember who from. It'll come to me, though. It always does. This old brain forgets nothing, even the shit I want it to."

"Do you think this glow is what's driving the sludge toward me?"

"It's not only the glow. You've got a strange feel about you too. An odd type of magic. Where'd you say you were from?" He took his fingers and opened my eye wider.

"My mother was a Plaguer. That's where I get my magic."

"You have the feeling of human, but not entirely." He was staring into my one eye as if it opened up into my soul.

Bitters leaned back, and his eyes rested beyond my right shoulder. "There's some sort of something here. I can feel it."

"Do you think it might be the Death Spell? Callon said you didn't—"

"He doesn't deal in them," Callon said, shaking his head, as if I'd said something drastically wrong to Bitters.

Bitters didn't pay me any mind, ignoring my question completely. Maybe Callon hadn't lied?

Suddenly, Bitters jumped out of his seat. "Wait! I know what to do."

He was telling us all to wait as if we weren't sitting here hanging on his every word. Where did he think we were going? He was my last chance at answers because no one else had any. I wouldn't be leaving until I got them.

He began rifling through tubes and papers, which created an avalanche at his feet. He continued undaunted.

"I got it!" Bitters held up a bag of what looked like salt.

He grabbed a long oval dish full of ashes, then turned it over and dumped it on the floor. Dal was whacking at Dax's arm and pointing. Dax gave a shrug, as if he couldn't do anything with him.

"We incurred a debt," Dax said softly.

"How long is it going to take to get paid?" Dal asked.

Dax shrugged.

I lost interest in their domestic squabble as Bitters dumped the white grains onto the empty plate. He made two small piles before motioning to me. "I need blood. Not much. Just a couple drops."

I turned to Callon, who was staring down the old wizard as if he'd asked me to slit my wrists. I ignored the expression and put my hand out. "I need your blade. Mine is dirty." Mine was *always* dirty.

"A lot of things can be done with a person's blood," Callon said, as he continued to stare at Bitters.

"I vouch for him," Dax said. "He's crazy, a complete slob, nearly burned the house down five times already, but he's loyal."

I kept my hand out. "This is why we came. If he can give us answers, I'm not leaving without trying everything."

Callon didn't budge, and neither did I. The tendons in his neck were strung a little too tight, the line of his mouth too straight, and there was that flare in his eyes. It didn't matter.

"Fine. I'll use my dirty one," I said.

There was a small move of his head to the right. I was

fairly certain if we'd been alone it would've been a full shake and his eyes would've rolled skyward.

He drew out his dagger. "Give me your hand. You can't cut for shit, and unlike your knife, mine's sharp."

I gladly did. He was right. I was klutzy with a knife. I had a scar from when I'd helped Issy peel potatoes.

Callon made a slight prick on the tip of my finger.

Bitters smiled widely, a little too giddy for my taste, but I was all in at this point.

"Squeeze it onto the pile." He pointed, putting the plate right under my finger.

I'd only squeezed out a couple of drops, but the entire pile turned the color of my blood. This stuff was definitely *not* salt. What was he going to do with it? I tapped my foot a little faster as I thought about Callon's warning.

"Now you, Dal," Bitters said, waving her over.

I jerked my head to her, along with everyone else, as if she knew what was going on.

"Why me?" Dal asked, with the same look of confusion we all had.

"Why her?" Dax asked.

"Don't you want to do something with this and the mud?" I asked, all of us speaking over each other.

Callon was pointing at Dal as he asked Dax, "Wait, so you vouch for him when it's Teddy but it's not okay for Dal?"

"Only because it doesn't make sense. The mud doesn't want Dal," Dax said.

Callon stared at Dax for another second before turning to Bitters. "What are you playing at?"

Bitters seemed unfazed by all the aggressive energy

directed his way. "Do you people want answers from me or not? Dal is a Plaguer. Teddy was born from a Plaguer. I need to see if there's some sort of connection."

"So it still might be the Plaguer blood drawing the sludge?" I asked.

"I don't know," Bitters said, throwing his hands up.

I wasn't so sure he was as in the dark as he played. He knew something, or suspected, at minimum.

"Here." Dal strode forward, grabbing the knife that seemed to never leave her hip. She twirled the knife in her hand. She was squeezing out blood onto the other pile and I hadn't even seen her cut her finger.

Bitters took the plate and then turned as he placed it on the table. He began to whisper words I didn't understand, and the two piles of red began to rise. He continued to chant, and lines of red sand streamed upward and then began to circle each other. He continued, his words growing stronger, and a chill filled the air. The two streams of sand began to merge, and as they did, they glowed a light blue, like the heart of a flame.

"Look at that!" Bitters said, hopping up and down.

I looked back at Dal and Dax. He was their wizard. Did they know what he was so happy about? One look at their squinted eyes said no.

"She's your daughter." Bitters made a stabbing motion with his finger in my direction, before clapping and laughing as if he'd won a prize.

The sound of Bitters' hands slapping together was the only sound in the room. Even my heart had stopped beating. Thought was beyond me. All that existed in the place of my brain was muddled confusion.

"Bitters, our daughter is dead," Dax said. This was no gentle reminder but a verbal kick to the teeth.

So much for vouching for Bitters. It sounded like someone was going to die if he didn't stop with the made-up fantasy crap, or at least get evicted.

"That's what threw me off the scent. But no, I'm sure. She's your daughter. I'm positive." Bitters pointed at me again. If he didn't stop, I was going to break his arm.

I looked at Callon. He said nothing, but I didn't like the way his eyes had narrowed on me. He couldn't possibly believe this, could he?

I looked at Dal; her lips were parted and she had that damned hopeful expression on. Dax's expression was more of an *ah ha!*, which wasn't much better.

"You've all lost your minds. My mother lived half a world away from here and she sold me. You're not my parents." I turned to Bitters. "You were supposed to tell me about the Hell Pits. Does this have anything to do with why they'd be attracted to me, or was this some side amusement of yours?"

Bitters shrugged. "Mostly an amusement."

"Can you help me with the Hell Pit? Do you have any idea why it wants me?" I demanded.

"No," Bitters said.

What if Dal and Dax tried to cling to this bull and forced me to stay here? Then what? Suddenly, the basement was a jail I needed to escape. "I'm leaving."

I wasn't willing to be anyone's prisoner ever again. It didn't matter if they were trying to trap me with made-up family ties that couldn't be real. If Bitters wouldn't or couldn't figure out what was going on with the sludge stalking me, I was getting out of here.

I spun, looking to see how many people were between me and the stairs, hoping I wouldn't have to kill them on my way out. Either way, I was leaving. I'd had it with this place. I weaved around Callon. He could stay and continue to ponder Bitters' words and catch up with me later. I was getting my shit and getting out. I had a good five miles before I'd get stuck, and hopefully Callon would be following me by that point.

Dax shot in front of me. "I don't know what's going on, but we should look into this."

Dal got right behind him, her face still full of that hope stuff again in spite of what I'd told them. Stupid woman. I couldn't look at her. It was too sad.

"You said your daughter is dead. There's nothing to talk about. Let me pass."

Dax held out his hand. "I can't let you leave."

Callon grabbed my shoulder to pull me back. I was about to haul off and punch him when I realized his target was Dax. "Dax, get out of the way. She doesn't want to stay, and no one is forcing her to."

Dal grabbed Dax's arm. "Dax, he's right. We can't keep her here. Not after what she's been through. We can't force her."

Dax turned toward her. "What if—"

"It doesn't matter. We can't do it. We can't. Not after what she's been through." She clung to his arm as if he were the only thing keeping her standing. Dal looked over at me, glassy-eyed. "We force her to stay and she'll run the second she can, and we'll never see her again."

Dax stared at her for a moment before his hand covered hers. He nodded. She nodded back, as if to say it would be okay.

Dax turned to me. "I'm not letting you leave without some questions answered. After that, you can go. It's a fair compromise."

Callon turned to me. "What do you want to do?"

To run and not look back. I didn't know who these people were, but they weren't mine. I had Tuesday—that was my person. And Callon, maybe, as crazy as that seemed.

Dal was gripping Dax's hand so hard while she waited for my answer that he'd be bruised tomorrow. I shouldn't care what these people wanted, but he wasn't asking that much, right? And she was going to cry. I could see it. The longer I stood here arguing, the more her eyes filled. They weren't going to be able to hold that load too much longer without some tears springing free.

"Fine. For a little while only." I gave Callon a look that said, *And if they try to stop me after that, the gloves come off.*

He put his hand to my lower back again, letting me know he would back whatever play I wanted to make.

Dal and Dax led the way upstairs. They took a seat at the table, side by side.

I walked over but didn't sit. Callon didn't either.

"What happened to your child? You said she was dead. How can I be her?" I asked. It was brutal and to the point, but they were trying to latch on to me to relieve their sorrow. It wasn't my sorrow to fix. I had enough of my own problems without their two-decade-old grief to deal with. This wasn't why I'd come here.

Dal's head dropped forward. "I'm sorry about what happened downstairs. We're not trying to frighten you or force you to stay here, but we do have reason to think it could be true."

"Our daughter was only a month old when she caught a coughing sickness and died," Dax explained, putting his arm around Dal's shoulders.

"Then why would you think I was her?"

Dal reached up her hand, holding on to Dax's. "There is this place that can sometimes save the dead. It had worked for a dear friend of mine when I lost him. When our daughter died, we put her there. We checked on her every day for months, but it didn't seem to work. Finally, Dax thought we needed to stop. That it was destroying us. That we had to get past it."

"It was too hard, especially after our first loss. We had to move on before it broke us," Dax said.

"First loss?"

"Our son. I gave birth to him at five months, too small to survive on his own," Dal said.

No one spoke for a minute, as I could see Dal trying to gather herself.

Callon was the first to break the silence. "I don't know what kind of magic this place had, but after that long, I'd think it unlikely to have worked."

Dal was nodding rapidly, her head still dropped forward and with suspicious swiping action across her face happening.

Dax nodded, and I could see the logic hitting him. I wasn't their daughter.

"Who are your parents?" Dax asked.

"I didn't know them, but my mother was supposedly a Plaguer," I said. "Considering that I do have the sight, I believe it. She sold me as an infant to a man named Baryn. That's it. Every detail I know."

"Then you can't say for sure that you're not our daughter," Dal said, lifting her gaze to me again with that damn hope clinging in spite of the tears now flowing down her cheeks. "We need to go back to the grave. I want you to come with us."

"I'm not your daughter. We came for one reason only. To get answers about the Hell Pits." I would've left it there, except something about the smile being stripped from Dal's face hit some chord within me. Even if I'd decided to give up on hope, something about her losing it scratched and tore at my insides.

I wanted to tell them that I was done. I couldn't talk about it anymore. Maybe Bitters believed what he said, but that didn't mean it was true. Pretending as if we were family would only cause heartache in the end. I focused on Dax instead, on features that were set in stone. You couldn't wring an emotion out of him if you tried right now. He was locked down like granite.

Callon was standing a few feet to my right with a look that said he'd back me up either way. I was about to turn around and leave until I heard Dal take in a shaky breath. How many times had I done that very thing as I tried to hold it together because something in life had broken my heart once again? That shaking breath was my undoing.

"Look, once we have things under control, I'll come visit the grave if you want. But I can't do it right now." And later, I might be dead, but I wasn't going to tell them that. I'd never get out of this house.

Dax's mouth softened, and I took a glimpse at Dal. She didn't look happy, but at least her breathing wasn't choppy anymore.

"That would be good," Dax said. "We'll hold you to that."

Fuck. I'd been hoping for something closer to *We'll see you when we see you.*

"Will you stay the night?" Dal asked.

"If it's all right with you, yes."

I didn't want to. I wanted to grab my bag and hightail it out of this crazy house, but there was one last thing I had to handle before I left here.

TWENTY-THREE

"Twenty minutes out front," Callon said as he walked to the door with our bags in hand.

"I'll be down."

Twenty minutes? It was as if Callon had known I was up to something since last night. He hadn't gone for a run or a chat. I'd had to sit on my hands waiting for an opening. I watched out the window as Callon walked across the lawn, meeting up with Dax. Two down.

I heard the front door shut again, and a minute later, Dal was walking toward them. This was it. I had one chance to do this, and it had to happen now. I ran out of the bedroom and made my way downstairs.

The basement door was open, and a stream of funny-smelling smoke was wafting upward. I closed it behind me, hoping to muffle any noises the rest of the house might hear.

"Hello?" I said softly as I took a few more steps down.

"Come in," Bitters responded.

I spotted him around the corner, sitting at the table.

He got up and turned to look at me and then pointed his pipe in my direction. "Are you here to complain? I don't like complaints."

Even if I did want to rant and rave, I wouldn't right now. I still needed him.

"I'm here because I'm desperate and I need to ask you for one more thing." I barely took a breath before I continued, not giving him an opportunity to stop me. "The man I came with, Callon—there's a Death Spell that ties him to me that I'd like to get undone. And I know you don't like them, but I really need this."

"Death Spells are tricky things."

"So Dax did mention it to you?"

"No one needed to tell me anything. I can see it. There's a black rope that ties the both of you together."

Did that mean Dax had asked him or not? Did I press for an answer and risk alerting him? No. I needed this fixed. That was the important thing, and I was short on time because I had this hunch Callon didn't want it undone. Maybe he was afraid someone else would get me and use me. It didn't matter. I couldn't trust him. He'd already tried to shut me down once.

Bitters waved a hand next to me, and the image of a black rope appeared, leathery and thick. It disappeared into my waist, as if it were anchored to something inside me, then extended out until it faded into the wall in the direction of the front yard, where I'd last seen Callon.

"Can you sever it? I've heard Death Spells are harder to undo."

He nodded. It wasn't a vigorous nod but a gentle up and down.

"So you can reverse it?"

He took a deep drag of the pipe while he scratched his unruly hair. He blew out a few smoke circles before saying, "Yeah, I might, but it depends."

"On what?"

"How your magic reacts to it. If it cooperates, it'll work. If not, you might be stuck with it. And there will have to be payment." His eyes were narrowed, but I couldn't tell if this was some sort of swindle or if he'd gotten smoke in his eye.

"I'll pay whatever you want, but I need it done." Dal and Dax's conversation last night ran through my head. I now understood how someone could end up with a crazy wizard in their basement. If I was lucky enough to survive this and have a basement, he was welcome to it.

"Eh, I'll give it a shot."

He puffed on his pipe again, ashes falling about the floor, blending in with the others.

"Uh, what do you think the payment will be?" I asked.

"I don't have anything in mind now, but I'll come calling when I'm ready. You sure you want to break away from this Callon guy? I can't say he seems like a nice man, but that's not the important thing. He seems like the *right* man, and that's what counts."

"Shouldn't the right man be a nice man?" I asked.

"Sure, in fairytales maybe, but not in the world we live. You're better off with the man who can get the job done, by whatever means necessary. This Callon looks like that type." He stabbed his pipe at the air, emphasizing his point.

"I just need this done."

"Okay." With a shrug, he walked over and started moving things around on his table until he found a pair of scissors. He mumbled some words over them and then came to me and made a snip. The black rope dropped, hanging limply at my side.

"Done."

"That's it?" What the hell? A snip from a pair of scissors and the big, bad Death Spell is gone?

"Not sure. It might try to regrow, but you'll have a while before that happens. And if you're far enough away, it might not be able to. I'll call on you for the bill at some later point." He walked over to his table and went back to whatever I'd interrupted.

I didn't argue or question. I didn't have the luxury, as the clock was ticking and I needed to get out front before the house was searched. I took the stairs two at a time, left the house, and strolled across the lawn.

"Where were you?"

"Just getting ready to leave."

He didn't say he didn't believe me—aloud, anyway.

I turned away from Callon's all-knowing eyes and looked at Dax and Dal. "Thanks for the bed and the food. I'll try to make it back out this way after everything gets settled." I might need a place to crash while I was on the run from sludge, anyway.

They were looking at me the way Callon had. Was everyone going to call me a liar today? I hadn't even lied to them. I really might be back.

They kept staring, and I feared that, at any moment, Dal would try to embrace me.

"Okay, well, nice meeting you," I said with a quick wave. I walked away, heading toward the bike. Their desperate eyes burned my back, making me want to run, not walk.

The sooner I got out of here, the better. If I had to hang around and watch these people staring at me like I was their dead daughter, they might drive the final nail in the coffin of my sanity. I wasn't who they wanted me to be. That person was dead. They'd seen her die. The sooner they accepted that, the better.

I stood by the bike, waiting for Callon. He was taking his sweet old time as Dal and Dax continued to talk to him, while taking turns staring at me.

He finally made his way over, and I caught a glance of Dal and Dax from the corner of my eye. Dax put his arm around Dal's shoulder, giving her a gentle squeeze. She dropped her head and turned, walking out of his embrace and heading back to the house. Her head didn't lift.

Callon stopped beside me but didn't get on the bike. "You're sure you want to leave? We could stay another day or so. I don't think that place they're talking about is that far."

So help me, if he didn't get that disapproving tone out of his voice, I was going to ride out of here without him. And I could now, even if he didn't know it.

"I get that they're your friends, but that doesn't mean I should pretend to be their daughter. Don't you think there's something cruel about that? I do."

I stepped back, giving him room to swing his leg over the bike. He didn't.

"What?" I barked.

"Would it be the worst thing in the world to make sure? Let's face it, you could use some people on your side."

This from the man who'd nearly bitten his friend's head off? "Excuse me, but you weren't very nice yourself not too long ago."

"It was different and Dax understands what was happening."

"Oh, so for you it's different? But when I try to save everyone from chasing a fantasy I'm an ass?"

"I didn't say you're an ass. What I'm saying is you're running scared. Would it really hurt to—"

"Yeah, actually, it would be excruciating, so back off."

He didn't say anything else for a few seconds. It looked like I'd actually won the argument.

Then he stared in that way that said he thought I was being an ass. He shook his head, punctuating the stare. It was worse than words.

I turned my head, silently letting him know what I thought about his disapproval.

He finally got on the bike.

TWENTY-FOUR

WE PULLED UP TO THE LODGE RIGHT BEFORE SUNSET the next day. I climbed off, legs stiff and butt sore from riding for too many days with barely a break.

Zink was walking out toward us before Callon killed the engine.

"How much did it move?" Callon asked.

"You're not going to like this answer," Zink said.

"Is it closer?" I asked before Callon could respond.

Zink looked at me with utter contempt. "No. It moved a little southeast."

What was opposite of northwesterly? Southeast. At least, I thought so. "That's the direction we came from, isn't it?"

"Yes," Zink answered with a bite to his tone that could've taken off a few fingers.

The stuff was following me. There was no denying it now. It would keep heading toward the lodge as long as I was there. It would head wherever I went until it finally got me.

The door to the lodge opened again, and Tuesday ran out. She took one good look at me and jerked her head back toward the lodge. Callon had already fallen into conversation with Zink over the exact coordinates of the Hell Pit, so I slipped away. I didn't need any more details on that right now.

Tuesday ran up the steps of the lodge and headed right to my room.

"What happened? You look like someone threw you in a barrel and rolled you downhill for miles," she said as soon as we were there.

She was right. I was shaken, and I didn't know which part of it was messing with me the most. "Did you know the Hell Pit turned directions while we were gone?"

She cringed but there wasn't any surprise.

"Yeah, well, that's not all." I filled her in on everything from Bitters eating the sludge and Dal and Dax thinking they were my parents, leaving only one important piece of information out.

She let out a whistle of sorts after I finished. Koz was really the whistler. Tuesday was merely in training and hadn't quite nailed the knack or finesse of the gesture, but I appreciated the attempt.

"Did they feel like they could be your parents?" She asked.

"I don't think so? Neither of them look old enough to have a kid my age, that's for sure. That weird wizard is the one that started it, and he might've been making it all up. He was definitely crazy. Maybe he had the wrinkled-brain disease." I flopped back onto the bed, wondering if I'd be able to get any sleep tonight. I really hoped so.

"You mean like Betty back at the village, where she kept asking the same questions over and over again and never remembered your answers?"

"Actually, no. More like just making shit up."

"Maybe it's an elaborate setup with all of them? They know what you can do and they want to win you over somehow by being your lost parents."

I shook my head. "No. They're good people. I could tell even when I didn't want to. I've spent years watching and listening. You learn to see the signs."

There hadn't been too many people who'd wanted to interact with me at the village, even before Baryn had ruined my existence thoroughly. There'd been even fewer willing to chance his anger by engaging in any kind of contact. It had taught me one very important thing: how to really listen. When you really listened, the world opened up like a book. People showed you their true colors, their motivations, their hates and loves. It was all there to be learned if you could just shut the hell up for a couple of minutes.

Bitters might be crazy, but he'd believed what he said, whether it had any truth in it or not. Dal and Dax wanted to believe. And when I saw Dal's face at the mention of her lost daughter, I saw an agony that surpassed my own misery when I'd been chained to Baryn.

"They might've been misled, but if they clung to the idea, it was out of desperation to get back something that had broken their hearts. Almost made me wish I could be this person for them." I needed to stop thinking about them, or what it might've been like to grow up there with them for parents. They were the type that would've loved me no matter what I was or did. Made me wonder what I might've been like if I had? But I hadn't had that life, and dwelling on it accomplished nothing.

"You know, even if they aren't your people, your people might still be out there somewhere," Tuesday said wistfully.

Sometimes it seemed she would've rather her father be missing than dead. Then she could pretend she still had a living parent somewhere, waiting for her.

"No. My people stopped being my people when they sold me. You're my only people."

"Don't get me wrong, you could do worse than me. But Baryn said they sold you, and how many times did he lie? It's not as if he'd be above stealing a child or paying for one that was stolen. Come to think of it, instead of focusing on what this mud is, maybe we should be focusing on what exactly you are? What is it about you that it wants? Maybe if we could figure out where you came from, it would help?

"You need to go back to the village and get as many details as you can about who sold you. There's still someone around that would know Baryn's secrets. Baryn might be dead, but Turrock is still alive. He'd know where you came from. You might be able to negotiate for answers, or the guys could torture him instead." She shrugged, as if it didn't matter.

There was no faulting her logic. But if Turrock was tortured for a year, it wouldn't be enough to make up for what he'd done through his lifetime.

Tuesday was right about going back, but the idea gave me chills and made my stomach heave. Sweat was breaking out on my forehead and my room hadn't seen a fire in days.

I sat up, clenching the bed cover in my hands. "I don't know if I can do it."

"It's different. Callon won't let anyone hurt you, and I'll come with you." Her skin was about three shades paler than before we'd had this discussion. Not one part of her wanted to set foot back in that place either.

If I didn't go back, I'd have to leave Tuesday, the only family I had. I couldn't make her leave this place with me. I couldn't even tell her she had the choice. It would tear her apart. If I had to leave, I was leaving alone.

She had a life here, and a decent one, like we'd always hoped was possible. I wouldn't let her come with me and throw it away to live a life on the run.

"Hey, you didn't tell me if Bitters could break the Death Spell." Tuesday was already gnawing at a cuticle like it was an eight-course meal after a week-long fast.

I sucked at lying to her, so I stuck as close to the truth as I could. "Callon found out from Dax that Bitter didn't deal in those kinds of spells."

She stopped chewing. "I'm sorry, but I'm relieved that didn't work out. I don't think leaving is the right answer."

"Yeah, I can see your point," I said, smiling.

TWENTY-FIVE

For the first time since I'd lived there, I didn't head straight to the great room for breakfast but went into the kitchen. I didn't want to see anyone, and I'd rather they didn't see me either. I was running on fumes when it came to keeping a stiff upper lip. I'd used the last of my energy not falling apart in front of Tuesday last night and hadn't gotten any replenishment with another sleepless night.

I found a few biscuits sitting on the island and some pieces of bacon that hadn't made it out to the rest of the crowd yet.

"A bacon sandwich?" Issy asked as she walked in.

"Yeah, I had one recently, and it wasn't half bad." I tried to scrape the bottom of my tank to give her a smile.

She stopped in front of me and her brows drew in. "I heard the trip didn't go so well, but you look even worse than I imagined."

"No, I'm fine," I said, giving her a wave of my hand.

She grabbed it and pulled me after her toward the root cellar.

"No one can hear anything down here," she said, pulling up two crates for us to sit on. "Me and you, we've got a link. You saved my life, and if I could save yours, I'd do it in a heartbeat, but I don't know how to save you from this."

I got up. "Issy, it's fine, really."

She grabbed my hand again and tugged me back to the crate. "No. You have to hear me out because it needs to be said. I'm going to pretend not to know what's probably coming for you. Callon is still trying to fix it, because he can usually fix everything and he can't believe otherwise. Tuesday, well, she's going to think it'll be okay because that's how she thinks. But me and you, we know how things might work out, and I've heard whispers of things I shouldn't."

I turned my head and swiped a hand over my cheek, catching the only tear that had slipped away from me. That was it. I was cracking.

"It's okay to let a little steam out. It'll make it easier to hold it together later when you need to," Issy said.

I gave a short laugh. If I let out what was bubbling up, there'd be no holding it together of any sort. Keeping a lid on it was the only thing saving me, because once I blew, it was going to be epic.

"So, what are you thinking? I can see something brewing," she said.

I sniffed so that I didn't end up a teary, snotty mess. Then I pulled it together because I had to.

"If we can't find a solution to the Hell Pits soon, I'm going to have to leave, and I'm going to do it alone, one way or another. This stuff, it might follow me to the ends of the Earth. I can't make anyone else live that life with me."

She nodded as she looked down at her folded hands, devoid of shock. She let out a sigh. "I won't try to talk you out of your choice, but know that I'd gladly go with you. I've lived most of my life here. Would've died here if it weren't for you. I'd be happy to go see some more of the world."

"I thought we were dealing in realities? I won't have you give up the best place I've ever heard of to live like a nomad with me. Plus, the people here need you. No. I can't have you come." I shook my head, never surer.

She reached forward, gripping my hand hard. "You already undid the spell, didn't you?"

"Issy, don't ask me a question you don't want the answer to. It'll put you in a bad spot."

She nodded, but her smile slipped and she leaned back. "I figured you might try. I guess I was kind of hoping that you wouldn't be able to."

"Like I said—"

"You won't burden me with secrets. I know. Is there anything I can do?"

"Yeah, not act depressed while I'm still here and try to be a friend to Tuesday when I disappear."

"I can do that." She nodded, keeping her grip on my hand. "Just know I'd take your place if I could."

"Come on, I'm sure you've got other things to be

doing today." I stood, knowing this wasn't going to get any less emotional the longer we talked about it. If we kept going, I really might start bawling, and that was pointless. I'd keep trying to find a solution until I couldn't. And then I'd do what I had to.

She didn't try to stop me and stood with a new determination. "Actually, I do. If you're not going to be here too much longer, I'm going to make sure you have the best days possible." She strode up the stairs and back into the kitchen.

She was already talking to Hess before I made it all the way up.

"We're having a roast tomorrow. Spread the word," she said.

I could tell by their expressions that this was a good thing.

"We are? We don't usually do that for another month," Hess said.

"We're doing it early."

Koz appeared a couple of seconds later. "Isn't it early in the season for a roast?"

Issy wiped her hands on her hips, making her way over to Koz like a warrior.

"This place might not be here much longer. I want a roast, and I'm throwing a roast."

"All righty, then. I'll spread the word," Koz said, smiling.

"What exactly is a roast?" I asked Issy after they'd left.

"It means we're going to roast something while

everyone gets completely fall-down drunk and has a good time."

"Oh. That sounds interesting." I'd never gotten to go to any of the parties back at the village. And drunk? I'd never done that either. My life was going to shit. That was what people did when they hit hard times, right? Get drunk? Issy was brilliant.

TWENTY-SIX

THE LIGHT IN THE GREAT ROOM WAS THE BEST TO read at night, but I was regretting my choice. I looked over the edge of my book, watching Zink as he leaned against the other side of the mantle. He was watching Koz and Tuesday. He tilted a bottle to his lips and shook his head, a deep scowl on his face. The pair was oblivious, but my blood was boiling and it wasn't because of the fire beside me. I wasn't sure if it was the laughing Zink found so offensive or their happiness in general.

Him scowling at them lit the fuse on a powder keg, and I was having a hard time smothering it. I might be leaving here soon, and Tuesday would only have Koz. If Zink thought he was going to ruin it, I'd kill him before I left.

"Is it all happiness that upsets you, or that she's someone near and dear to my heart that you find it so offensive?"

Koz and Tuesday didn't blink in my direction, so absorbed in each other that they didn't hear.

Zink narrowed his eyes as he turned my way. He took another swig.

It appeared as if he were going to ignore me until he said, "Despite our mutually low opinions of each other, my current distaste is not their happiness but that it is not the time to be marking a mate."

"Marking a mate?" I looked back to them, and they didn't seem to be doing anything other than snuggling and kissing.

"Yes. He's fucking marking her, and we have enough problems. What if..." He shook his head and took another sip. I didn't need to be a mind reader for this one. If they had to kill me, Tuesday might not be so content here after that.

"If marking is anything like a dog pissing on something, I'm sure she can wash it off," I said, hoping Zink took the insult I'd intended.

He huffed. "Yeah, you think you're so clever. You don't miss a thing, do you?" He took another sip.

I shook my head and went back to my book, pretending Zink wasn't in the room. If he was worried about how Tuesday would take my death, it meant she was probably safe enough, or he wouldn't care at all. Fighting with Zink right now wouldn't do me any good, even if it did feel fantastic.

I tried to read the words of the next paragraph. Then I had to keep rereading them, because I couldn't get past his stupid face in my peripheral, agitating me. I slammed the book closed. I was better off with less light and no Zink.

Zink narrowed his eyes as Koz darted his tongue out

and licked the skin on Tuesday's neck. His fingers grew whiter where he gripped the bottle.

Wait a second, was that part of marking? Was he putting his scent on her somehow?

Holy *fuck*. Callon had licked me right after the mud had gotten on me. I wouldn't have remembered if the guys hadn't gotten all weird about it, but they had. It had cemented the action in my memory.

No. It couldn't be. Why would he have done that? Now I really couldn't concentrate on anything else.

"What exactly does marking entail?"

Zink looked over with a smugness that made me want to rip his face off. "You mean you don't know? I thought you had it all figured out."

The look in his eyes, the taunting. Zink wasn't going to come out and tell me directly, but it was all there if I wanted to open my eyes and see the truth. Callon had marked me as his before we'd even made it back here. But why? He'd hated me, especially back then. Had it been to protect what he thought was an asset?

No. This couldn't be. Zink was screwing with me.

I looked at him again.

He laughed in a way that was meant to belittle me. "Yeah, you don't miss a trick, do you?"

No. I'd offered myself to Callon and he'd ignored me, completely. This made no sense.

Either way, I was done with the current company. I was going to get some answers. Zink laughed again as I walked away. Callon was here somewhere, and I was going to find him.

I barged into his office first because it was closest.

When he wasn't there, I made my way up to his room. The door was open and Callon and Hess were standing in his room. Both of them spun to look at me.

I took a single step inside but then froze in deliberation.

"Did you..." This was almost more awkward than when I'd asked him to sleep with me. It was ludicrous, too. Zink was probably fucking with me, setting me up to get laughed at, and I was walking right into it.

Except Callon had licked me, just like Koz had done to Tuesday. My gut screamed that meant *something*. I had to put it out there and be damned if I was a spectacle. I'd been one before and I'd surely be one again.

I crossed one arm around me and pointed into the air with the other. "You didn't do anything I didn't know about, such as marking me as a mate or something? I know it's an odd question and it sounds bizarre, but I've seen some things that are making me wonder, and..."

Why weren't they laughing or looking at me like I was ridiculous? Why did Hess look nervous? Why did Callon look at Hess and nod toward the door, as if we were going to need some privacy?

He had.

Hess kept his eyes on the floor as he walked past me, as if I had a headful of snakes and he'd turn to stone if he so much as peeked at me. It was a smart move. At that moment, anything was possible.

I heard the door shut behind me. I took two ragged breaths before asking, "You marked me, didn't you?"

"Yes." He stood there calmly. The calmer he was, the more I wanted to march over there and beat him silly.

The only thing that stopped me was fear that I'd accidentally suck his life from him in my anger. I wasn't at that point—yet. Maybe later, though.

I nearly fell back into the wall as the full scope of it hit me. The way he never actually asked me to go somewhere but always touched me. How he sometimes "cuddled" and spooned me when we slept together. He'd been marking me with his scent. I'd made a joke of them being like dogs, but that was exactly what he'd been doing. The joke was on me.

"You rub your scent on me all day long, don't you? You don't touch me all the time because you're bossy. You do it to mark me as yours." I stayed with my back against the wall.

"After what you went through, I thought you needed time, and I was making sure you got it. I was helping you." He waved his hand in the air as if what he'd done were nothing.

"You act like you hate me. I offered to have sex with you and you ignored me. *And yet you marked me as your mate?*"

That was it—I was going to kill him. It was official.

"I'm protecting you," he said as if he had the right to get annoyed.

"You're not protecting me. I'm not a girl. I might not have slept with anyone, but my innocence is long gone. I'm not looking for someone to come save me and build me a castle. I didn't ask for a savior, and I don't need one. Go find someone else to protect." I walked closer to him, my hands fisted because I wanted to hit him so badly.

I screamed instead, turning and walking from the

room because I might actually commit murder in this moment.

"Teddy," he called after me.

"No." I left his room and didn't look back. When I walked into my room, Tuesday was sitting on my bed, shaking her head.

"You don't need to tell me. First Hess came down looking rattled. I came up here to see what happened, and even I could hear you."

I sat on the bed beside her and leaned forward, hands still fisted, head shaking.

"You need to do something drastic. You can't let him get away with this. He's acting like he owns you." It was clear by her expression that if she didn't have to whisper because of all the ears, she would've been pacing and screaming herself.

"Like what?" Easier said than done.

"Flirt with someone else. Show him he doesn't get to corral you."

I huffed. "I don't know how to flirt. I know how to avoid."

"You can do it."

"I'm glad you believe that." It was good that someone did.

Tuesday grabbed my arm, trying to impart the seriousness with which she took this matter. "You have to do this and you need to do it where everyone can see. It must be done. Callon needs to know he doesn't own you. He's walking all over you, and not even like they do on the good rug in the front hall that people feel bad wiping their feet on. He's stamping all over you like that banged-up mat in the kitchen."

I sucked in a breath. That thing was a mess. It couldn't be that bad, could it? "Really? The kitchen mat?"

She gave me a knowing smile. "Yep. That filthy thing that people use when they don't want to mess up the other floors. That's what you are, and all the guys probably know it."

"I refuse to be the kitchen mat." Fuck Callon and his protection.

"Don't be the kitchen mat."

TWENTY-SEVEN

THE NIGHT OF THE ROAST WAS WARMER THAN USUAL, as if the lodge and the weather had decided they wanted to give me as good a send-off as possible. Tuesday was by my side as we walked out to the large gathering. Everyone in the nearby cabins had come out for the roast.

Callon was already there, across the field. We'd been avoiding each other since last night, and I planned on continuing tonight. He looked across the gathering, and I turned without so much as a nod.

"Good," Tuesday said from beside me. "He can't have it both ways just because you love him."

"What? I don't love Callon. Don't even say that." I glanced around, hoping no one had heard her crazy talk.

"No, of course you don't," she said with a shake of her head. "I was confusing you with me and Koz. You two *hate* each other."

"By the way, did you know Koz was marking you?" It hadn't occurred to me to ask yesterday.

"I suspected. It's the only reason I don't care that he

hasn't said that other thing yet. If he cared enough to do that, then I figure it's only a matter of time."

Koz had better say it before I had to leave. It was going to be hard enough to disappear on Tuesday. I needed to know she had someone committed by her side.

We skirted the crowd, avoiding people I hadn't come in close contact with before. It was easier than expected, since there was a chunk of people giving me the cold shoulder.

"There's my girl!" Issy said. She'd told me people got drunk at these things, and it looked like she'd started earlier than most. She gave me a big hug that I tried to not shrink away from, before she was on the move again.

Tuesday was still scouting the men. "Well? Anyone catch your eye?"

Even with a lot of them snubbing me, there were still quite a few eligible bachelors, men who didn't seem hostile. Maybe they didn't believe what they'd heard or didn't think I should be blamed for something out of my control? Didn't matter. I'd take it. And it had to be a normal man. It couldn't be a beast that might've picked up on Callon's marks. I knew there were a few more of them lingering around the lodge. I hadn't met most of them, though, and now I knew why. They'd been steering clear.

I scanned the crowd, and the top of a blond, curly head caught my eye. His name was Timmy and he was a man, mostly. In his early twenties, he didn't have that same filled-out look that Callon had, but he was still fit. He might not carry the same air about him either, but he was human. You couldn't expect him to have the same presence as a beast. His jaw didn't have any stubble, but he was blond—maybe it was hard to see? Either way, none of that mattered. He'd always been friendly and kind. I could do worse. I'd feel him out, maybe start with a kiss and see where it went from there. After all, this might be my last chance to be with someone in any normal capacity.

"Timmy?" Tuesday whispered as she followed my line of sight.

"He's nice enough, don't you think?" I asked.

"Oh yeah, he'll do. He won't push. You'll be able to set the pace. It's a solid pick." She gave me a literal pat on the back.

Timmy looked our way, as if he'd felt the two sets of eyes measuring him up.

"Smile a little," Tuesday said under her breath.

I did. He smiled back. He turned to the guy he was talking to, said a couple of words, and then got up and began walking over toward us.

Wait, what had happened? Was he coming over because I'd smiled?

"That was so easy. Is that how it's supposed to work?" I asked.

"Normally, yeah." She nudged me with her elbow. "I'm going to bail over to Koz. Good luck, but you won't need it. He's already putty. I can smell it on him."

"Do you have to leave..." She was already ten feet away from me.

Oh no. I guessed I was flying solo on this. I would prefer he were approaching to fight with me. I knew how to do that. This? Flirting? Hooking up? I had no experience in this arena.

He walked over and then stopped a couple feet from me. "Hey."

"Hi."

We nodded. We stared. We looked elsewhere and then back at each other. We were the picture of awkwardness.

"Want a sip?" he asked, holding out his bottle.

"Sure—"

I reached to take it, but before I could, an arm wrapped around my waist. I was tugged away from a gaping Timmy. I didn't have to look at my assaulter. There was only one person who felt they owned me and would pull a move like this.

"Did you not hear me last night? You are not allowed to touch me anymore. No marking. No scent. Nothing." I tried to pull his arm from my waist without making a scene. It stubbornly wouldn't move.

I was pulled up to a wide tree, thick enough to offer a small amount of privacy.

My back against it, Callon leaned a hand beside my shoulder. "Are you trying to prove a point? Don't use that boy to get back at me, and don't pretend for a second you want him."

"Not everything I do is about you." This might be a little about him, but I'd cut out my tongue before I admitted it. Mostly, this was about filling my life with as much normal stuff as I could before I had to walk away from here and live the rest of eternity alone. I had no future, so I was damned well going to have a present.

He tilted his head and raised an eyebrow.

"At least admit what *you're* doing, and it's not about protecting me." I shoved at his chest.

"I am protecting you."

"From big, bad Timmy? Would his kiss be lethal to me? Maybe I'd have sex. Would that be the end of the world? Would I die? The only thing you're trying to protect is you and your interests. I'm sure another man in the picture would fuck that up royally, so you're putting me on a shelf, whether I want to be there or not. Guess what? I won't allow it."

He straightened and had the nerve to smile. "Really? I think I've been doing pretty well."

"So no denying it? That's who you are and you're fine with it?"

"You're the reason you're stuck with me in the first place. I don't care if it's fucked up. You did it to yourself."

I had done it, but I'd also undone it. It cost me all the control I had in me to not tell him that, too. But I wouldn't. That knowledge needed to remain a secret. When I left, I didn't want anyone knowing. It would be a clean break.

But I wasn't leaving right now, and he'd find out he wasn't going to control me, not now, not ever.

"We'll see how stuck I am." I walked past him, not sure if he'd try to stop me. He didn't, but he did follow me. There was something about the way he walked past me with a determination in his stride that gave me an unsettling feeling in my belly, as if I'd bluffed my last game, and he was about to call in an IOU I couldn't afford.

As soon as we hit the outer perimeter of the group, I made a right in Timmy's direction. Callon made a left. Good. Maybe he was going to have a drink on the other side with his pack of dogs. He was going to have to accept that I could do as I wanted. He couldn't put me in a box and save me for later.

Timmy had been lingering on the outskirts of a group. It was obvious he'd been hoping I'd return by the way he turned back to me the second I approached.

"Timmy, do you have a minute?"

He wasn't Callon. He couldn't turn into a beast or rip someone apart in seconds, but he might be able to punch. Lack of fangs shouldn't be a deal breaker. Right?

Right. Yeah, definitely. Callon was wrong. I could be into Timmy. He didn't know me.

"I'm sorry about that. We were having a little argument that carried over from yesterday. He didn't mean to interrupt. I was hoping you might want to still share that drink with me?"

"Of course I would." He held out his bottle with the hint of a grin as his eyes flickered across the way, toward Callon.

"It's okay. We don't have anything romantic going on. You don't need to worry." I took a nice, long swig of whatever the acid in the bottle was and then handed it back, coughing a bit.

"You're sure?" His eyes kept flickering back and forth between Callon and me.

"Positive. I'd know, right?" I shot him a grin so big that my cheeks hurt.

His lips hinted at a tentative smile. His fingers

brushed my wrist and then he wrapped his hand around mine, pulling me forward a bit. "Want to come grab a seat with me?" He nodded toward one of the logs that had been rolled out and was unoccupied. It sat off by itself a bit, with a tree giving it a little coverage.

"Sure," I said, letting him continue to hold my hand as we walked over.

I took a seat on the log and tried to ignore Tuesday giving me a thumbs-up from her vantage point, about thirty feet away. Then she held up a hand and pointed toward Callon behind it. She scrunched her nose and made a stabbing gesture. Koz, who was standing beside her, grabbed her hands and stopped her.

I didn't see what happened next because I was startled as Timmy decided to move in a little too close.

No, not too close. If the side of his leg brushed mine, that was a good thing. That was what I'd been planning. This was living, right?

"I wanted to tell you before—you look absolutely stunning tonight."

I had a harder time forcing my lips to form some imitation of a smile this time, even as my stomach clenched. He didn't know any better. He probably thought I wanted to hear that. Most girls would, right? Unfortunately, I hated it. I wasn't pretty, not really.

"Thanks," I said, sounding stiff.

"I mean, not that you don't always." He must have picked up on my tone. He was trying to fix something he couldn't understand. I should've felt bad for him. A small part of me did.

"I mean come on, you're too beautiful to ever look

bad." He laughed, thinking his flattery would win me over.

It was getting harder to smile when all I wanted to do was run from him. I didn't want him to look at me anymore, and I didn't want to hear another word about how beautiful I was. It made me want to drag my fingers across my skin and scar it again. He didn't see me at all.

"You must know I've wanted to talk to you from the first moment I saw you."

I got to my feet, and he followed me. I felt his hand reflexively tighten around mine, trying to stop my departure. It made me want to run even farther and faster.

And then all eyes were drawn to Callon as he said loudly, "I need everyone's attention."

I used the moment to yank my hand from Timmy's. I tucked my arms around my waist to avoid him grabbing me again.

While I was at it, I might as well use Callon's distraction to take a few more steps away. Tuesday and I were going to have to regroup. I wasn't sure this was going to work out.

I edged away even farther. If Timmy's hand made any sudden movements, I didn't care how bad it looked— I was bolting.

"You all know Teddy by now," Callon said, his deep voice crisp and clear, even where I stood all the way on the other side. My eyes jerked to his, Timmy no longer a concern.

What was Callon up to? That bad feeling I'd gotten in my gut when he followed me was back; it was laughing at me now for being a dumbass and not listening. Telling me I should've followed Callon and that Timmy wasn't the priority right now.

Callon stared at me with a look that said he'd be getting the last word. Now what? Could I ram into him, take him down, and stop whatever he was planning? Yes, it might work, or I might make it worse. I was going to have to stand down and wait out whatever was about to happen.

"So we're all clear, she's off-limits. I don't care who you are or what she says. That's all." Callon gave me a last look that said, *Now what do you plan on doing?* Callon's gaze shifted to Timmy. The guy scrambled away from me as fast as he could. Real nice.

Callon smiled and walked back into the lodge. Koz's forehead fell into his palm, hiding the grimace that had started. He looked the way I felt, except I didn't have the luxury of squirming with all the attention on me, and other than Zink's, they were *all* on me.

Did I (A) run after Callon like a ninny, (B) give my own speech, declaring his speech to be bullshit, or (C) do absolutely nothing until they got bored of watching me?

Giving my own speech to counter his would never work. I sucked at public speeches. Waiting the stares out wouldn't work either. Even Tuesday was gaping, frozen in her spot beside Koz. She took a step forward as she started to come out of her shock. I gave her a shake of the head, telling her to not run over to me. It would only add to the spectacle, and these people were waiting for part two and seemed quite convinced they were going to get it.

I had only one choice. Run after him like a ninny.

That was too hard to swallow. I'd march off like a woman to be reckoned with and see if I could pull it off.

I cleared my throat, something similar to Callon but a few octaves higher, and a little squeaky. "If you'll excuse me. I have something I need to handle."

I didn't walk away immediately, as if the crowd would give me some response. I'd lost it. It was confirmed.

Tuesday stepped forward. "Sure. You go handle your business," she said, trying to cover the silence.

A few pairs of eyes shifted her way, but not enough to call her a supporting cast.

I walked away, leaving a chorus of whispers that were growing louder as I went.

Callon wasn't in the great room or his office. I took the stairs two at a time until I was down the hall and pushing open his door. He was standing by the window, his hands on his hips, and turned to look at me as if I'd wronged him.

I shut the door behind me, a mask of calm merely coating the surface. Shutting the door wouldn't keep our words private from any of the shifters, but it gave me an illusion of privacy. That would have to be good enough for now, because what I needed to do couldn't wait.

"You bastard. How could you do that in front of everyone? How? That's what you call protecting me?"

"You're right. I wasn't protecting you. I was protecting Timmy, because if he continued to touch you, I was going to kill him. If you don't like the way things are, then I'm not sure what to tell you, because I. Will. Kill. Him."

The blood was pounding in my ears so loudly that I wasn't sure I'd hear him if he said anything else. What was this? What was he saying?

"I can't do this," he said.

Did he just agree with me? No. He didn't look like he was agreeing. Not at all. He still looked pissed. I was afraid to ask but couldn't not. "Can't do what?"

"Leave you alone. I don't know what to do with you." He was talking as if he were angry, that I'd done this to him somehow.

He didn't? If he'd wanted to stump me, that had done it. I was still in stunned silence when he continued.

"I can't kiss you or sleep with you or 'use' you, as you put it. I don't steal kisses in a closet or behind a tree. That's not how I work. It won't be on your terms. If you give yourself to me, *you give yourself to me*—you're mine. *That's* how it works."

I might've stayed in a haze if that didn't have one huge gap. "Are you saying you're a virgin, then? Because here you are, single, alone? Clearly that's not how it works."

"It is with you," he said, and then his hands were in my hair, pulling my head back, and his mouth was covering mine. He was pressing me against the wall, tilting my head so his tongue could dip deeper.

My hands went from pushing against his chest to gripping his shirt. I twisted my head to the side, my breathing ragged.

His muscles tensed underneath my fisted hands.

He pulled back, his hands still in my hair. "You still want this?"

I knew what he was asking, and it wasn't if I still wanted to sleep with him. That would've been an easy yes. He wanted me. I wanted him.

But committing to him? Saying I'd stay until who knew when? Maybe forever? Could I stay with him forever? Would he be forced to move around with me? Would I want him to? Could I willingly tie myself to anyone at this point? The idea felt like iron bars slamming down all around me. It sucked the oxygen from my lungs.

I turned my head to the side, needing a minute, needing space.

"That's what I thought." He stepped back.

My hands fell from him. The space between us grew into a chasm as I walked out.

TWENTY-EIGHT

CALLON WAS ON THE FAR SIDE OF THE LODGE'S LAND the next morning, right where the ground dropped off and the stream turned into a small waterfall.

After last night, seeing him was going to be tough, but there were other things that needed to happen. I couldn't put life on hold because of a kiss, and a scene in front of *a lot* of people, no matter how much I wanted to. Things were spinning out of control in every direction, and time was slipping by quicker than whiskey in a drunk's hands. There were hard choices to be made. I needed as many answers as I could get before I made them. When I left here, I needed to know without a shadow of a doubt it was the only option.

That meant I had to go back to the village and question Turrock, and I'd need Callon for that. If that made me weak, then so be it. There were certain hurdles I wasn't ready to jump alone—not yet, anyway. I'd be jumping them on my own soon enough.

I stopped on the bank six feet above him. "Hey."

He'd probably heard me approaching about a mile back. "Hey," he said, barely breaking his stare from the creek and dirt to glance at me. I didn't know if the terrain was that interesting or the idea of looking at me was that distasteful.

How could I know his feelings when I couldn't decide upon mine? I was bouncing between elated that he wanted me and mad because nothing was simple with him. He couldn't only take what I was willing to give. In typical Callon fashion, he had to have it all. Sex wasn't good enough. I needed to give him all of me. I didn't have all of me to give anymore. Maybe if I'd lived a different life, had a different past, *we* would've been different. But that future had died at least a decade before at Baryn's hands.

"What are you doing?" I asked, looking for some way to bridge the gaping chasm between us. I crossed my arms as he took longer than normal to answer.

"The Hell Pit is moving steadily closer. I'm surveying the land for our final stand." His voice was distant. His eyes were colder. He was shutting me out. I hadn't realized until now that I'd been *in*.

I looked for the best way down, trying to find a perch on a root. Callon fixed the issue for me when he reached up and lifted me off the side of the small cliff. His hands didn't linger. He touched me as little as possible to get the job done and that was that.

I'd told him last night not to touch me anymore, and I was already wishing I could rewind the clock.

I made a little circle about the area. "This is it, I guess?"

He nodded. "The stuff flows uphill, but it does seem to slow it down a little. If we do have to leave, this might be the last thing in between us and it. I want to trench out around it and maybe buy a little more time."

He stopped talking and walked a good ten feet away to look at a different spot that was conveniently farther away from me.

I kicked the rocks by my feet as I said, "When this is over, it might be best if I find somewhere else to go—that is, if we can break the spell binding us." I feared his reply the way some feared the return of the plague. I wasn't sure why I was telling him this. I didn't need to anymore. I could simply leave.

He finally looked at me for more than a passing second. "If that's what you want, I'll help you get settled. I have connections with a lot of different communities and villages. They aren't all bad."

As soon as he said those words, I knew exactly why I'd told him. I'd wanted him to fight for me. Because if there was any chance that I could have a normal life with someone, that person would have to be all in, every ounce of him willing to battle it out, because it wasn't going to be easy. I was fucked up and broken and knew it. He knew it too, and he was ready to throw in the towel.

He might've been relieved that I was taking the initiative. I couldn't blame him. No one should have to get stuck with someone as fucked up as me.

There was only one move left to make, one possibility for answers. If I was going to leave here, it would be better if I could find a way to stop the Hell Pits from destroying whatever life I could make. There was only one place left to go.

"I need to go back to my old village."

The hard edge softened. "Why would you want to go back there?"

Just because you know a tough conversation is coming, that doesn't make it any easier to have. I'd witnessed enough of them to know.

Someone might as well have tied my tongue into a knot for how useful it was. I leaned on the nearest tree, my brain needing every ounce of energy available to explain. Plus my spine seemed to have disappeared at the thought of returning there.

"There are a couple of reasons. I was talking to Tuesday, and she made a good point. There might be a reason in my past that's drawing these things to me, and there are people at the village that might know more about where I come from."

He'd walked closer to me. "You said a couple reasons. What else? Is this about Dal and Dax?"

I shrugged. "I wouldn't mind ruling them out, but that's not it."

He didn't say much as he watched me, and I started to fidget. Didn't he realize how hard this was?

He leaned on a nearby tree of his own as he waited.

"I don't know who exactly I used to be. I don't know who I am now, either, not really. I can't seem to decide if I'm a victim or a survivor. I want to know deep down what I'm made of, and part of that might be facing the place I don't want to go and tell the people there that they can't hurt me anymore. They have no power."

"You don't get it. It doesn't matter what those people think or know."

"But I still need to go. They might have answers."

He looked off into the horizon, not answering.

"What is it? Why don't you like my plan?"

It was another few minutes before he turned back to me, the sun setting casting a glow on his skin. When his eyes met mine, I saw that flare of red. Something had put him on edge, and it must have been me.

He let out a long, slow breath and then said, "Because for the first time in weeks, you're reminding me of the first night I met you."

"What's that supposed to mean?"

He took a couple more steps away from me. "Nothing. When do you want to leave?"

"Tomorrow morning, if we can. I want to get this lousy shit over with."

He let out a soft laugh. "Spoken like a true survivor."

TWENTY-NINE

WE'D BEEN TRAVELING FOR TWO DAYS AND NOTHING was going well. Callon no longer slept next to me. Even around camp, when we settled in for the night, Callon kept his distance and his words to a minimum. This put Zink in a chipper mood. Zink's happiness made my mood even fouler. I shared a tent with Tuesday, who would rather be sleeping next to Koz, so they were both unhappy as well.

If that weren't enough, Tuesday was barely eating, and this time it wasn't a show for Koz. The green hue of her skin was the biggest tipoff that she couldn't stomach anything. She'd been getting worse each meal since we'd left, and tonight was no exception.

We were almost back to the village, and in spite of insisting on coming, everything about her screamed that she wasn't ready to walk back in there.

I made my way over to the fire and sat beside her on the log. Koz was eyeing me up as I did, probably hoping that I could fix her. Even Hess seemed to be interested in the outcome. I was going to nudge her in the right direction, but there was only one fix: her not going.

I leaned in until my shoulder was bumping hers. "You don't have to come. You can wait behind."

"I'm going. I have to." She wrapped her arms tighter about herself as the cold sank into her unfueled body.

Or maybe it was just freezing out. I leaned closer to the fire, holding out my hands. "I have to go. *You* don't."

"We're sisters. We do these things together. I go where you go."

"Maybe this time you stay near where I go? What do you think?"

She laughed. That was a start.

It faded quickly.

"It was my idea," she said.

That was when I knew I had her. She needed a little cajoling, maybe, a couple of solid excuses to hang her hat on, but she was cracking.

"I know that you say that place wasn't the same hell for you that it was for me, but we're still talking about hell. Being on an upper tier of hell doesn't mean it wasn't still God-awful."

Tuesday shuddered beside me. It might have been the memories this time. Couldn't be sure, but I was wearing her down. Now I had to finish this off, even though I didn't want to. In truth, I wanted her with me, but not like this.

I leaned back again, making sure she really heard me. "You're missing one thing. When I go in this time, I know I can kill anything that comes near me. That's an awful big safety net to carry around, and one you don't have."

Koz cleared his throat from across the way, as if he'd swallowed a bug.

I knew what bug it was too. "I'm not saying you wouldn't protect her. If I didn't believe you would, I wouldn't like you so much. But it's still different."

Koz gave me a shrug. It was the only admission of being right I was going to get, but that was okay.

Koz's gaze moved back to Tuesday and softened. His lips turned up slightly as his eyes heated. "Just as long as we're clear I'll always have her back, we're good."

If she didn't know he loved her after that, she was deaf and blind.

I glanced to my side and saw Tuesday staring at him like the sun didn't need to rise in the morning because Koz walked the Earth. I got it. She liked him. Strike that. Loved him. Still, this amount of worship might've been overkill. You shouldn't worship any person. All it did was raise them up and give you a crick in your neck. Eventually they'd tumble down, possibly falling right on top of you. And it was inevitable that they fell, because that was what humans did, even the beast variety. I'd rather walk beside a person. If they leaned a little, it was easier to support them when you were on the same level and by their side.

"Look, if I couldn't do what I do, I'd never go back there," I said, trying to move back to the subject at hand before she left to go pray to Koz.

"Really?" she asked.

"Really."

Callon stood slightly in the shadows, out of Tuesday's view. Right now he was giving me a look that said I was full of shit. He was right. I hadn't used my gift in months. I didn't know if I could still do it, but I was going back either way.

But I didn't need Callon to believe me. I only needed Tuesday to buy the story, and she wanted to. That was half the struggle. She'd believe it because she wanted to.

"Are you sure?" she asked.

"I'm positive. Honestly, it might work out even better if you wait outside the village. Stay back with Koz and you'll be able to identify who's coming and going; Koz can't. Callon mentioned something like that already." I turned to Callon, and so help him if he didn't back me up. He could ignore me all day if he wanted, but he better say the right thing now. "Isn't that right?"

"Said it to Koz earlier today," he answered.

She nodded. "Okay, I can do that."

Koz looked at me as if I'd been deemed the newest deity in the group. Callon glanced my way, but spared me any such revealing emotions of adoration, before he walked off into the woods.

A few minutes later, Tuesday disappeared into our tent with Koz. Hess retired next, and Zink followed him just so he wouldn't have to be stuck alone with me. I wouldn't be getting any sleep tonight, so it didn't matter much to me where I sat.

About an hour later, I was throwing another log on the fire when Callon returned. I didn't bother looking at his eyes. It didn't matter anymore. He walked over but kept a buffer of a few feet between us. I'd noticed he'd been leaving that same amount of space ever since the night of the roast.

"You should try to get some sleep," he said, more a matter of fact than overflowing concern.

"Tent's occupied." It was an excuse, but it was also true.

"You can take mine. I'll sleep outside."

For a split second, I'd thought he was going to sleep beside me. I hadn't realized how fast relief and happiness could spike inside, or how fast they'd fall when you realized you were wrong.

"I'm fine here." A week ago, he would've picked me up and dragged me in there with him anyway. Tonight, he stood next to me as if he didn't care at all.

I was so pathetic that I was happy he hadn't gone into his tent yet, even if we both remained silent.

THIRTY

We left Koz and Tuesday hidden in the forest behind us as we walked toward the village. Callon was on my right, Hess on my left, and Zink covering my back. I'd never appreciated Zink's cold edge quite as much as I did now. He might try to kill me himself next week, but the battle lines for today had been drawn, and I was on the right side of it at the moment.

Callon hadn't tried to talk to me before we'd arrived. He didn't try to take my hand and make everything better, and I wasn't delusional enough to think things had changed. But when we paused in front of that rusted metal door, and I took in a few long, shuddering breaths, pulling myself together, the back of his hand grazed mine. I turned to him, and his look told me everything I needed to know. We'd fight and bleed and kill as one. We'd walk out of here together, even if we didn't talk while we did it.

A metal window slid open and a guard's face appeared. "Who are you and why are you here?"

I couldn't see the face and didn't recognize the voice.

"Tell Turrock that Teddy is here to see him." I squared my shoulders like there was a rod in them and stood like I had steel for bones.

Even from where we stood, I could hear raised voices, but I couldn't make out the words.

"They're fighting over whether it's really you," Callon said, his voice barely above a growl.

There must've been a little more flavor to it, because his eyes were flaring red.

"Your beast is showing," I said. I didn't care if the beast made a full-fledged appearance, but not until after they opened the gates and gave me answers. Then he could go all savage and rip them apart with my blessing. If he turned now, we'd never get Turrock to talk.

The gate, rusted and patched, began to grind open. The sound alone sent chills through me. How many times had I heard that sound, wondering if I'd ever escape? If I'd die in that hell? And here I was, willingly walking back into it. My heart pounded, stealing the blood from the rest of my body, leaving my face white and my hands cold and clammy.

My pack edged in closer. I could do this, even if I had to kill every motherfucker in there. I could do it.

Callon's arm brushed mine as we walked toward hell.

The gate groaned its way open far enough to reveal a man standing in the opening. He was a giant, or as close to one as I'd ever seen, with his hair of bright red and a flowing beard. Ivan. I knew him well. Too well. He'd done Baryn's dirty work many times. The night I escaped, he'd been the last person to drag me out to the pole and chain me there.

Blood came pounding back into my veins with a vengeance. My bones filled with iron as rage flooded every cell in my body. I walked forward. I wouldn't leave this place without this man dying, and by my hand.

Ten more of Baryn's thugs idled behind him. No, they were Turrock's thugs now. I marched forward, the guys keeping pace.

"No matter what is said, don't get riled. Don't do anything until we get to Turrock or he'll go into hiding," I whispered before we reached them.

"We're not idiots," Zink said from behind me.

I didn't look at Callon.

Ivan smiled, ignoring my entourage. It might've been bluster, or maybe he was confident in his superior numbers. He shouldn't have been; I recognized most of the men behind him. He was going to die a miserable death, hopefully today. I saw it as I stood there.

"Didn't believe it was you without the droopy eye. You're walking all straight and normal now. Too bad Baryn is gone. He'd have an awful lot of fun, seeing as how you're a clean slate and all."

I heard a low rumble, but it didn't come from Callon. It came from Zink. *That* I hadn't expected. The guy didn't even like me. I might've underestimated Ivan. He did have a way of rubbing people the wrong way.

Callon was frozen, possibly not breathing anymore.

Ivan popped his head up, finally looking beyond me.

Not good, not when I didn't know whose eyes might be glowing red.

"Where's Turrock? My business is with him." And I

had to see him before things went south and I lost my chance. Don't *look at the boys*.

"Which is?" Ivan asked.

"Which isn't any of yours." Ivan's attention was fully back on me, which was what I needed. He couldn't die yet. I needed to get to Turrock first.

"You're awfully haughty now, aren't you? Too much time off the pole, if you ask me, but we'll be fixing that real soon."

Ivan reached out toward me, and I knew exactly what he was going to do. He'd done it many times in my past. He'd grab a hank of my hair and then wrap it around his fist. Then he was going to die, because *I* was going to kill him.

There was a blur of a movement. When it was done, Ivan's hand was lying on the ground in front of me and I was getting sprayed by the blood shooting from his stump as he screamed. Dammit. I'd wanted to kill him, and now he was going to bleed to death.

For a few seconds, there were no other sounds other than Ivan's screams. It didn't last long. Suddenly, the entire village was screaming. I hadn't realized how many people had been looking on, hiding behind buildings or bushes. Maybe even hanging in the trees. Now they were all running and yelling as they stampeded toward the gate.

I didn't have to look far or rack my brain to know why. I was surrounded by fur and fangs. Three of them. All three had changed. Not one of them had listened to me, despite what I'd said or Zink's words. What happened to "we're not idiots"? Apparently they were, because it was chaos and there was no way I'd be able to get to Turrock. He'd probably been watching on and was hightailing it out of there right now, and who could tell with all the people running around?

I spun on them. "What did I tell you people? Don't do anything no matter what is said. Did you not hear me?"

I got a growl in response. I wasn't sure who growled, and I didn't care. They could fuck off too. I had to act quickly. I didn't have time for this. I ran in the direction of Turrock's house, hoping I'd catch him. The beasts following me weren't helping matters, but at least they kept the path clear so I could cover ground faster.

By the time I got there, the door was swinging on the hinges. Turrock was gone, and so fast he hadn't bothered to shut the door.

He hadn't made it past us, which meant he was either still in the village somewhere or, more likely, had left by another route. There'd always been rumors that there was another way in and out. I'd never been able to find it, but I'd believed it.

I walked over and punched the door.

"We're too late."

THIRTY-ONE

WE WALKED THROUGH THE NOW-EMPTY VILLAGE. I was no worse for wear, except for my mood. I couldn't say the same about Callon, Hess, or Zink. They'd shifted so fast that they'd torn their clothes. There wasn't a large selection of fine clothes for them to choose from, especially when you were built like them. They looked a bit ragtag, but it served them right. What were they thinking?

"Just tell me one thing." I stepped around Ivan's dead body, lying in a pool of blood. No one had bothered to get the idiot a tourniquet, and there was a boot print on his cheek. "Who took off the arm?"

I didn't care that he was dead. I was pissed off royally that he hadn't died when I'd determined he should, which would've been after I'd talked to Turrock.

"I did." Callon gave me a stare that dared me to say something about it.

Oh, I'd dare, all right. "Why? You couldn't hold back for half an hour? You knew how important this was."

He stopped walking and planted himself in front of me. "No. I couldn't."

"The guy was annoying. He had it coming," Hess said.

It was idiotic, but no one was going to agree with me if that meant disagreeing with Callon. I took a deep breath, telling myself to drop it. The opportunity was lost for now, but not forever. Turrock would come back here and I'd get my answers, if I was still alive. I might have to sit and wait him out, but he'd be back.

We walked through the gate that was left wide open. I didn't know where everyone had taken off to, but there wasn't a body to be seen.

We hadn't gotten too far when someone whistled. It could've been a bird, but I'd heard these signals before.

Callon gave an answering whistle.

"What's that mean?" I asked, barely getting the words out as Callon picked up the pace.

"Koz caught someone. They're not alone."

I began jogging toward where we'd left Koz and Tuesday. When we got to them, Turrock was on the ground beside them, passed out, knocked out or plain dead. Wasn't quite sure which. Then I saw his chest move. Tuesday was beaming like she'd given him the knockout punch. Koz was beaming at her as if she had.

"What happened? How'd you get him?" I asked.

Koz pointed his thumb in Tuesday's direction. "I didn't see him with all the people running. I was looking in the other direction. Next thing I know, she's yelling for me as she's launching herself onto his back. We think he hit a rock on the way down, but he's alive, with a steady pulse."

I closed the distance and hugged her. That part only lasted a couple of seconds before we began jumping up and down together.

"You did it!" I said.

"I know! I did it! I did it!"

The guys might've thought we were overreacting, but they couldn't understand. She hadn't *just* caught Turrock for me. She'd tackled him to the ground while avenging herself. She went from being so terrified of going back that she could barely eat, to slaying her dragon. What she'd done was broken free of the fear she'd lived under her entire life.

"Let's take him a little farther away for more privacy," Callon said, before hefting Turrock over his shoulder.

We didn't get much farther than a mile or so before Callon dropped Turrock onto the ground, leaning him onto a boulder with shrubs all around. Dammit. I knew this place. It matched his death scene. He'd been leaning on that rock right there, and the rest? It was too gory to think about. Would we do that to him? We were either sick fucks or really desperate. I hoped we were sick fucks, because this couldn't get screwed up again.

I had to take control of this situation before what I saw happened. "I have something to say. This is very important."

They all actually turned to listen to me. I couldn't let that get to my head, though, because there was a huge, gaping distance between listening and following. These people did not follow well, or follow me, anyhow.

I pointed at Turrock. "This man is going to die in this field." Nobody blinked an eye over that statement. One thing about beasts: they weren't faint of heart. Tuesday was smiling, looking like she wanted to do a little war dance around the clearing.

"He can't die until I get my answers. This does not end the way it did in the village, right? No one touches him without my say-so."

I got a couple of noncommittal shrugs from the guys. Callon gave me nothing. Tuesday was frowning.

"This is important," I said.

"We'll try. Best we can do," Hess said.

Unlike when I spoke, he got a round of nods.

I turned to Callon. He didn't like me much right now, but he was a reasonable man. He had to see the logic in my request. "Callon?"

His arms were crossed as he stared at Turrock. His eyes were nearly flaming red. "Answers or not, he won't live to dawn. That's the best I can give you."

I turned to Tuesday. With enough pressure applied, she'd back my play, and then Koz would follow suit. I wouldn't have the majority, but I'd have a stalemate. "Tuesday, you know we need answers. It was *your* idea."

She looked down at Turrock's limp body, his gut over-hanging his waist, a line of drool hanging from his bottom lip. He was as disgusting as his soul was dark.

"I can't help. I agree with them. We wake him up and he's either going to give you answers by dawn or he's never going to tell you anything. Keeping him alive isn't going to do anything but make the world a shittier place." She took a few steps toward him while taking a swig from her canteen. She spat through her teeth into his face.

Turrock groaned in his sleep.

"That's the most help I can offer, because the truth of it is that he deserves to die. I watched him torture you for years, and I won't let him string you along for days on end. He shouldn't be allowed to see dawn."

What the hell had happened to Tuesday? She was more bloodthirsty than the guys. I watched her turn back to go stand with them. Callon patted her on the shoulder as she neared.

I had to get to work, and fast. I grabbed my canteen and splashed some more water on Turrock's face, trying to bring him the rest of the way to consciousness. His eyes opened as if he had sandbags weighing down his lids. They passed over me as if he didn't know who I was. They shifted to the guys and then paused on Tuesday. They shot back to me, as if Tuesday had confirmed my identity.

"So it's true." He leaned back his head and laughed.

"Shut the fuck up, you bastard." Tuesday, who'd never hurt a fly, walked over and kicked Turrock in the ribs.

Turrock grunted and rolled on his side.

I grabbed Tuesday's arm. "I know you're upset, but can you please not kill him?"

She pursed her lips but nodded after a second. I'd thought the guys were going to be the problem, not my hundred-pound friend.

She took a step back.

I kneeled in front of Turrock. "I have some questions for you. After you answer, we'll let you go."

The dark eyes of the devil narrowed on me. "Bull. I'm not stupid, girl. You're going to kill me. Why should I tell you anything?"

Most of the guys were looking on with *I told you so* expressions. Tuesday had bloodlust emanating off her. Callon's eyes were still blazing red.

"I'm the only thing between you and them." I pointed behind me. "I suggest you start talking. Who did you buy me from?"

He stared straight at me then opened his mouth before closing it again. Then he shrugged. The fucker was screwing with me.

Still, I kept trying. "Did my mother sell me? Did you meet her?"

His eyes flickered. I waited.

"You know, I miss the days when you were chained to the pole, silently weeping. Do you miss them?" he asked, sounding completely genuine.

Callon walked over, and a fist crashed into Turrock's mouth. Turrock's head lolled on his shoulders before it rolled back. He laughed, blood spraying from his mouth. He was happy. He knew he was going to die, and he wanted it quick. He wasn't going to get what he wanted this time.

I turned and looked at Callon. "I need him alive."

Callon reached to grab my arm but stopped short. He pointed instead. "Over there."

I walked far enough away that Turrock shouldn't be able to hear and turned to Callon.

Callon gave Turrock a glance before turning to me. "He's not going to talk. He knows he's dead either way. He knows you're going to kill him because he knows what he did to you. He won't give you anything. If we'd managed to talk to him in his village, we might've been able to trick him into speaking. But not now."

He went to walk back, and I jumped in front of him. "Maybe we let him go free. We bring him back to the village. I'll get my answers and kill him another day when we can convince him he's safe and trade for the info."

"No. People like him shouldn't be allowed to live."

"I'm the one he wronged." I laid a hand on Callon's arm before forgetting we didn't touch anymore and jerked it back. I crossed my arms in front of me so I wouldn't accidentally do it again.

He looked over my shoulder. "And I'll be the one who kills him." His tendons were strung tight and his hands were fisted.

Why had I believed I could keep him under control? It wasn't like anyone could control me. Why would I be able to control Callon when he was just like me? His beast being so near the surface only enforced that.

The vision I'd seen of Turrock's death was finally fitting together. I grabbed the knife I'd tucked into my boot, knowing what I had to do.

"I've got an idea."

I turned, knife in hand, hoping I'd be able to pull it off. I knelt beside Turrock, knife in plain sight by his face.

"I'm never going to tell you anything. You might as well get it over with or let your animal do it," Turrock said, then smiled as if he'd won.

"You are going to tell me everything. Do you want to know why?"

"Sure. Why?"

I waved Callon over, making a quick tweak to my plan because I wasn't sure I could do what was needed, not the way it had to be done. I might have the anger, but not the know-how or the stomach.

Callon came and stood beside me. I held my knife out to him, and he took it. Everyone else watched closely, wondering where I was going to go with this.

"This man here is going to torture you, the way I was tortured, but worse. With that knife, he's going to gut you; he's going to open up your belly and then pull out your intestines until they're sitting on the dirt beside you. You're going to die a long and slow death. But that won't be the end.

"See, you knew I had magic when you bought me, but you didn't realize what I could do. The thing of it is, I don't only see death, I can save you from it. All those years, you wasted me. You could've used me to conquer countries. With me, you could've been immortal. Now, I'm going to use my magic to give you the worst end anyone has ever had. Every time you die, I'm going to bring you back to life so he can kill you all over again. I'm going to keep you here in agony until I get my answers. I'll keep you at the brink of existence, where you'll writhe in pain, the way I did, for as long as it takes. And you know what?" I leaned closer and smiled. "I'm going to enjoy it."

"You're a liar. You can't do anything of the kind." His

words were confident, but the shudder in his tone told me
he was on the verge of pissing himself.

I stood to make room for Callon. "Gut him."

I forced myself to watch on, trying not to throw up, as
Callon did exactly that as if he'd been born a butcher.
Tuesday backed away. Even Hess was watching a spot in
the forest above the spectacle instead of looking on. Koz
pretended he needed to comfort Tuesday, but I knew
green when I saw it. Zink was fine.

I focused on Turrock's face. The yelling I could
handle, but the rest was rough. I couldn't turn away,
though. When Turrock looked my way, he had to see an
immoveable stone. But watching him get disemboweled
made my lunch repeat, and I wasn't sure I'd ever eat
another piece of sausage again. Callon reached into
Turrock and dropped his intestines into the dirt.

I cleared my throat. Turrock's eyes shot to me, his
nose running and tears streaming.

"Callon, cut his throat to speed things up. We can go
slower on the next round. I want him to see what's in
store for him." *Please, don't make me do this more than
once.* Even to him, I wasn't sure I had it in me.

Callon dragged his knife across his throat. I gripped
Turrock's hand, afraid to let him get too far into death. I'd
never actually brought someone back. I'd only kept them
from crossing over. I wasn't sure I'd be able to do that
right now, as it hadn't been thought out any of the times
before.

I closed my eyes. *Please come back. I need answers.
Don't die.*

My hand warmed. The slit at his neck began knitting

closed and Turrock's eyes flickered open. I dropped his hand immediately, afraid to give any more of myself. Every other time I'd done this, I'd had a recent death, something to transfer. This time? Yeah, I only had my own, and I'd just given a little to Turrock.

"Now give me my answers,' I said as firm and tough as I could. If he didn't, there wouldn't be another go around or I'd be dead. I already felt like I had a couple toes in the River Styx as it was.

His forehead was dripping sweat and he was looking at me as if I were the devil come to collect him. I'd won.

"I'll die quick?" he asked.

"Yes."

"It was a man that brought you, not your mother. He showed up at our gates and said that your mother died and you needed a home. That she'd been a Plaguer so you'd have magic. Baryn was the one there. He bought you for a sack of rice. That's all I know."

"That's it? Everything? I don't believe you."

He began sobbing, trying to reach for me, but he was too weak to grab my hand. "That's it. I swear it. Please..."

I stood. I couldn't take it anymore, and I didn't see a reason to. I believed him. He reeked of desperation.

"I think we're done," I said, about to drop down beside him. Tuesday was quicker, though. She marched over with knife in hand. It was a quick swipe right across his throat, reopening the wound that had knitted closed.

I dropped to the ground not far from him. Fuck!

"Thank the Wilds that shitshow is over," Hess said. "I know I'm a beast and all, but I didn't have the stomach for his guts all hanging out in the mud."

I heard some more talking, but I didn't have the energy left to listen.

Callon was kneeling beside me. "What's wrong with you?"

I leaned my head on my elbow. "I'm not sure." How was I supposed to tell everyone Tuesday had just screwed me? Maybe I could pretend I got a sudden flu?

Callon came closer and cupped his hand behind my head, forcing me to look at him. "You can't just give, can you? You need to take in order to give."

I let out a sigh. "Maybe."

He straightened. "Dammit, Teddy."

"What's going on?" Tuesday asked as she was walking over. "Teddy, why do you look like you're the one about to die?" I didn't have time to answer before she looked at Callon. "Why does she look like this? What's wrong with her?"

"She gave some life but didn't have any to give other than her own," Callon said, his jaw shifting.

Tuesday turned to me, and I watched as confusion turned to comprehension, then to horror, as what she'd done struck her. "Oh, fuck!"

"Now what?" Koz asked, coming to stand beside us. Tuesday was hysterical and turned into his arms. Zink and Hess edged closer. Zink had the nerve to shake his head at my stupidity. Hess was scratching his, as if it couldn't quite compute.

I tried to lean up a bit. It wasn't a good move, because I wavered, and Callon grabbed me underneath the arms and dragged me over to prop me up by a log. It was wholly undignified. I didn't have to see myself to know it.

Tuesday pulled out of Koz's arms and waved her hands in the air. "It's okay. We have to find someone for you to kill and it'll be fine."

"Watch her. I've got to go get a person," Callon said.

He was about to walk off when I attempted to yell, "I'm not just killing someone to live. They've got to be bad."

He turned back around, his brows an inch lower. "I saw plenty of men back there standing behind Ivan that I'm sure the world wouldn't miss. Give me a name and a description, because I know there were others there that helped Turrock, and enjoyed it, running around this forest right now."

"I don't—"

"I'll go with you," Tuesday said, running over to Callon. "There were a bunch of sadistic fucks there. I'll ID them. I don't have a problem with this at all."

"Watch her," Callon said to the guys before the two of them left.

THIRTY-TWO

Koz squatted next to me, holding out his canteen. "You're not going to be weird about it when they bring the person back, right? You know you've got to do this."

"I know." I accepted the offer, taking a long swig. All my water had ended up on Turrock's face.

"Because you can't get picky." Koz took the canteen back and closed it up. "If you end up all fucked up because of what Tuesday did, she'll be devastated, and we can't have that."

Hess and Zink were standing a little ways away, but they were listening too.

"I know, and I'm going to try. As long as it's a bad enough person, it'll go fine." Hopefully Tuesday would pick a good victim. If they were one of the worst offenders? I might be able to kill in cold blood. There were plenty of people back in the village who'd relished doing horrible things at Turrock's command.

Then there were the others who fell into the grey

zone. Some had committed the same atrocities, but out of fear. If they brought back one of them, I wasn't sure I could do it. Who was I to steal their life when I'd wronged people out of fear? I'd tied Callon to me because I'd been afraid.

"We should start a big, warm fire near her. I think that would help," Hess said.

There was a look that passed between the three of them that was off. Did they think I was going to die? I wasn't. I wouldn't win any races at the moment, but I'd make it.

"Isn't that dangerous with all the people from the village being out in these woods now?" I asked.

Koz waved a hand toward me. "Nah. No one is going to bother you with us here."

They built up a pile of wood in front of me that could've been enough to burn for months. Koz lit it and slowly arranged the wood while Hess and Zink piled more logs beside him. It was freezing out, but I didn't think we'd be staying long enough for the bonfire they were creating.

"Isn't this overkill?" I asked, after the flames reached Koz's waist.

"No. I think we could use it a hair bigger, to be honest. You're not looking so good, and it's freezing out here. You die on us and Callon's going to be pissed. Bigger the better." Koz grabbed another log and carefully managed to get it onto the heap without getting burned.

The heat it cranked out was nice. Like he said, it was cold out here, and the chill seemed to be sinking deep into my bones. Who knew how long it would take for

Callon and his murderous accomplice to get back? It was their fire. If they wanted to keep building it, so be it. I closed my eyes, listening to the crackle of burning wood, knowing I was safe with three beasts around me.

I was on the verge of sleep when I heard the crows cawing loudly. They didn't usually carry on unless I was doing something stupid that they could get a good laugh at. Well, maybe today had qualified, considering my current state.

Someone grabbed at my jacket. I jerked back but didn't make it far, as the man over me wouldn't release it.

"I'll be taking that," he said, ripping the jacket from my body as I was sent rolling. I knew him. He was from the village, used to tend the lumber and fires in the winter. I used to watch him walking back and forth with wood, his hair greasy, and his eyes always had a sneaky look to them. He'd always steered clear of me. He must not recognize me now.

I looked about, but none of the guys were there. These assholes had left me sleeping beside the biggest damn fire they could build and taken off? Really? They might as well have wrapped a bow around me for the first murdering bastard to come along.

"I need these, too," he said, tugging my boots from my feet.

"Get off me," I yelled.

Boots and jacket torn from me, he paused to take another look at what he could get. He smirked as he looked me up and down, discovering something else he was interested in.

He dropped my jacket and shoes beside me as he

knelt down. "Might as well have a sampling of all the goods while I'm here. Don't like to be wasteful."

I shoved weakly at his hands, as they moved to my pants, and yelled, "Koz." My voice barely carried, but they had good hearing. He'd hear me. Someone would.

I looked to the side. A small girl stood in the distance, long red curls framing her face as she watched. She must've run from the village with the rest of the residents. Had she gotten lost in the chaos?

"Go," I tried to yell to her, but my warning came out a whisper. She shouldn't see this. She probably had enough mental scars from that place already.

He clamped a hand over my mouth, yanking my head away from the girl. "Your friends took off on you fifteen minutes ago. I watched them gather their shit and leave, but let's not push the issue. I'm going to take this knife and hold it to your throat. If you don't fight me, you get to live. If you give me a problem, you don't. Either way, your body will still be warm while I fuck it. Are we clear?"

I was going to kill him. In my vision, I saw his eyes go wide before he dropped dead.

I nodded under his hand, and he lifted it.

"I don't want trouble. As long as you don't kill me, I'll help." My weakness made it easy to fake acceptance for what he was going to do to me.

I must've really looked the part, because he didn't hesitate as I reached out, laying a cold hand on top of his. His head jerked to mine at the soft gesture. I smiled, knowing I was going to kill him. I locked my fingers around his.

There was a flicker in his eyes as he felt the odd

sensation of his life force draining out of his body, weakening him, the transfer of strength so subtle, so foreign, that he didn't understand what was happening. He didn't try to pull back, believing he was the one still in command. By the time he realized something was terribly wrong and tried to pull his hand from mine, it was too late. I had sapped him of his life, and he was falling over.

I watched the light leave his eyes as life flooded through my veins. I shoved him away from me as I stood, buttoning my pants and grabbing my jacket from where he'd dropped it on the ground. The girl was gone, and I hoped she hadn't seen what I'd done.

I sat on the log, pulling my boots on, not nearly as cold as I'd been. Footsteps approached from behind. I turned, watching as the three of them made their way closer. Zink gave the body a kick before he nodded. Hess went straight to the fire, outstretching his hands. Koz joined him.

"I'm assuming you were all watching?" I asked. Just because I knew why they'd done, it didn't mean I liked them for it.

"Of course. We wouldn't leave you out here alone," Koz said, almost as if the situation amused him.

"How far would you have let that go?" I asked.

Koz shrugged. Hess didn't look at me.

Finally, Zink answered, "Until you did what you had to. We all live at the lodge and pretend we're civilized, but deep down, where it counts, we know what it takes to survive this world. You know it too. You're too strong to get a free pass."

"What if I didn't want to kill him?"

Zink gave the dead body another nudge with his toe. "You think this guy was going to improve this world? I sure don't."

"You want me dead. Why bother?" I asked him.

He shrugged. "You still have your uses right now."

He wouldn't go against Callon yet, not until it was past the critical point.

I'd finished tying my boots, but I didn't get up. I stared at the body a few feet away from me instead. What kind of monster was I? Yes, the guy had wronged me, but the way I could so casually deal out death? This was the second man I'd condemned to die in less than a day. I was now a confirmed killer, and I was no closer to answers than before. Maybe that was why the Hell Pits followed me. Maybe they'd killed the Magician because he was evil and I was too.

My veins were pumping with life, and I felt like I could run miles. And yet I couldn't get up from where I sat on the log.

Hess stopped beside me. "Don't be ashamed of what you are. You might be a killer, like us, but you're also a savior. You do what we can only dream about, pull someone who deserves more time from the brink of the River Styx. You can save the people who deserve saving."

Callon rushed back into the clearing as if the giant bonfire built by his men was a call to battle. His eyes scanned the area and landed on me, then the dead body near my feet. He walked over to the dead guy, rolling him over with his boot for a better look.

Tuesday ran to my side. "What happened? You look better physically, but like shit otherwise."

I waved a hand at the dead guy, shrugged, and shook my head. I couldn't talk about it. It was too much, too quick.

Tuesday nodded, putting a hand on my shoulder.

"Is this why we have a bonfire?" Callon asked the guys. He was a lot quicker to pick up on what their plan had been than I.

"You want her alive. She's alive," Zink said.

Had Callon looked at me the way he was cold-eyeing Zink, I'd be reaching for the nearest weapon. Callon's gaze shifted to me. "You okay?"

"I'm fine," I said, hoping that would be the last question about it. I got to my feet, grabbed my water canteen, and left in the direction of the stream.

THIRTY-THREE

FROM THE MINUTE I WALKED INTO THE GREAT ROOM for breakfast, I sensed the shift in people's attitudes toward me. Eyes glazed over me, as if they wished they hadn't seen me. Now that they had, they didn't know exactly what to do about it. No one would snub me outright, because Callon had pretty much tattooed his name on my forehead the night of the roast. It didn't matter. I could feel it. After days of traveling, and now no better off than when we'd left, it was the last thing I wanted to deal with.

I could deal with direct hostility. I wasn't used to handling the nods of artificial courtesy. I took a plate from the pile and loaded it up with eggs. I headed straight to the seat next to Tuesday, the only friendly face in the room.

"Did something happen while we were gone?" I asked softly. I didn't care if they heard me, but damned if I'd let them know it was bothering me.

"Apparently the Hell Pit had started moving away

again while we were gone. By this morning, word was already spreading that it's back to heading this way again."

"Well, that explains the warm welcome home." If warm was a frigid winter. Tuesday cracked a tiny smile. At least I could amuse someone.

It wasn't like I could blame them for hating me. I could've made it easier if I went upstairs, but I had a limit to what I'd do to accommodate their distaste.

A guy that worked on repairs around the lodge inched in closer, trying to be discreet about his eaves-dropping.

"Hey! Back up!" Tuesday yelled at him. She turned back to continue our conversation. "The people here are a bunch of assholes. Have nothing better to do than to stare and listen," she said, not so quietly.

The guy's face went red as he backed away.

Issy walked in and took the seat on the other side of me with her mug of tea. "You look like you could use some reinforcements." She took a sip of her tea. Issy got up with the sun. It wasn't a surprise she'd already heard the news.

"It's true, by the way." I didn't whisper or worry who was listening. What was the point? They knew. And if they didn't, they'd find out soon enough.

"You mean about you being confirmed as the reason we might be run out of our home? It was all they could talk about before you came down, until I told the lot of them to shut the hell up. I'd be sleeping in a dirt bed if it weren't for you, and I know it."

Issy's time of ignoring what I'd done for her seemed

to have officially passed, even if I would prefer a little more subtlety. I'd liked it so much better when we didn't discuss what had happened. I gave her a quick smile and hoped she'd move on to a different topic—even going back to me drawing the Hell Pits here was preferable.

"No matter what happens or what people say, you're a good person. I'm not certain how you managed to save me, but you did. And I'm not asking right now, either. I'm not sure I want to know." She was smart enough to figure out she probably wouldn't like the *how*.

Tuesday leaned forward so she could see past me to Issy. "It's for the best you don't."

If the subject bothered Tuesday, the feeling didn't make it to her stomach, as she moved onto a muffin. She had a lot of calories to make up for with all those missed meals on the road.

Issy didn't say another word after Tuesday's warning. Telling her that I'd sucked up one person's life and given it to her wasn't a conversation I wanted to have over breakfast. There were too many other hard subjects I needed to tackle today. I was going to have to leave here, and soon. My days were numbered. I needed to make a plan as best I could.

I couldn't look at Tuesday when I thought about it.

Hess ducked into the great room. "Callon is calling a meeting on the back lawn," he said loudly to the room. Tension spread through the crowd like a palpable wave.

Most people didn't waste any time getting up and exiting. Tuesday grabbed a couple of muffins and gave us both a *let's go see what this is all about* look. Issy grabbed her tea and followed. I was the last in line. News didn't tend to be good these days, so I didn't see a need to rush out there.

Callon was on the back porch as people gathered around him. His eyes passed over me but didn't pause. I took that as a good sign. Maybe this would have nothing to do with me for a change.

Callon cleared his throat, signaling he was ready. "Most of you here know about the poison pits. There's been word that they're shifting positions. One seems to be moving quite steadily in our direction. I'm looking for a team of people to help build a trench between here and it. It'll be quite a bit of work, but it might be our only option to slow it down."

A man near the front raised his hand. I vaguely remembered his name being Levi. I was positive he'd die from a heart attack in about five years as he was digging a hole somewhere else.

"Levi is our first," Callon said.

Levi waved his hand again. "No, that's not what I meant. We've all heard that the Hell Pit is coming because of her. Is that true?" He turned and pointed at me.

Callon's eyes went hard. "We don't know for certain why it's heading this way. Only that it is."

"But that's not what my sister heard," another woman, who lived in one of the surrounding cottages, said. "She told me that everyone knows it's her."

Callon's shoulders straightened. "Then she was wrong, because nobody knows anything."

I weaved my way up to the front of the group, even as

Callon's eyes shot to me, then flickered back to the corner where I'd been.

I ignored the suggestion. I wasn't going to lie to these people. It didn't matter what he wanted. Everything they'd heard was true, and there was no denying it. All they had to do was go look at the jar that was in Callon's office and then watch me walk across a room. The sludge didn't lie, that was for sure. I wasn't going to either.

I didn't stop until I was standing in front of Callon, who was crossing his arms and frowning at me.

"Callon is right. We don't know for sure if it wants me. But it does appear that way."

"Can't you go?" Levi asked.

To give the man credit, it wasn't said maliciously, more like recommending the best course of action. As much as I was about telling the truth, this wasn't the moment I was going to come clean and tell them it was my conclusion as well.

"She can't. The next person who suggests that should go pack their things," Callon said from behind me.

A hush settled over the crowd.

No one else said a thing. I could see on their faces what they wanted to say, and none of it was nice. I straightened my shoulders and kept my head up.

Callon stepped in front of me. "Back to the purpose of this meeting. Who's volunteering? This might be our only shot."

But it wouldn't save this place. It would buy a little time and that was it.

Slowly, hands began to rise. I walked away from the group before they were done counting numbers.

I'd barely hit the bottom stair in the hall when Issy was behind me and tugging on my arm.

"Did I ever show you around all the camping gear that was stored here?" Issy locked elbows with me and steered me in a new direction.

"Camping?" I'd never heard of camping, but it seemed Issy was going to show me all of this gear, as she pulled me with her.

"It's what they used to call living outside. There's all sorts of stuff. It's fun to look through when you need a distraction." She smiled and continued to tug at my arm.

Her explanation had me picking up my speed. "Thanks. I'd love to see it."

"It's in one of the basements. Not the one where I keep all the dried meats that'll last us through winter, but the one next to it. Do you know where I mean?"

"No." God, I loved this woman. At least I'd have a chance of surviving.

"I'll show you. It'll be fun going through all of it with you. Always good to learn about the old ways, just in case." She patted my arm.

THIRTY-FOUR

It was three a.m. and I hadn't gotten a minute of sleep. Tomorrow was the day I left. Tuesday might never forgive me, but that didn't matter. She'd stay and make a life. It would be all right, and maybe someday I'd be able to come back here. At least there'd be a here to come back to if I did this. If I didn't, there'd be nothing.

There was only one thing I needed to do. I got up, put on my boots, and left my room. I made my way downstairs, not as careful to be as quiet as I normally would. I opened the door, letting the fresh air wash over me, and then stepped outside, breathing deeply. Was I really going through with this?

I turned toward where Callon's room was. There was a glow of light coming from his window, defining his silhouette. He was watching, waiting.

I looked back at the trees. I wanted to run free through them, feel the air flowing through my hair. Most of all? I wanted Callon with me, beside me. Tomorrow and yesterday didn't exist. There was only this moment as I took another step.

And then another.

It was wrong. He wanted more. I didn't have it to give and yet couldn't stop the need I felt, driving me forward. I took a few more steps and then glanced toward his window again. He was still there. Maybe this was the time he wouldn't follow me. I was about to find out either way.

I ran.

Once I started, I couldn't seem to stop or slow down. I tripped on a branch, launched forward, and skidded to a halt. I got up again and continued to run to the one place I wanted to be, nearly crazed.

Finally, his steps sounded behind me, louder than usual. I turned, knowing what I'd find. He was here, his beast, standing in front of me.

Then his shape shifted. He'd never changed before. Every other time he'd remained a beast and then carried me to his den. Why was he changing?

Callon stood before me naked, human, every muscle in his frame tense, as if he was warring with himself.

"Go. Back. To. The. Lodge." Each word was ground out.

For what? To lie there alone? This was my last night here. Whether he knew it or not didn't matter. *I* knew. I'd made my choice, as terrified as I was. He wouldn't unmake it for me. I didn't want to be alone anymore.

He stood before me, nothing but hot flesh and coiled power. I stepped closer, my breathing as shaky as the rest of me.

My lip trembled as I said, "No."

He fisted his hands, the tendons in his neck tensing into a sharp V.

"Go," he said.

I could do as he asked, walk back. I could remain standing here as he slowly regained his control, until he dragged me back with him. Or I could unleash the part of me that wanted to run as wild as he did and untether us both, damn the consequences.

I spun, running from him, knowing I'd trigger the predator, the part of him that was so close to the surface that I could taste the power he barely held in check. I ran toward the place he brought me when he was the beast.

It happened so fast that it was a blur. One second I was running again, and then I was tumbling with him, turning as we fell until he landed underneath me. Turning again, until the length of his body was pressing against mine.

His arms caged me in, his eyes feral.

Still, he held back, his frame rigid as he fought himself. It made me want him more, and I hadn't thought that possible.

I arched up, rubbing against him.

"You don't know what you're doing," he said.

"I know exactly what I'm doing. I knew it the second I ran." I leaned my face closer to him and ran my tongue up the sensitive skin of his neck, marking him as he'd marked me.

The last bit of his control snapped. He stood, yanking me up with him and then tossing me over his shoulder. He ran through the forest, but not toward the lodge. He climbed, carrying me up the cliff until we were in his cave. He dropped me onto the pile of furs but then stepped away, still warring with himself. Still fighting what was going to happen.

"Sleep," he demanded, backing away.

"No." I got up and followed him. "I need you. I need this. I can't be with anyone else. They'll never know me. They didn't see me as I limped my way to freedom and then crawled when that didn't work, scarred and disfigured. They know this." I stabbed at my face, the one I saw every day that didn't belong to me anymore.

"It's not me. You know me. You're the one who didn't flinch. I know how men looked at me before, but you didn't. You never cared." If I was going to have one last night here, I wanted everything, including Callon. I wanted it to be true and not some boy who wanted me for a face that didn't feel like mine. "I need you tonight. Please."

He stood still as I moved closer. I grazed the ridges of his abdomen with my hands, afraid of moving lower, scared he'd pull away from me.

"I need you."

"Whether anyone else saw it or not, you were always beautiful." His hands went to the edge of my jacket, yanking me to him. My length pulled against his, his lips covered mine as his tongue plunged into my mouth. I grabbed his hair, afraid he'd change his mind.

He pulled my jacket from me. The rest of my clothes followed in short order as he walked us backward, dragging me down to the pelts with him. His body covered mine from shoulder to the tips of my toes. He cupped my face with his large hand, a callused thumb fanning back and forth across my cheek in a gentle caress that was in sharp contrast to the way his mouth dominated mine. His other hand went on a trail of discovery. Its callused palm traced a line from my throat to between my breasts, pausing to test the weight of one before continuing its journey. He dipped his hand lower, smoothing over the quivering flesh of my stomach. Nerves had nothing to do with the tremors. It was anticipation, the knowledge that, for the first time in my life, I wanted sex with a man. Not any man, but this one, only this one. He pressed his fingers against me, and I arched into him.

He broke from our kiss to shift his arms to either side of me, rising above me on his elbow. His knee rode the inside of my thighs, pushing them farther apart until he could settle his hips in between. The hard length of him rubbed against my center, and I pressed farther, ready, wanting, knowing exactly what would come next.

He shoved inside of me, and a wash of pain had me jerking stiffly, but it was barely anything compared to the pain I'd felt in my past. He paused, resting his forehead against mine, waiting for it to fade. A restlessness took over my body at his continued stillness. I arched into him, asking for more, and he gave. He withdrew, and the friction sent tingles of pleasure through me. He thrust back in as my hips met his, each movement building the pressure within until I was digging my fingers into his back, feeling as if I'd die if I didn't have even more of him. His thrusts increased until I was exploding from within; he followed me over the edge with a final thrust and a growl that no human male's throat could produce.

No matter what came tomorrow, this moment was right. I'd never been so sure of anything in my life. I was meant to be with this man. And even if it only lasted tonight, that would have to be enough.

THIRTY-FIVE

I FOUND MYSELF ALONE IN MY BED THE NEXT morning. Callon had returned me to my room and left. I was relieved he'd not stayed, even if it meant I wouldn't see him one last time. It was better this way. The ache in my heart would've only been worse if I'd woken beside him. What if I chickened out because he'd been here? No. Definitely better.

I got to breakfast late, knowing he'd be gone. Tuesday had disappeared with Koz, as was their morning routine. There was a note waiting in my room for her. I'd written five different notes to Callon, but none of them seemed right. Last night would have to stand on its own.

Leaving the lodge in the middle of the night would've drawn much more attention, so I lay low in my room until late morning. Activity around the lodge was at its peak, and no one paid me much mind as I walked with a pack on my back. It was filled with everything I'd need—some weird, metallic-looking blanket and a tent stuffed into it with the rest of the supplies. There was enough dried meat to fill my stomach for weeks. Plenty to live on, but part of me couldn't imagine a future as I walked away from the lodge—or not one I wanted to think about.

I told myself not to cry, but as usual, my body wouldn't listen. The farther I walked, the faster the tears fell. The crows cawed as they flew overhead, always mocking. I'd been walking for close to thirty minutes, now sobbing, when I was suddenly stopped by what felt like a rope around my waist.

I tried to take another step. It didn't work. I took several steps back and then ran forward. Instead of getting farther, I fell to my knees.

Bitters hadn't cut the tie between Callon and I. It had been a bunch of bullshit. I should've known it wouldn't be that easy. What was wrong with me? He'd taken a plain old pair of scissors and snipped. Was I a complete idiot? Yes. All evidence was pointing to that conclusion. Now what did I do? I walked over and kicked a tree a few times for good measure, since I had nowhere else to vent my frustration.

Standing in the middle of the woods wasn't going to fix anything. I'd have to come up with a different plan. I had no other choice. I had to go back to the lodge.

And I'd slept with Callon. It was bad enough I had slept with him, but then I ran off the next day without a word? The entire scenario was groan-worthy, epically bad. The only way to possibly salvage it was to get back before he knew I'd tried to leave.

It was freezing out, but I'd broken a sweat with my pace, and it didn't matter. Callon was waiting for me, leaning against a tall oak, right before the line of trees gave way to the field around the lodge.

"Didn't realize you were the love 'em and leave 'em type," he said.

Now I was sweaty *and* red. Of course there had been no way he'd let this go without saying something.

His forearms corded where they crossed in front of his chest. He didn't get cold like a normal human, so his lack of jacket might mean nothing. Or it meant he'd felt our connection being tugged on and left in a hurry.

"I thought maybe it wouldn't still hold. I had to try." The idea of telling him that Bitters had duped me with his magic scissors was too much humiliation to pile on top of the current load.

Plus, Callon was visibly fuming. I didn't need to add fuel by telling him the whole story right now.

I used to wonder if Callon wanted me dead. Now I couldn't figure out what he felt. Was it possessiveness over my unique talents? Did he simply want me the way a man wanted a woman? Was his ego bruised because, like he said, I loved him and left him? Or did he not know how he felt?

I definitely didn't know. Tuesday thought I was in love with him. If loving someone meant you wanted to kill them most of the time and yet you couldn't bear the idea of never seeing them again? Yeah, maybe she was right. This was love. But if that were true, who the hell wanted any part of it? I couldn't afford love, and neither could he. We had something more important. Obligations.

"You should've waited a week. You would've had

company," he said, before he turned and walked in the direction of the lodge.

"What are you talking about?" I asked running after him.

He turned his head slightly toward me. The longer I had to wait for him to answer, the worse I felt.

He stopped and let out a sigh that had the ring of defeat. It wasn't something that he wore well or often.

"I'd hoped that as the Hell Pit continued to flow uphill, it would eventually slow down and then stall out. It's not. It's crossed onto our lands. We're running out of time."

Callon, who'd been so sure we'd find an answer, was on the verge of defeat. I'd expected to fail this entire time, but hearing it from him was the last nail in the coffin. "What about the trenches?"

"Working on them, but I don't think it's going to be enough."

"I have to leave here, even if you come with me. You have to get me away from here." This day was getting worse and worse. He had to see the logic of it now, or we were done.

"It won't work anymore."

"Why not?"

He was already grabbing a stick from the ground and drawing in the snow.

"That's us." He pointed to a small circle. There were two larger circles to south and the west. "The western one is the closest, but it's neck and neck right now. The people I have watching them tell me the two of them are about to merge into one larger one. Once it does, we only have two directions left to go. North and east. Even if we were to leave tonight, it wouldn't matter, as it would still draw them closer to the lodge." He tossed down the stick.

Because if the Hell Pits wanted me, they'd have to travel over the lodge to get to me.

"Then we leave and head southwest. You said they haven't merged yet. There's got to be a way to thread the needle in between them before they do and draw them away."

"Last word was that it was close to joining, so it might've already happened." He turned and began walking again. I wasn't sure if he was still mad at me or the defeat was getting to him. I didn't care either way. I couldn't. We were down to our last option.

"What if it's not?" I yelled.

"I'm expecting an update soon. We'll reassess then. By the way, Tuesday was looking for you," he said, then made a point of looking at the bag on my back.

Oh, shit. The note. I had to get inside before Tuesday got nervous and found the note in my room. I abandoned Callon and ran the rest of the way to the lodge, ignoring the looks I was getting. I dumped my supplies outside. I'd fetch them later when it was dark out and no one was watching.

I burst into the back door. Issy looked up from her seat at the counter where she was drinking her tea.

"No good?" she asked. I shook my head as I ran past. "Can't say I'm upset by that," she called after me.

She said that now. Wait until she was traipsing through the world with no shelter and no food and her tune might change. That was another day's problem, though. If Tuesday found my note, there would be absolute hell for weeks.

Running was too conspicuous, so I walked as fast as I could straight to my bedroom. She was in the hall, hand on my doorknob and about to go in.

"Where've you been? I've been looking for you for an hour," she said.

"Went for a walk to clear my head."

She walked down the hall toward me until we were both standing on the top landing. "I wanted to see if..." She turned her head toward the window over the main door. "Who are those people? Not a great time to visit, that's for sure."

I looked out and groaned.

THIRTY-SIX

CALLON WAS STANDING ON THE LAWN WITH ONE dark-haired man and a woman with flowing red hair, also known as my "long-lost parents." It might be easier to play into the ruse. Only issue with that was I didn't think I could act well enough to get past the finale when they discovered they were wrong and left.

Tuesday turned to me. "You know them? Is that..." She sucked in the loudest breath I'd ever heard.

"The people who think they're my parents." I wasn't sure if I should go get my bag and try to escape again or march right up to them and tell them to leave. I *was* sure neither would work. These people were stubborn as hell. I couldn't escape. Only one thing left to do: see why they were here and try to scare them away. It would be less painful for all involved if no one got attached.

"You didn't tell me your dad was hot. Whoa. If I wasn't in love..." She made a very disturbing humming noise as she fanned her face.

Callon was talking to them and smiling as they

walked toward the lodge. "I've got to get out there before he invites them to stay."

"I should come too," Tuesday said, walking beside me.

"No. Stay here. I'm not looking for a welcoming committee. I don't want them to stay." She was already looking happy about this situation. I didn't want happy. I needed mean. *Real* mean.

She pointed to the door. "But I want to meet the fake parents."

"No. They aren't staying. Now don't come." I opened the door and shut it before she could try to come with me. Hopefully she wouldn't just open right back up and follow.

I walked out the door. It was entirely possible they were here for something else. It wasn't what I'd bet on.

Callon inched closer to me as I approached. I wasn't sure if he was giving me a buffer or was afraid I'd tackle them to the ground.

Dal said, "Hi, Teddy. So happy to see you again. We came to talk to you."

Even the phrase "ready, set, go" didn't make me want to run the way those words did. They boded nothing but bad. I needed to limit exposure before we all got sucked into an emotional tsunami that left no one standing.

Dal stepped forward, clearly itching to reach out to me before she crossed her arms in front of her.

Dax stepped up next to her. "After what happened at the farm, what Bitters said, we went back to the grave. It was empty. We felt that we needed to tell you."

Crazy. They were completely bonkers. "It's been

years. Are you sure you went to the same spot? Are you sure an animal didn't..."

My words died as they all looked at me aghast. What the hell? It wasn't like animals didn't eat dead bodies sometimes. I didn't know when all these beasts got such delicate sensibilities. Didn't they realize I was doing them a kindness? This relationship was doomed. They were wrong. I wasn't their daughter and they didn't really want me. They just didn't know it yet.

Dax cleared his throat. "Either way, we know you're having some trouble here, and we wanted to see if we could help."

Sure they did. Now I was never getting rid of them.

I turned to Callon and tilted my head to the side. "I need a word with you."

"Why don't you go get warm in the lodge?" Callon said to them.

We walked until Callon stopped. I hoped that meant we were out of earshot, but this discussion was happening either way. There were enough problems. I didn't need these two staring at me while we sorted through the mess that was going on here.

I paced in front of him. "When are they leaving? You didn't leave it open-ended, did you? I hope you told them we didn't need their help. They're only here for me. Do you see the way they look at me?" I crossed my arms to stop from pointing at them. Then I uncrossed them, thinking of how Dal had done the same thing two seconds ago. They didn't need anything else to support their crazy notions. They'd take an innocent gesture like that and use it.

He stood still as he watched me move back and forth. "Parents or not, they're offering to help. I'm not kicking them out."

"They stare at me weird, like I'm going to fix them. I'm not. I'm going to break their heart again." I glanced over at the lodge and saw a glimmer of them through the window. I wasn't so sure how mine would be faring either. "They're doing it now. I can't have them here."

"They're curious. They'll get over it."

I shook my head and stopped pacing. "I hate when people look at me."

"It's not *that* bad."

"It. Is. For someone who wants a..." I pointed a finger back and forth between us, because I was not saying *relationship*. "This behavior doesn't infuse confidence in you being a good..." I wasn't saying *boyfriend* either. "You get my point."

He tilted his head toward me. "You're going to play *that* card after you tried to run away the day after without a word?"

Yeah, I sort of had. I had a good reason, like trying to save everyone's home, thank you. But it didn't look too good on the relationship scale. If he was flunking, I didn't know where I was right now.

He leaned forward. "You want to kick them out, *you* do it."

He headed off toward the lodge before I could argue further. Some boyfriend he was.

I could still see Dal and Dax through the windows standing in the hall. They stared at me like I had three horns and purple hair. I'd rather walk into the middle of the Hell Pit than go inside that lodge right now. But it wasn't like I could leave.

I caught a glimpse of Tuesday standing next to them, smiling. That got my feet moving. She better not be telling them anything about my life. Distance was what was needed.

By the time I got inside and close enough to hear, it was already getting weirder.

She stood too close to Dal. "You know, Teddy and I are pretty much sisters. I guess that would make you my parents, too."

She *wanted* my fake parents. Unfortunately, no one was going to be able to keep them, so she shouldn't just move it along.

"Hey, sis, I need you." I wrapped an arm around her and dragged her into the kitchen. "What are you doing? Don't encourage this."

"You said the farm was nice. Maybe me and Koz could honeymoon there with our new parents?"

"You can't have them."

"I shared with you."

"I can't have them either. They're not mine, and nothing good is going to come from pretending." I gave Tuesday a last warning glance to keep her greedy hands away from the fake parents as I headed back.

She crinkled her nose and stuck her tongue out at me as I left.

By the time I walked back into the hall, Callon and the fake parents had moved into the great room. Callon was talking to Dal and Dax when I walked in. He glanced my way, and I could've sworn I saw guilt. Was he telling them to stay as long as they wanted? Maybe he'd told them to lay off the staring? You could never quite pin him down.

"So, how long do you think you might be staying?" I should be telling them to get out but couldn't seem to get my lips to form those words. They'd lost their only child and gone insane. Since I didn't have the guts to say it, couldn't get Callon to say it, I was stuck dealing with it for a little bit. It wouldn't be too long. A Hell Pit was heading our way, about to wipe out the lodge. There was always a silver lining.

Dal smiled and shrugged. She didn't seem to care whether I wanted her there or whether I even wanted to be in the same room with her. All she wanted to do was smile at me like I was a Christmas Day feast. What was wrong with this woman? Did she not know I wanted nothing to do with this charade? She should *not* be smiling.

Dax didn't have any of his wife's smiling attitude. "We're staying until this situation is settled. Until you're settled." He stated it like he was about to go out back and chisel it into the side of the mountain if I didn't get the message.

"Well, you might be waiting quite a while. I don't think I'm going to be settled for weeks, possibly months."

Dal continued to smile. Dax looked ready to find some more mountains.

"It might even be years. I could end up having to go from place to place for a long time, the way this stuff is hunting me down. It's not a pretty picture. It's a real disaster." The only thing I didn't say was "you should run for your lives," but that was clearly implied if they were sane enough to hear it. It was time they went and found themselves a new fake daughter.

"That's fine. We can wait," Dax said.

I glanced at Callon. "Could even be decades, right?"

"Sure. Decades. Maybe even a millennium?" Callon shrugged. And this was who I'd slept with? *Asshole.*

I was never going to...

No. Don't say that, even in your head. You might be stuck here for a while. You'll never stay out of his bed now that you know what you can have while in it. Lying to yourself would only complicate things and add unneeded guilt.

With no way to fix this, only one option left: retreat. "Well, I've got a lot of stuff I need to get to before dinner."

Dal smiled. Dax looked rooted to the ground.

I left and went outside. Tuesday followed me as we walked away from the lodge.

She didn't press me for information, but she looked like she wanted every detail.

"You know all that food I snuck you? I might have to go into hiding, and you'll have to return the favor by bringing me dinner."

"They seem nice enough. I think you should embrace it."

That suggestion made me walk faster. "There will be no embracing. They will eventually realize it's a mistake, and then it'll be done."

"Okay," she said, her voice a little higher and faster.

The crows took that opportunity to caw and fly overhead.

"Are there more crows?" Tuesday asked, looking upward.

"I think they made friends or something." I didn't have time to worry about the damn crows.

We hiked a little farther up the mountain. When I turned around, I sucked in a breath.

"Tuesday," I said, pointing in the distance.

"Oooh, shit."

For the first time, we could see the Hell Pit from a lookout point close to the lodge.

I CHEWED ON A PIECE OF ROAST AT DINNER. DAL AND Dax were sitting across from me. Tuesday was beside me, eating daintily as she smiled at them. Callon was to my left. Issy and the guys were all the way at the other end of the long table, leaving some seats in the middle as buffer.

"How far did you have to travel from your normal route to get around it?" Callon asked, talking about the Hell Pit. It had been the main topic of dinner, rehashing everything that had happened.

"About a half a day," Dal said, glancing at me. No matter how hard I tried to not participate, it didn't matter —their attention was focused on me.

I shoved the last of the meat on my plate in my mouth. I chugged some water down when it nearly got stuck and then stood.

"Really long day. I'll see you all in the morning." I

gave the table a wave and then exited the room before anyone could stop me. I got out of there fast, but not before I noticed Tuesday slide into my chair. If only she could take my place.

There would still be tomorrow and the next day, but if I could limit exposure, eventually they'd leave. We might all be leaving.

That didn't help me sleep. This time it wasn't just fear that kept me awake, but Callon. There was only one thing that would wash my mind clear for a precious few moments. *Don't do it. You can't give him what he wants, and you shouldn't pretend you can. You're too messed up and you know it.*

Although maybe I could. Or I could pretend to? I couldn't leave him anyway, and it wasn't as if I wanted anyone else. Was there really any harm in continuing this for a while?

After ten minutes of hard internal debating, I gave up caring about what was right. I got up, one destination in mind.

I opened my door to see Callon already heading my way. He stopped in front of me.

His eyes slipped lower, looking at the ragged t-shirt I was wearing to bed like I'd covered myself in honey.

"Do you want me to leave?" he asked, his voice gravelly. That was it, a dip in his pitch and I grew breathless. What had become of me that he could undo me so easily?

"No," I said, as I took a step back, inviting him in.

He followed, shutting the door behind him.

In one last flare of panic, I asked, "This doesn't mean anything, right?"

"Do you really want to discuss that?"

It did mean something to him. And I'd be lying if I said it meant nothing to me, but that didn't change anything, did it? If we talked about it, it would ruin this moment, and that would be very, *very* bad.

"No, Definitely not."

He put an arm around my waist and lifted me, and I wrapped my legs about him like I'd done it a thousand times as he walked back to the bed.

THIRTY-SEVEN

I GRABBED SOME BISCUITS IN THE KITCHEN AND headed outside. I'd skipped breakfast and lunch. There was no denying it. I was a chicken avoiding my fake parents. If they didn't see me, maybe they'd leave. I was so consumed in my thoughts that I nearly mowed Levi over as he was walking toward the supply shed.

"Sorry," I said, jerking away from him.

He gave me a nod in return, not openly hostile but a few pegs down from friendly, as he kept on his way.

I didn't move. Levi was supposed to die from a heart attack, and not for years. Today, I'd seen him die of a fever while lying in some worn-down shack. He was wearing the same shirt he had on today. Something had changed.

I went straight for the kitchen. Issy was busy rolling dough. "Any idea where Callon is?" I asked, keeping my distance. I didn't need to see another death, especially hers, or I might pass out before I found him.

"He was out front earlier. Not sure where he went off

to." She glanced up, took one look at my face, and squinted. "You okay?"

"I'm good," I said, trying to keep space between me and everyone I saw as I made my way out of the kitchen. "Or I will be. I just have to talk to Callon."

I looked out the front door before shooting into his office, and then taking the stairs two at a time.

Tuesday was making her way down the hall.

"Did you see Callon?" I asked.

"No. Why? What's going on?"

"Not sure."

Tuesday came to stand in front of me, and I nearly fell over.

Tuesday's death had been the same for as long as I'd known her. She'd die in her bed after living decades longer, if her wrinkles meant anything. It had never wavered, not once. I could set my clock by it, and I'd taken solace from it many times. No matter what happened, she'd be okay, even hanging around me. She'd live a full life.

Or that used to be the case.

Today she was dead in a ditch, her body twitching as the last of her life left her. Her chest still. Her face youthful.

"Teddy, you okay?" Tuesday reached out to place a hand on my arm, and I jerked away.

It took a second before I could get my words back. Tuesday was getting more and more concerned as she watched.

"Yeah, I just..." My words dried up again.

"What? You look white as a ghost."

"I'm just freaked out, and it hit me, is all. I'm okay. I swear. Just on edge." I couldn't let her know the changes I was seeing in people's deaths. Especially hers.

Her face softened. "Yeah, I know. I think every sane person is on edge at this point." She rolled her eyes as if it all made sense, turning to head downstairs. Before we took our first step, the bell rang. That meant either there was food to be had, which wasn't likely at this time of day, or there was something important about to be said. The idea of an announcement filled me with so much dread that I nearly couldn't walk.

By the time we got a few steps down, people were already piling through the hall and into the great room. I couldn't see any more death visions and hold it together through that meeting.

"Go get a seat. I'll be down in a second. I want to drop off my jacket in my room." I waved her ahead.

I ran back upstairs and deposited my jacket to keep up my cover. The room was packed by the time I got back. I didn't go in but lingered in the doorway, where I could make a quick exit.

Callon was standing off to the side in front of the crowd, waiting for everyone to settle down.

He glanced over at me. I shook my head slightly, begging him not to say what I feared. He paused long enough to give me a glimmer of hope and then moved to the front of the room, not looking at me again.

"Thanks for coming. I've got some bad news that can't hold. The Hell Pits are getting closer and seem to be picking up speed. We're going to have to evacuate in three days."

A murmur spread through the room.

"It's unavoidable," Callon said, raising his voice over the din. "Pack only what you think you can carry. If you want to stay and take your chances, that's up to you. This isn't a forced move. You're free to do whatever you want. But you will be on your own."

The room erupted into full-blown panic. Several people asked, "Where are we going to go?" Others had already moved on to "What about our things?", "How are the children going to manage the move?", and "How far are we going to go?"

He was swarmed with people as I ducked out the front door and threw up in a bush.

He walked into his bedroom. I looked at him from where I was sitting on his bed. I'd been waiting nearly an hour for him to get done answering questions. We couldn't leave this place, and by the time I was done, he needed to understand that too. I glared at him a little harder with each step he took, throwing down the gauntlet with my expression.

He looked back at me, silently accepting the challenge.

"You knew this was coming. It's not like it hit you out of the blue, which is more than I can say for most of the people who live here." He moved to the far end of the room, staring out the windows of the horizon, where there'd been a clear sightline to the Hell Pit since this morning.

"This morning, two people's deaths changed," I said.

There was a split-second pause before he replied, "Then we'll be careful of those two people."

"We don't know how many more there are." My voice was harsh and stilted. He wasn't hearing me.

He turned from the window, as agitated as I was. "There's no other choice. We. Can't. Stay."

He was right. We couldn't. This thing would follow me to the ends of the earth. I was sure of that. But they might be able to if I didn't.

I jumped to my feet. "Then we should leave, right now, while we might still be able to." We. Could I do that to him? Condemn him to a life perpetually on the move? There was no other choice right now.

"We can't. The two Hell Pits have merged into one. There is no saving this place. It's over."

"There's got to be—"

"There isn't."

I grabbed his arms, and then I whispered when I would've rather screamed. "Tuesday will die. I saw it."

Another pause, this one long enough to give me hope. Then his eyes shuttered off his soul. "I'll warn Koz and we'll protect her. There's nothing else to be done."

I turned and then sat back on the bed. Now what? What did we do now?

"I need to go help organize. We don't have much time," he said. He stared at me for another couple of moments before he walked out of the room.

He was wrong. There was one thing that could be done.

THE PLACE WAS ASLEEP AS I WALKED THE HALLS. Callon was out staring at the Hell Pit. Dal and Dax were hopefully sound asleep in their bed. Tuesday and Koz were otherwise occupied and definitely not worried about what anyone else was up to, if the moans coming from their room meant anything.

I walked until I came to the door at the end of the hallway. Zink was already out there on the deck, leaning on the railing. I stepped outside and wrapped the blanket around me as I took a seat on the bench.

"Thanks for meeting me."

He tipped his head in acknowledgement. "Can't say that curiosity wasn't partially to blame. What's with the clandestine vibe? I was fairly certain that secret meetings and notes under the door weren't our thing."

He was still leaning, but his body was tilted toward me now.

The seconds ticked on by as he watched. Once I said it, it would be set in motion, real. As soon as I told Zink my plan, I wouldn't back out.

What did it matter? I wasn't backing out anyway. There was only one way to stop the encroaching monster, and it was to give it what it wanted.

I looked down at my fingers where they fidgeted with the blanket and let a single tear escape. That was all the softness I could afford. What came next would require nothing but cold, hard strength, or it wouldn't be done.

"Zink, you're a pragmatist. You know what needs to happen."

He straightened, turning fully my way now, his back to the forest.

"Are you saying what I think?"

I notched my chin up, shoving the pain and loss aside and focusing only on the plan. "This stuff, whatever it is, will never stop. My life is not worth everyone else's here."

His eyes dropped from mine. If it were possible, cold-hearted Zink was thawing slightly.

"I'm going to need your help. I won't be able to pull it off without you," I said.

"What do you need?"

"Callon has people watching the Hell Pit, monitoring it at all times. If I know Callon, they'll have orders to keep me away from it. They might spot me before I get close enough. All I need is for you to get me to the edge fast enough that I can do what I have to do before anyone can stop me. I also need you to be there to stop him if he tries to follow me in."

His gaze dropped to the floor. "When?"

"Not tomorrow, but the next day." Two days would be soon enough, and I had to put some things in order tomorrow. Goodbyes that needed to be said, in some manner or other. This trip would be different. There was no chance of a return.

He looked back up at me. "I don't know what you feel for him, but I know he'll never forgive me for this."

"But he'll be alive. So will everyone else. Anyone on the run with me will be easy pickings. There are deaths already changing."

"You're right. You're not worth all the lives here."

I nodded. It wasn't a surprise. This was why I'd picked Zink.

"But for what it's worth, you're good people, Teddy. If I could find some way to change this, I would."

"Thanks. But now you can kindly shut the fuck up, because I can't have you making me soft before I do this. If I thought you were going to get all weepy, I would've asked Koz."

In one of the rarest moments for us, we laughed together.

THIRTY-EIGHT

Easiest to hardest, I'd knock them out one by one. That had been my grand plan when I woke this morning. I'd stood at the door and realized there weren't any easy goodbyes. They'd all twist my insides up worse than they already were, even Dal and Dax.

They deserved a goodbye too. They'd come a long way to see me. They'd offered to help in any way they could. If a person could discover long-lost parents, those would be the ones you'd want. Plus, they hadn't gotten much of a goodbye with their real daughter. It was the least I could do for them.

My plan already trashed, I decided to go with closest to farthest. I'd knock them out as I found them.

That put Dal and Dax up first, if they were still in their room and not down at breakfast.

The door was open, and Dax turned to me before I set foot inside. Dal turned, sensing me there.

They had that look on their faces again, like I was an angel that had descended from heaven. They knew what

I'd gone through, the way that I'd lived, and yet here I was, floating on air.

Neither of them spoke as they waited to see what wondrous words I had to utter, wondering if I meant to grace them with my presence, scared that if they spoke first, I might run away. It was too much.

"Do you have a minute?" I asked.

"Of course, come in," Dax said. Dal lit up like a daffodil on the first day of spring.

I moved into the room, and Dal glanced at the spot on the bed beside her. Normally I'd ignore that. But since this might be the last time I'd see them. I swallowed hard and sat beside her.

"There's been a lot going on lately, so we haven't been able to spend that much time together. But I wanted you both to know that I really appreciate the effort you're putting out in my direction. And whether or not I'm your daughter, I know you've tried to do the best by me since Bitters said I was."

Ah, fuck. She was going to cry. I could see the tears starting to well up. This was nice stuff. Why was she crying now? Did she have some sort of endless supply? How could someone cry this much?

Double fuck. My eyes were starting to water. This was not going well, and it was only my first goodbye.

I stood so fast that I got lightheaded. "Yeah, so I just wanted you to know that."

"Maybe after all this settles down, we could spend some more time together?" Dax said, putting his hand on Dal's shoulder. She looked incapable of words right now.

"Definitely." I wasn't lying. Not really. I might live.

Death wasn't a foregone conclusion, even when wading into a pit of poison. There was a small chance I'd make it, like maybe only one or two percent, but that wasn't zero. If I did, I would spend some more time with them. I'd give them a chance. They'd lost a lot too, after all. Who knew? Maybe I'd let them adopt me if things worked out.

I gave them a wave goodbye and headed to my next stop.

Issy would be in the kitchen, drinking tea about now. She'd be the trickiest, as she didn't miss a thing. I had to be bland, get my point across, and get out before she caught on. But I also had to keep my distance. I didn't want to know if she'd die anyway.

She was in the kitchen, drinking tea as she went over a list.

"Is that for packing?" I asked, pointing.

"Yes. Trying to figure out what will travel the best but has the densest nutrition." She bit the end of her pencil, looking at the sheet.

"Issy, I hope you know how much I appreciate you looking out for everyone. I'm not sure what any of us would do without you."

She waved a hand at me. "It's just a list. No need to overdo it. We'll find somewhere else nice, right? Callon will see to it."

"Yeah, I know. Plus, you always take care of us." *And Callon might need you after I leave.* Of course, I couldn't say that, but she'd be there without a word asked.

She smiled as she bit the pencil.

"I'll see you later."

It took me a while to seek out Tuesday. I knew she

was up in her and Koz's room, but there was pure terror as I approached her. If my decision hadn't changed things, there was nothing left to do.

The door was cracked, and I pushed it open the rest of the way. She was standing in front of the bed, things laid out on it.

"I don't know how much to bring. Callon said as little as possible, but how little is too little?"

I was glad her attention wasn't on me as I neared.

The second I got close to her, I knew her death had shifted back to dying peacefully at a ripe old age. I couldn't decide whether I wanted to hug the breath out of her or drop to my knees and cry with relief. It didn't matter, since I could do neither. She hadn't known how close to death she'd gotten.

Years ago, Maura, her mother and my adopted one, had shielded me from Baryn's sickness and proclivities for longer than I'd realized. I hadn't known myself until I thought back to my childhood years with an adult's eye. The way she'd come back from Baryn with a glazed look. The way she'd step in front of me and drape herself over him whenever he'd come near—she'd been the only reason I'd had a childhood at all. I'd never gotten to thank her in life. Telling Tuesday of my debt would cause her more pain than good. But I'd finally found a way to repay her, at least in part. Not that I wouldn't have done it anyway. Tuesday hadn't lied when she said she was my sister.

"What's going on? Why do you look so relieved? Figured you'd be in a pickle of a mood today. Is it all that sex you're having?"

"You know, I was in a bad mood, but I think somehow things will work out. I think we'll get to come back somehow."

I sat on an empty corner of the bed. "Sometimes I imagine how happy Maura would be if she knew this was where we ended up. I don't think I would've survived as long as I had without her and you."

"You're getting a little weird on me now," she said, folding a couple of things up.

"I'm just happy we ended up here, is all. You deserve a place like this—you know that, right?"

"And so do you. You're freaking me out now." She stopped folding.

I smiled and got up. I'd overplayed my hand. I needed to switch gears to something that would utterly absorb her. "Where's Koz? Isn't he helping you?"

"He's out in one of the sheds trying to figure out which wagons we should take. Been out there half the morning."

"I'll go ask him how much stuff he thinks we can bring. It'll be more than what Callon suggests for sure."

She laughed. "Good idea."

I laughed with her and then shot into my room instead, shoving my head in my pillow so no one would hear me cry.

———

It didn't take me long to find Koz a little while later still looking over wagons.

"What's up? Don't you have packing to do?" he asked as I walked into the largest shed, more of a barn.

I marched up to him. "Are you going to marry her?"

"What?" He jumped like I'd slapped him.

"You heard me. I need to know if you're going to marry her. I need to know you're not going to get bored." I shoved his arm.

"Teddy—"

"I need to know." I shoved him again. "We're going to be traveling around to who knows where, and I need to know you'll take care of her forever, no matter how bad it gets out there."

He threw his hands up as he took a few steps back. "I can't talk to you about this."

"Why?" I asked, following him until I had him pinned down in the corner.

"Because you're too close to her. When I do it, I'd like at least a small element of surprise."

When, not if.

He cringed a little as I reached forward and patted him on the arm. "You're a good man, Koz." I walked out of the barn.

"I'm not a good man. I'm nothing. This talk never happened," he yelled.

"You got it."

CALLON WALKED INTO MY BEDROOM AT MIDNIGHT. He stood at the foot of the bed.

"I've been waiting for you," I said.

"I won't change my mind."

"I know."

"I have to tell you something else. I told Bitters not to undo the spell. I knew what you were going to do and got to him first."

"And you say *I* do stupid things. Are you crazy? Why would you do that?"

"Because I know what you would do, and I can't let you."

"Why?"

"Because I can't let you go, not to that. If you were going to be happier, maybe I could. But not to that life."

Callon loved me.

I got up on my knees and made my way to where he was. I wrapped my arms around him and buried my face in his neck. "You're doing what you believe is right. I won't fault you for that."

I hugged him tighter. *Just please don't fault me when I do what I think is right.*

THIRTY-NINE

Where the hell was Zink? Of all the people I thought would measure up to the task, it was him. There was a rustling in the trees, and he stepped forward fifteen minutes late.

"Where have you been? He's going to realize I'm missing. He's already on edge. I need to be gone before then." It was midday, and Callon would be looking for me at lunch. I just knew it.

Zink opened his mouth, but it took another second for the words to make it out. "I can't do it." He threw up his hands.

What? No. I was ready. I'd geared up for this, and it had to happen now, before I lost my nerve.

"What do you mean? Of course you can. You don't even like me!"

"My sleepless night might indicate otherwise. Apparently I don't hate you enough to deliver you to your death. I think you should take your chances."

"We can't do this. That stuff will be at our doorstep,

and it's the middle of winter. You *need* to do this. This has to happen. You need to help me."

"I'm sorry." He shrugged. "He loves you. I can't kill the woman he loves. I just can't."

"He'll get over it." I grabbed his arm and tried to drag him in the right direction.

He yanked his arm back. "He won't get over it. I know him. He doesn't love in half measures."

I'd have to try on my own. There was nothing else to do. I wouldn't take everything from him.

"Fine. But don't try to stop me. I don't want to have to kill one of Callon's best friends, all right?"

His chest swelled before he let out a long breath. "I'd considered it, but I won't. We each make our own choices in life, and we each live with the consequences. I'm choosing what I can live with. I won't stop you from that same choice."

I shook my head and took off. I didn't have any more time to waste. I ran so fast that my lungs burned.

Callon had posted guards around the Hell Pit as it had gotten closer. I wouldn't doubt for a second that they'd been warned to keep me far away. As soon as they saw me, they'd yell. Callon would hear, and he was lightning fast.

I kept running. As soon as I got in sight, it happened exactly as I feared. The guards saw me running toward the edge of the Hell Pit.

"Stop!" they yelled. When I didn't, they charged me from both sides. I ran faster, but I was never going to make it. The Hell Pit was too far, and they were faster and closer.

Then there was a tinkling noise, like the sound of a thousand wind chimes all at once. A golden mist filled the air. Dazed by what was happening, I slowed. The men who had been running toward me looked like they'd slammed into an invisible wall on either side of me.

I heard yelling and turned to see Callon crashing into the same invisible wall behind me. And then Dax was there with him, trying to break through. Dal, Tuesday, and Issy, who were slower, were running toward them. I could already see Dal crying.

"Don't do this!" Callon screamed. "Teddy! We'll find another way." His voice sounded muted, though, as if he were screaming through a thick piece of glass.

Tears streamed down my face as I yelled back to him, "I love you."

Hess and Zink stepped forward, pulling him away from the wall that he was battering himself against. I saw him struggle against their hold, my vision blurred by my tears. I finally understood Dal's endless supply. When you loved someone, truly to the depths of your soul, there were no words for the agony of loss. Losing someone you loved defied any other pain you could feel; it changed who you were, who you would be. It darkened your world for the rest of your life.

Callon was the reason I could do this. Had to do this. I wouldn't ruin his life, running and hiding. It would destroy him eventually, and everyone who went with us. I'd stolen from him before. I wouldn't do it again.

"It's all right. You need to do this."

I jumped at the sound of the little girl's voice. "I saw you in the forest. Who are you?"

The little girl took my hand, walking me toward the mud. The muted screams dulled further as we made our way. "Tiffy. I came here to help you. You need to go into the mud. It's what you're supposed to do. You're the only one who can help it. You need to go to it, give it what it wants. It's the only way to heal it."

We stopped by the edge.

"Are you part of it?" I said, looking at the mud and then her.

She giggled. "No, but in a way, I've known it for a very long time. We're friends, sort of." She stepped into the mud, our arms outstretched now as she urged me forward. "Come, I have things to show you."

"Will it hurt?"

She smiled. "No."

I followed her in, letting it ooze in around my feet. And then we were no longer wading through a Hell Pit. We walked through a field of flowers. In front of us, Dal and Dax knelt, sobbing at a freshly dug grave.

"Was that me? Is it true?"

"They buried you here to save you, but this place changed you and your magic, gave you the gift of taking and giving life that you would need to heal things when the time came. But you wouldn't be ready until you were older."

"Do you know who took me? Why would they do that?"

Dal and Dax faded from view. Faceless robed beings appeared, and lifted a wriggling baby from the ground.

"My people did. They didn't do it to be cruel. They did it because it had to be done. You had to remain hidden until you were strong enough. Once you were changed, you weren't safe there. No one could know about you."

"So they brought me to hell and left me there?" I asked.

"The first time you met the Magician, you nearly lost everything. If he had found you sooner, you wouldn't have won. So they left you to Maura until it was time for people to hear the whispers of a girl who could work a miracle."

We were standing in front of the gates of the village now. A man was passing a baby through the gate.

He turned and, not long after, disappeared into a golden mist.

"They left me in hell," I said.

"Some people are born in heaven. Others are born in hell, clawing their way out from the day their life was cursed. Heaven isn't worth anything if you haven't seen hell first and know what you have. I'm not saying that justifies what they did, but you'll know what you have."

"I'm dying. I won't have anything," I said.

"No, you'll have more happiness and joy than you ever dreamed of."

She let my hand go, and I was waist-deep in the Hell Pit. The field of flowers had been a hallucination. This stuff was playing with my mind. I wished it had continued. I didn't want to die like this.

Either way, this had to end quickly. I knew the scars I'd leave for the people watching while this all played out. I could hear my mother crying, the image of her collapsed on the bank scarred into my brain.

I'd feared what having the mud swallow me whole would be like, but now I worried it would take too long. What if one of them broke free before I died?

"Take me already," I said, moving deeper until I was up to my shoulders in it.

Why was I still standing here alive? I tried to move, and it flowed around me, just like water would. I wasn't frozen like the Magician had been. It wasn't even uncomfortable. It felt more like a warm bath.

As I waited, the mud right around me began turning colors. The muddy brown turned blue, then clear. Why wasn't it swallowing me whole like it had the magician?

"Don't you want to kill me? Just do it already."

The blue water around me spread wider until it was a few feet out. Then the water closest to me turned green, and that began to spread out. Finally, it was replaced by sparkling gold where I stood. It began to fizz where it touched my skin, like some sort of carbonation was happening, tingling wherever it touched me.

Then it got even stranger. This glittering fizz touched me everywhere, seeming to seep into my skin, and I felt a sense of relief and calm and serenity. It was as if I were feeling the emotions of whatever this thing was, and it was nothing expected. Malice and anger weren't a glimmer. Whatever was happening to me, whatever was filling me, it wasn't evil. It was beautiful.

I could feel magic flowing through me. I lifted my arms, my hands glowing in front of me, tingling and glittering like the gold of the water.

I was so enraptured by what was happening that I didn't realize right away that everyone had grown quiet.

No one was crying anymore, at least not that I could hear. A quick look showed stunned faces.

I looked back to my hands, at how they glowed. I shoved up my sleeves, to see my arms were the same. I shed my jacket, the cold completely gone.

The intensity of the relief filled me until I felt as if I were about to burst with happiness. I felt like someone who had been living in hell was about to walk through the gates of heaven. Tears of a joy that didn't belong to me streamed down my face. And just when I thought I was going to be completely overwhelmed by the magnitude of emotion, streams of glittering silver and gold were trailing out of me and rising like smoke.

Hazy forms of people started to appear all around me, slowly rising, all smiling as they looked upon me.

Soft words traveled across the air. "Thank you" from one. Then another, until it was a chorus surrounding me.

This thing hadn't been trying to harm me. It had been seeking release. The souls of the wronged had been stuck here, attached to the discarded magic and rotted skins, waiting to be freed. Waiting for my strange gift to release them. One day I was going to die, maybe violently, but hopefully peaceful in my bed, Callon lying beside me. But that day wasn't now.

At the bank, no one was holding Callon back anymore. He stood, watching with everyone else. Even from over there, Callon's beast ears could hear the thank yous.

The mud was now almost completely changed to a glittering lake of brilliant blues, greens, and golds that began to lower. I don't know how long it continued, but finally there was nothing but regular mud under my feet, the shadowy figures were gone, and the crows who'd haunted my every step for years flapped their wings and flew away. They'd been trying to signal the need for the passage of souls for too long.

By the time the last of the lake disappeared, and the last shimmer faded from the sky, exhaustion overtook me. My knees gave out. Before I crashed to the ground, Callon was lifting me in his arms.

EPILOGUE

I dug in the garden beside Dal on a warm spring day. We were planting it on the south side of the lodge, in spite of there being a larger garden that was tended to by the gardener and his helpers not even thirty feet away.

She stopped digging, sitting back on her heels. She stared at me more than she gardened. I didn't mind anymore, or not as much. Sometimes I stared too now. Since her and Dax had been here awhile, I'd been forced to adjust. They'd been leaving "next week" for months.

"How many Hell Pits are you going to go to?" She dug another hole for a tomato plant. I'd found out those were her favorites when she'd determined that half the garden was going to be tomatoes.

"Callon is gathering information, and we're plotting out a map. Figured we'd leave in a couple of weeks." The map had actually been finished a week ago, but I'd been putting off the departure. Part of me hoped the rest of the

Hell Pits would come to me so I didn't have to leave here ever again.

"Maybe I should stay here while you're gone? Bookie won't mind running the farm for a while longer. Otherwise, who'll tend the garden?" she asked.

"That would be great. It might be hard to find someone otherwise." I purposely didn't look at the other, larger garden being tended not far from us.

She smiled and went back to digging.

"While you're here, maybe you could help Tuesday with the wedding? She wants to get married after she gives birth." I wasn't sure if Tuesday was happier about the baby or the fact that she could blame the baby for the nonstop eating.

I didn't have the heart to tell her that Koz knew she had a healthy appetite, and half the time it was him leaving cookies in their room, not me.

"I know she'd want you involved. She's becoming very attached to you."

Dal leaned closer. "She knows we're not actually her parents, right?"

"She doesn't care."

She leaned back. "Okay, then." She pulled out a missed weed before she made a new hole and put a few seeds in it. "How's it going with Bitters? Is he still refusing to leave Issy's cellar?"

"Yeah, but I think it'll be okay. I caught her smoking his weird pipe last night and giggling."

"Yep, that's how he gets his foot in the door before he takes over."

"How long do you think he'll stay?" I was the one that stopped digging this time.

"Callon owes him a debt? Decades."

"Yeah, but it was to *not* do something."

She was shaking her head. "Doesn't matter. He takes his debts seriously."

"Shit. Do you think there's any chance—"

She watered a couple of holes as she said, "You're my daughter. I'd give you my life, but I'm not taking him back."

I knew it was too much to ask. Life was easier.

The sound of raised voices carried onto the lawn as Callon walked out the front door with Dax on his heels.

Callon turned toward Dax. "You're her father, so I'm not going to punch you, but *back off*." He turned and kept walking.

"Do you think this is going to keep happening?" I asked.

Dal tossed down her shovel and leaned back, letting the sun hit her upturned face. "No. It'll settle down. Dax really does like Callon. He's just mad about a few things."

"It's been months of this, though."

Dax smiled as he headed our way. At least he hadn't chased Callon down.

"It'll take him some time, but he'll get there," Dal said.

"Callon didn't do anything that anyone else wouldn't have done. I mean, I did sort of torture the guy a little and chain him to me."

"I know, but he feels that Callon should've been

gentler with you." Dal smiled widely as she watched Dax walk over. She'd been with him close to twenty years, and she looked like she was still crushing on him.

He stopped in front of her. She held out her hand, and he pulled her up, wrapping an arm around her waist as they kissed each other hello. Seriously? It had been decades. Weren't they a little bored?

"How's the garden coming?" Dax asked me.

"Good. Everything okay?" I pointed vaguely in the direction Callon had disappeared.

"It's fine. Just laying some groundwork. Nothing to worry about."

"All right, then."

Dax smiled and then turned back to Dal, who was winding her hand through his hair.

I knew where this was going. I'd seen it too many times before. I stood, brushing the dirt off my pants. "I'm going to go check on some stuff."

"Sure, see you later," Dal said, pulling out of Dax's arm and tugging him in the direction of the lodge. At least they were going inside this time.

"See you in a bit," Dax said, following her.

I walked into the forest. "Callon?"

An arm went around my waist, and then I was turned and pressed against a tree, his mouth covering mine.

He pulled away after a few minutes.

"I've been waiting to get you alone all day. I swear your father stalks my every move," he said.

I ran my hands through his hair. "Is he driving you crazy?"

"Yes, every minute of the day, but it's okay." He dipped his head, nipping at my lower lip.

"You sure? Do you want me to talk to him? Try to get him to lay off?"

He laughed. "No. If I were him, I'd beat the shit out of me. He's letting me off light."

"What do you mean?"

He brushed the hair from my face.

"I felt something for you the first time I saw you. You were beaten down but not beaten. All that you'd gone through, and you kept on fighting. I should've tried to help you right away, not abandon you."

"Well, I fixed that problem," I said, laughing.

"I'm glad you did. You're a survivor. You've got this burning soul inside of you that won't go out, no matter what. If I have to get chased by your father every day for another year, you're worth it."

"Only a year? I'm not sure they'll be going back that soon." I wouldn't be surprised if they never left.

"Then he can chase me all day for a lifetime, as long as you're in my arms every night."

"You can't get rid of me, remember?" I pulled his head to mine.

Actually, twenty years didn't seem so long when you thought about it. Tiffy had been right. I had more happiness and joy than I'd ever dreamed of.

Sign up here to be notified of new releases by Donna Augustine.

http://www.donnaaugustine.com
Twitter
Facebook
Facebook Reader Group
Follow me on Bookbub

ALSO BY DONNA AUGUSTINE

Ollie Wit

A Step into the Dark

Walking in the Dark

Kissed by the Dark

The Keepers

The Keepers

Keepers and Killers

Shattered

Redemption

Karma

Karma

Jinxed

Fated

Dead Ink

The Wilds

The Wilds

The Hunt

The Dead

The Magic

For Ashleigh, who saved my ass on this one!

ACKNOWLEDGMENTS

I cringe to think of what my books might turn out to be if I didn't have these people helping me along the way! Thank you, Camilla, Christine and Lori. Special thanks to Donna, who always goes above and beyond. It's noted and appreciated every single time.

www.ingramcontent.com/pod-product-compliance
Lightning Source LLC
Chambersburg PA
CBHW061537170626
46811CB00001B/8